A bad day

T he small man looked down on Joe Don and Bobby Lee, who were trying to cry for mercy, attempting to beg for a chance to explain. But the wads of cotton in their mouths made speaking impossible. Animal-like moans were the only sounds able to escape their writhing, naked bodies. When there was no response to their efforts, Joe Don and Bobby Lee began shaking and waving their hands.

Their freaked and feeble minds had given up hoping for the best. Instead, they had reached the point of trying not to think at all.

Judith thought she heard a few words from the distance, but wasn't sure. She was still in her own state of shock, but also relieved that the worst for her was over.

Silently she watched as the two kidnappers who had violated her for three full days were stretched out in the small grassy circle in front of the house. Their legs and arms were extended as far as possible, crucifixion style. Their wrists and ankles were tied with thick, plastic cord to metal stakes that had been driven into the ground.

"Whr . . . Whr . . . Whrill! WHRILL!!!"

Also by Ed Okonowicz
from Myst and Lace Publishers, Inc.

Spirits Between the Bays Series

DISAPPEARING DELMARVA
Portraits of the Peninsula People

POSSESSED POSSESSIONS
Haunted Antiques, Furniture and Collectibles

POSSESSED POSSESSIONS 2
More Haunted Antiques, Furniture and
Collectibles

STAIRWAY OVER THE BRANDYWINE
A Love Story

FIRED!
A DelMarVa Murder Mystery

DelMarVa Murder Mystery #2

HALLOWEEN HOUSE

Ed Okonowicz

Halloween House
DelMarVa Murder Mystery #2
First Edition

ISBN 1-890690-03-1

Published by
Myst and Lace Publishers, Inc.
1386 Fair Hill Lane
Elkton, Maryland 21921

Printed in the USA
by Victor Graphics

Photography, Design and Typography
by Kathleen Okonowicz

Dedication

To my wife, Kathleen,
who makes everything happen.

Acknowledgments

It's important that I thank those who took their precious time to read this book in its initial and final drafts, and also mention those who made important suggestions. In particular, I am indebted to John Brennan, Joyce Buker, Barbara Burgoon, Marianna Dyal, Peggy Mason, Sue Moncure, Mark Okonowicz, Ted Stegura and Monica Witkowski for their fine proofreading and editing suggestions.

Cecil County historian Michael Dixon provided fascinating information on DelMarVa history and Elkton's interesting past. Wally Jones, a retired member of the Pilots of the Bay and River Delaware, graciously took me on a container ship cruise up the Delaware from Lewes to Philadelphia one evening and later reviewed the nautical sections of the book. The real Ron Poplos, an old friend from the IRS, provided insight into law enforcement weapons. Eddie Okonowicz, R.N., provided information on drugs and medical procedures.

Thanks also are extended to Jay and Eileen Milburn and the owners of Milburn Orchards in Elkton, Md., who allowed photographs to be taken of their annual Haunted Barn and other decorated structures. Each fall, this popular DelMarVa attraction is visited by thousands of families.

Any errors in this book are the sole fault of the author.

Comments from the critics

About *FIRED!*

". . . this is Okonowicz's best book so far."
—The Star Democrat,
Easton, Maryland

". . . an entertaining, if gory, murder mystery."
—The Aegis,
Harford County, Maryland

". . . full of action, mystery, intrigue and excitement. To call it a page turner would be an understatement."
—Linda Cutler Smith,
Mystery Group Coordinator,
Borders Books,
Wilmington, Delaware

About *Halloween House*

"DelMarVa 2009 - Even in the best of places, unimaginable evil can happen. Discover Halloween House *wherein breeds the darker side of mankind."*
—Tish Murzyn,
Atlantic Books,
Dover, Delaware

Table of Contents

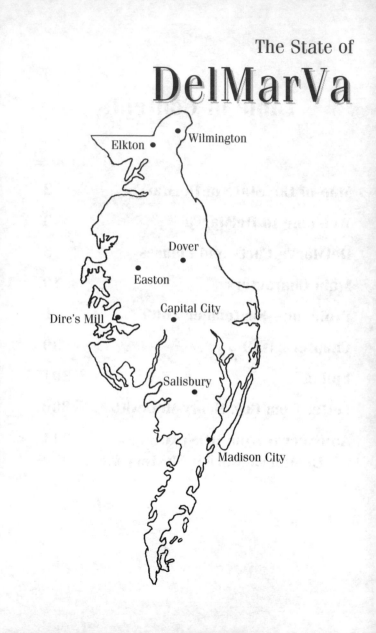

The State of
DelMarVa

Elkton •   • Wilmington

Dover •

• Easton

Capital City •

Dire's Mill •

Salisbury •

• Madison City

Welcome to DelMarVa

For three and a half centuries, the DelMarVa Peninsula—the elongated, diamond-shaped land area surrounded by the Chesapeake and Delaware Bays and Atlantic Ocean—included the people in the former state of Delaware, the nine counties that previously made up Maryland's Eastern Shore and the two northeastern counties that had been part of the Commonwealth of Virginia.

From the time of the region's discovery in the 16th and 17th centuries, the residents of the water towns, farm villages and cities existed interdependently, with families, businesses and politics crossing the borders at will. State lines never restricted political allegiance, family traditions, commerce, recreation, religion or common interests.

Long-time DelMarVans know each other's families and many have friends and relatives in common. Newcomers are constantly amazed that residents can't seem to go anywhere on the peninsula without running into someone they know.

For centuries, many peninsula residents believed the region should have been established as one sovereign state—extending from Claymont to Cape Charles, from Conowingo to Crisfield and from Cambridge to Chincoteague. In this book series, that logical event finally occurs. While this novel is fiction, in a few instances, well-known Mid-Atlantic sites and prominent historical figures are mentioned, but those are this book's only connections to reality. All of the characters are imaginary. Any similarities to persons or actual events are strictly coincidental.

In *FIRED!*, the first DelMarVa Murder Mystery of this series, this unique geographic area and cultural region became a separate state. Following the presidential election of 2004, the state of Delaware and the Eastern Shore counties of Virginia and Maryland were united.

Taxes were eliminated and crime—primarily because of the swift and just use of fatal punishment and the whipping post—was reduced to the lowest level of any state in the nation. But DelMarVa is not immune from the problems faced by every other metropolitan and rural area of the country.

In 2008, the only blemish on DelMarVa—Gov. Henry McDevitt's utopian kingdom—was a string of highly publicized crimes committed by serial kidnapper and killer Charles Bettner—detailed in *FIRED!*

But, in the fall of 2009, following the resolution of that terrorizing crime spree, life in DelMarVa returned to its peaceful normal state. But evil never rests. It appears from time to time, to remind the good that there is another, darker side of life.

In *Halloween House*, a new, sinister criminal disturbs the calm of the ideal, showcase state.

—Ed Okonowicz
in Fair Hill,
at the northern edge
of the State of DelMarVa
Spring 1999

State of DelMarVa
Facts and Figures

Capital: Capital City, near Federalsburg

Governor: Henry McDevitt, Victims Rights Coalition

Vice Governor: Lydia Chase, Victims Rights Coalition
    (both elected to 6-year terms)

Entered Union and Rank: 2007 (1 and 51) and the first state (Delaware) of the original 13 colonies to ratify the U.S. Constitution on Dec. 7, 1787

Present constitution accepted: July 4, 2006

Motto: Liberty, Independence and Swift Justice

Nicknames: First State, No Nonsense State, Diamond State, Peninsula State

State Symbols:
- Colors—Blue (Del.), red (Md.) and gray (Va.)
- Flower—Peach blossom
- Bird—Blue Hen chicken
- Dog—Chesapeake Bay retriever
- Tree—American holly
- Fish—Rockfish
- Shell—Oyster shell
- Crustacean—Blue crab
- Boat—Skipjack
- Insect—Checkerspot butterfly
- Sea Serpent—Chessie
- Song—*Our DelMarVa!*
  (modified from *Our Delaware!*)
- Poem—(See request from Gov. Henry McDevitt on page 306.)

Number of Counties: 14

Accomack	Northampton
Caroline	Queen Anne's
Cecil	Somerset
Dorchester	Sussex
Kent	Talbot
New Castle	Wicomico
North Kent *	Worcester

*Formerly known as Kent, when it was part of Maryland. Name was changed to North Kent to avoid confusion with former Delaware county of the same name.

Length: 215 miles—from Smith Bridge in the north, bordering Pennsylvania; to Fisherman's Island in the south, at the Chesapeake Bay Bridge Tunnel.

Width: 67 miles—from Taylors Island on the west, at the Chesapeake Bay; to Fenwick Island on the east, at the Atlantic Ocean.

Origin of Name: Named to signify the merger of all 3 counties of the former State of Delaware with the 9 counties of Maryland's former Eastern Shore and the 2 counties of Virginia's former Eastern Shore, to form the regional peninsula state in 2007.

•Delaware—from the Delaware Bay and River, named in honor of Sir Thomas West, Lord De La Warr, first English colonial governor of Virginia

•Maryland—in honor of Henrietta Maria, Queen of Charles I of England

•Virginia—to honor Elizabeth, "Virgin Queen" of England

10 Largest Cities: Cambridge, Cape Charles, Capital City, Dover, Easton, Elkton, Newark, Ocean City, Salisbury and Wilmington.

Professional sports teams: In Wilmington: Blue Rocks, baseball; DelMarValous Demons, soccer; and Blue Bombers, basketball. In Salisbury: Shorebirds, baseball; and DelMarVa Diamonds, football.

Six casino hotel complexes: Christina Hotel and Casino, Wilmington Riverfront Plaza; Chesapeake Casino, Cambridge; Delaware Park Racetrack and Slots, Stanton; Dover Downs, Dover; Oceanfront Casino and Resort, Rehoboth Beach; and the Wild Pony Casino and Entertainment Center, Accomack County.

Theme park: Pirate's Cove, in Accomack County, larger than the size of Disneyland in California. Offers more than 28 rides, as well as live entertainment in four theaters. Six four-star hotels and camping facilities are located nearby.

Professional auto and horse racing: Dover Downs International Speedway offers NASCAR and Indianapolis auto racing and also harness racing. Harrington Race Track in Kent County and Ocean Downs, located between Berlin and Ocean City, also offer harness racing. Since 1937, thoroughbred racing has run at Delaware Park in Stanton, located between Wilmington and Newark, with top purses and world-class horses and jockeys. In recent years, the Delaware Handicap has begun to rival the Kentucky Derby, Preakness and Belmont Stakes in interest, primarily because the DelMarVa track's purse size has exceeded the other three contests that are part of racing's Triple Crown.

Outdoor recreation: The state park system and private enterprises offer hiking, camping, crabbing, bay and ocean fishing charter trips. There are hundreds of miles of beaches on the Atlantic Ocean and Chesapeake and Delaware Bays. The barrier islands, south of Chincoteague, are a natural wonder and under state and federal protection. The DelMarVa State Fair is held in Harrington each July.

Cruises: Boat excursions originate from a new deepwater port in North East, located on the Upper Chesapeake Bay near the Susquehanna Flats. The cruises head south to the tip of the peninsula and then north, up the Delaware River to Wilmington. Modern rail service transports passengers back to North East after the end of the cruise.

Special Attractions: A short list of some of DelMarVa's top rated attractions include the

Brandywine Arts Festival	Garrison Days at Fort Delaware
Chincoteague Pony Swim	DelMarVa Poultry Festival
Rehoboth Sea Witch Festival	Crisfield Crab Races
Georgetown Oyster Dinner	Chestertown House Tour
Punkin' Chuckin'	Old Dover Days
St. Michaels Skipjack Races	Hardley: Civil War Spectacular
Elkton Mass Marriage Ceremony	St. Anthony's Italian Festival
Shepherd Muskrat Dinner	Ocean City Sunfest and
Bridgeville Apple Scrapple Fest	Easton Decoy Festival Show

Scenic rail tours: Six privately operated steam trains take passengers through rural areas of the state. Tours range from 2 to 6 hours. Some include dinner and entertainment. Holiday programs are popular. The Wilmington and Western Railroad, west of Wilmington, and the Parksley Railroad Museum, in Accomack County, are popular sites for train buffs.

Mass transit: An extensive mass transit train and monorail system carries commuters north and south the length of the state. Construction is under way to connect other major population centers across the state via rail.

Criminal justice: Criminals avoid DelMarVa because of its reputation for swift justice and harsh punishment. The whipping post was reinstated in 2002 (in the state of Delaware). The state's death penalty is administered either by hanging or lethal injection. In March 2003, during the celebrated execution of child murderer Elwood "Sugar Daddy" Looney, at the state prison in Gumwood, then Delaware Governor Henry McDevitt, himself, sprang the gallows trap door.

Political parties: One, the Victim Rights Coalition controls all three houses of the state legislature—the House of Representatives, Senate and People's Representative Assembly (PRA). This last body is made up of citizens from various occupations who have input into legislation and oversee the work of elected representatives, to restrict influence by paid lobbyists and organized political pressure groups. The PRA members also insure that the state representatives and senators carry out the people's wishes.

Main Characters

Detective Darryll Potters

Melinda and Craig Dire V

Rolph Kunralt

Angeleen

Maurice Knowles—Mo the Know

DelMarVa Gov. Henry McDevitt

DelMarVa First Lady Stephanie Litera-McDevitt

DelMarVa Police Commissioner Michael Pentak

DelMarVa Vice Gov. Lydia Chase

Sgt. Randy "R.J." Poplos

Bobby Bottles

Mammo Marguariete

Judith, Tina and Nannette

Moses Abraham Neigel Jefferson—Ol' Mose

Theo Athanor

Diane Kramer, WDMV-TV's *Your Eye on DelMarVa*

Joe Don Huckelby and Bobby Lee Groves

Snarky Jack

Charlotte Meredith Ann Dire

Sheriff Saxton Dire

Deputy Sheriff Wallace J. Smythe

Elrod Dire

Ape the Bartender

Tsu Chan Wrie

Salisbury Barracks Chief Dean Lively

Pennsylvania Gov. David P. Hornsby

New Jersey Gov. Sharon Kannedie

Prologue

September 2009
Philadelphia, Pennsylvania

It was four o'clock in the morning on the first Saturday in September. Angeleen pulled back the ornately sewn, white lace curtain and stared out the second-floor bedroom window of the Society Hill townhouse she shared with her soulmate Christie. Below, the narrow street was empty. Tall lampposts cast a soft glow on the gray, round-topped cobblestones.

In the distance, a pair of footsteps passed over the uneven, red brick pavement. The clipped, repetitive sounds traveled above the empty sidewalks and rose toward the black sky, passing and entering Angeleen's screened window. The accompanying scampering indicated that a tiny dog was moving quickly, trying to keep up with its master's rapid gait.

Soon noisy, box-like, delivery trucks would begin to navigate their daily, maze-like route, dropping off bundles of freshly inked newsprint at wooden street corner stands and mom-and-pop storefronts. As the daily information chain commenced, groggy readers would leaf through floppy pages of headlines, words and phrases, looking for stories that would make them forget they were on their way to work.

The first stop for sports fans was the Phillies' score.

Many others anticipated good news, until they read their lottery numbers and realized they had missed the jackpot by one digit or a country mile. Either way, it didn't matter. They were still losers. But . . . there was always tomorrow.

Older readers looked to see who they knew in the obituaries, often smiling that they had lasted another day and were not yet mentioned. But . . . there was always tomorrow.

Everyone eventually took in the front page, reading about the unfortunate souls who had been maimed, shot, stabbed, burned out or run over in the City of Brotherly Love during the past 24 hours.

Angeleen smiled, satisfied that she had completed another night on the job and happy she had increased her bankroll. With every additional day she was closer to the time when she would leave the city for good and head back to the country—back to a calmer lifestyle, perhaps in a small town setting similar to the locale where she had been raised. But, she would never want to relive the horrifying parts of her past that she had left behind.

For the last seven months, since Christie had hooked up with her bouncer boyfriend—appropriately named Bruiser Butch—Angeleen had been living pretty much on her own. But that wasn't a concern. Both 23-year-olds worked from 7 p.m. to sunrise, and there had never been a lot of time or interest in socializing. They had met on the job, hit it off enough to give house sharing a try and, surprisingly, the arrangement had worked out.

That was more than four years ago.

They were both still alive, hadn't killed each other—or been injured by anyone else. Under the circumstances, Angeleen figured they were beating the odds.

Their routine was set in stone, 12 months a year, six nights a week. The women would return home early in the morning, take extra long, very hot showers, activate their answering machine and put the telephone ringer on mute. During the next 10 hours, they tried to sleep and run a few errands before they reported back to Chez Cheveux.

The popular, top of-the-line escort service was located in a nondescript warehouse in South Philly, not far from Veterans' Stadium and the old Navy Yard. To passing delivery vans and tractor trailers filled with meat, produce and furniture, the nameless building— protected by a rusted, chainlink fence—was just another vacant machine shop that had been unable to secure a suitable tenant.

Inside the compound were spacious offices that would rival the headquarters of any successful commodities trader on Broad and Chestnut. In the large, empty chamber, two dozen stretch limousines—all black, late-model Lincolns—waited to deliver stylish, young, beautiful women to the dining tables and hotel rooms of visiting conventioneers and corporate executives who passed through the Big Scrapple.

Chez Cheveux was managed by Theo, a tall, dark-haired Austrian. His impressive size seemed out of place with his soft voice, impeccable manners and refined taste. His employees assumed he was the front man for a group of unknown and unseen investors. The all-female staff considered their on-site supervisor fair in his assignments, understanding and patient in times of stress and equitable when it came to pay.

Obviously, catering to more than three dozen vain, spirited and independent-minded women was not an easy task. His customers' demands also had to be addressed with aplomb, and Theo never seemed ruffled or out of sorts.

Chez Cheveux's clients, of both sexes, included city and state politicians, highly respected judges, top-level police officials and even a few prominent members of the clergy. Discretion was the agency's trademark—that and a stable of magnificent women who were known to entertain each client to his or her complete satisfaction. Of course, it was understood when applicants were admitted into membership—for a hefty $20,000 inauguration fee—that money was of no object to those who were entitled to utilize Chez Cheveux's services.

Angeleen dropped the bedroom curtain back into place, walked across the candlelit room and sat on the edge of her mahogany, four-poster bed. The smell of vanilla spice filled the attractively decorated chamber. It was the same scent that her mother had used during her rituals, but that seemed like ages ago—not a mere five years. As she breathed in the aroma, Angeleen fingered her tattoo, the symbol that her mother—Mammo Marguariete—had carved into Angeleen's palm with a kitchen knife and outlined in black ink. The "devil's talisman"—good luck charm—Angeleen had been told.

The marking was an indelible memory of the life Angeleen had escaped, but it was a world she could never forget. If it wasn't for the help of a naive social worker, Angeleen would be in a solitary cell on Death

Row, down the corridor from Mammo. But, that was another time and another world that Angeleen pushed aside, for the time being.

Finally, she had a chance to get ahead. Angeleen smiled as she thought of her financial plan that was right on schedule. If her body held up, if she stayed away from the drugs and booze—and if she wasn't knifed or beaten into a coma by a crazed client—she would be able to get out of the business and start a new, more traditional and respectable life.

She laughed at the thought, thinking about all her "respectable" clients, who lived in half-million-dollar homes, had a wife and a few kids, and what appeared to be a great job. But, if it was all so wonderful, why did they pay to have Angeleen and her colleagues bang their brains out for top dollar.

What a world, she thought. But, when she left she wouldn't be on the receiving end. She'd be in charge, setting the rules and in control. That's what it was all about—power. But, patience first, she reminded herself.

When the time came, no one would know how she got her money. She would settle far away, in a small town—in a quiet place where she could smell pine trees, hear the ocean, listen to gulls again. Just like before, but without the horror and abuse and murder.

In five years she would only be 28, still young enough to start over.

She leaned her head back on the pale blue pillow.

Closed her eyes . . . clenched her left fist tightly.

If she could just hold on . . . and if her streak of luck would just hold out.

Elkton, DelMarVa

It was just before noon on a bright, sunny Saturday in Elkton, DelMarVa. For nearly a century, the small town located at the northern tip of the Peninsula State—close to the Pennsylvania state line—was known internationally as *the place* to get married.

On this first weekend in September, traffic was restricted and news vans with satellite transmitters were double parked across several side streets near the large, impressive courthouse. On the normally empty Main Street sidewalks, print and television reporters from across the country jockeyed for a spot to report on the wedding of DelMarVa Gov. Henry McDevitt to former state psychologist Dr. Stephanie Litera.

Scores of photographers with lenses longer than shotgun barrels were perched in the county court-house's upper-level windows, hoping to capture a picture of the new bride and groom as they exited the ceremony.

The couple had been courting, and their wedding had been announced several months earlier, immediately after state psychologist Litera had escaped from the captivity of a serial kidnapper and killer in Madison City, a fishing ghost town north of Chincoteague. That sequence of sensational crimes in 2008 had been the only blight on DelMarVa's bright and shining reputation as a tough-on-crime state with the highest paid police force in the country.

More than 50 DelMarVa state troopers, clad in gray-blue uniforms with red and gold trim, formed two snake-like lines to escort invited guests into the ceremony and keep crashers a safe distance away. Whenever Henry McDevitt made an appearance, security always was a problem. His wedding ceremony only increased security problems for his bodyguards and the extra police who had been called in to provide much needed insurance. Adding to the bedlam was the presence of guests U.S. President Scott Woodyard and the First Lady.

Elkton's Main Street was a picture postcard of the past, the result of intense economic development effort that had started in 2000, soon after the turn of the century. At that time, three progressive town commissioners—over the heated objections of a handful of reluctant residents and self-appointed civic leaders—proclaimed the DelMarVa town the "Wedding and Romance Capital of the World."

Based on its well-known reputation as a site for quickie marriages in the early decades of the 20th century, Elkton decided to capitalize on its notoriety and build and license more than a dozen "new," old-fashioned-style wedding chapels that were gingerbread replicas reminiscent of the town's glory days.

On the evening of the final vote, one commissioner, who supported the town's effort to make the most of its romantic past, stated, "I am not asking for a reduction in the 48-hour waiting period, I am asking that we make the most of our history. Our town's wedding fame is even mentioned in the Broadway musical *Guys and Dolls*, and audiences of all ages still respond with a knowing chuckle about our fame—more than 60 years after our first golden wedding ring era ended. I say, bring back the days of Elkton's wedding bells glory. I, for one, would rather be known as the 'Wedding and Romance Capital of the World' than the 'Ghost Town That Time Forgot,' or the 'Town Too Dumb to Take Advantage of Its History.' "

The vote passed 4-1 and, within six months, commercial construction of inns and restaurants was rampant. Plus, couples were arriving from around the country to be wed, filling the county coffers with income from marriage license revenue.

On weekends, holidays and a fair number of weekdays, newly licensed storefront preachers did a brisk business, marrying DelMarVa residents and a large number of out-of-staters who came to the area for one reason alone—so they could be hitched in the same town as baseball legends Babe Ruth and Willie Mays, basketball star Charles Barkley Jr., U.S. Attorney General John Mitchell, boxer Jersey Joe Walcott, singers Ethel Merman, Billie Holiday and Maxine Andrews (of the singing Andrews Sisters), actress Joan Fontaine, comedian and Cowardly Lion Bert Lahr, Broadway producer David Merrick and thousands upon thousands of average Americans.

By 2004, seven hotels, several associated with major chains, had built Victorian-style bed and breakfasts in the town to conform to its residential character. Each establishment included a full dining room, gift shop and up to 12 attractive bedrooms or suites.

Visitors who could not find lodging near the downtown historic tourist district sought accommodations provided by a number of contemporary chain hotels located on nearby Route 40.

Florists, gift and antique shops, photography studios, a small theater and nearly 20 stylish eateries catered to a never-ending flow of downtown visitors. A new bus and taxi terminal, built near the old train station, provided public transportation for those who came into town using mass transit services over rail and road.

In the fall of 2009, Elkton—whose reputation in history had been established through its marriage business a century before—had achieved ultimate legitimacy the day 12 international news networks reported on the wedding of former U.S. presidential candidate Henry McDevitt.

Inside "We Gather Together" chapel, 48-year-old, red-haired Stephanie Litera—with her younger sister Monica standing as her maid of honor—said "I do," to 58-year-old Henry McDevitt, who had chosen DelMarVa Police Commissioner Michael Pentak as his best man.

The small chapel could only accommodate 60 guests. Among them were happy members of the Litera family from Wilmington; Vice Governor Lydia Chase and her husband, Ron; McDevitt's good friend and bodyguard Randy "R.J." Poplos; Senior Administrative Assistant Grace Welch; and members of McDevitt's cabinet and their spouses.

Other close friends and guests included the key advisers of McDevitt's 2004 presidential campaign. Seated in the second row were Baltimore developer Benjamin Bartolovich, Easton philanthropist Elyse Delmond, Retired Admiral John McDonough Jennings, Judge Clayton Ward of Greenville and founder of the Caesar Rodney Society, and Georgetown's Saundra Price, wife of DelMarVa's Chicken Czar Peter "Poultry" Price.

"This is Diane Kramer, live with *Your Eye on DelMarVa*. We're in Elkton, Romance and Wedding Capital of the World, reporting on the marriage of DelMarVa Gov. Henry McDevitt and Dr. Stephanie Litera.

"As many in our audience know, Ms. Litera, former state psychologist, was the last victim of Charles Bettner, a serial kidnapper who terrorized DelMarVa residents last year.

"She and the governor had been dating for several months when the kidnapping occurred. According to reports from the other victims, the new First Lady of DelMarVa played a major role in insuring the escape of the other captives.

"She has recently resigned from her position with the State Department of Health and Social Services to be with her husband and devote full time to her duties as DelMarVa's First Lady.

"Adding to the excitement in this sleepy DelMarVa village is the presence of a number of dignitaries, including President of the United States Scott Woodyard and First Lady Elisabeth Huber Woodyard. It was during the final days of the 2004 presidential campaign that Governor McDevitt withdrew from the election and pledged his support to the then Maine Senator, insuring President Woodyard's election.

"We've been told the simple ceremony has just been completed and that the new couple soon will be leaving the chapel. While we're waiting, let's focus on Michael Pentak, the best man, and Monica Litera, the bride's sister and maid of honor."

As two color photographs appeared on television screen, Diane Kramer continued, "Police Commissioner Pentak, 57, a former Philadelphia homicide detective and crime thriller author, was selected by the governor as DelMarVa's first police commissioner and the detective moved to the peninsula, in Fenwick Island, several years ago. He and the governor have become close friends and, it was Pentak, who personally supervised the serial kidnapping investigation last year that led to the rescue of state psychologist Stephanie Litera, now the First Lady.

"Monica Litera Witters, the younger sister of the First Lady, lives outside Newark and is a registered nurse. During Stephanie Litera's abduction last year, it is said Monica's strength held the Wilmington family together and that she never lost faith that her sister would be found. On a humorous note, we're told that when Stephanie began dating Henry McDevitt, Monica did not know the identity of her sister's significant other. Her only advice to her older sister was that she 'find a husband who liked to stay at home, was uncomplicated and that, if they got married, it be a simple wedding with just a few of the family present.' That," Diane Kramer added with a smile, "is certainly not what we're seeing here today."

Inside the small chapel, the smiling couple shared the nuptial kiss and two select photographers captured the special moment. As the bride and groom accepted congratulations from their relatives and closest friends, DelMarVa Public Affairs Secretary Sean Kelley exited the building and headed toward a temporary podium on the sidewalk. Standing before a score of microphones, Kelley prepared to release a statement to the press.

Diane Kramer was back on the air, live. "We're trying to get a picture of the new couple as they depart from the chapel," she said. "But, now we see the appearance of Sean Kelley, the governor's public affairs secretary."

As Kramer moved toward the sidewalk podium, she stretched her right arm, trying to advance her microphone toward Kelley's face.

A calm, experienced voice traveled across the air-waves. " . . . . to announce that the wedding ceremony has just concluded. The new bride and groom are very happy and will be leaving shortly for a private reception at Woodburn, the Governor's Mansion in Dover. However, simultaneous transmissions of the celebration will be broadcast to the First Couple's friends attending receptions at the DelMarVa Convention and Conference Center near Wilmington's Christina Riverfront Plaza, at the Convention Center in Ocean City, DelMarVa, and at the southern end of the state in the new Atlantic Visitors and Conference Hall in Accomack County.

"Tomorrow, they will depart for a short, one-week honeymoon at an undisclosed destination. The new couple wishes to thank all their supporters and well-wishers. They both look forward to serving the citizens of DelMarVa for many years to come."

Diane Kramer reappeared on the screen. "That's the latest news from Elkton, DelMarVa. We've been told that the couple will soon be exiting the front of the chapel. But, honestly, with so many newspeople and citizens here, it may be difficult for our camera crew to move close enough to get the couple in view. We'll break into our regular programming if that occurs. This is Diane Kramer, reporting live for *Your Eye on* . . . ."

Dire's Mill, DelMarVa

Craig Dire threw his brown longneck across the room and cursed at the same time the half-filled beer bottle smashed through the glass screen of his 63-inch television screen. As the projectile disappeared in the jagged mass of gray glass and black plastic, Melinda jumped from her barstool and raced across the spacious game room to comfort her agitated husband.

Melinda, with a train of jet black hair that seemed to bounce with every movement of her trim, athletic body, was 22 years younger than her 58-year-old spouse. Before becoming Craig Dire's second wife, she had worked as an Atlantic City cocktail waitress in Resort's Hotel and Casino. To many, Melinda resembled a young Elizabeth Taylor with thick red lips and an hourglass figure that still turned a lot of heads.

She was accustomed to Craig's tantrums and had learned quickly that there was nothing to be gained by complaining about his childish antics or trying to correct him.

Melinda knelt and took her position at Craig's feet. A good dose of unbridled understanding was what he needed and expected—and she was an expert at giving him the attention he craved.

"Baby," she cooed, rubbing his head, massaging his neck and stroking his beard, careful to avoid touching the pale white line that rose toward his eye. Most of the unsightly scar was hidden beneath his beard, but Craig was still sensitive about it being noticed. As she moved her smooth, thin hands back and forth, trying to relax her husband, Melinda said, "I told you not to watch that stupid wedding. All you did was get yourself all worked up and bothered. He's not worth it, Sugar Babe. Don't let him get to you like this."

Breathing hard, but remaining motionless on the overstuffed, black leather couch, Craig's words seeped through his clenched teeth like steam hissing from a sidewalk vent.

"I went to school with that guy. I send the bastard campaign contributions . . . ."

"That he sends back, Sugar," Melinda interrupted.

Craig glared at his wife and continued, "I am the richest, smartest, most well-known businessman in this half of the goddamn state, and that ungrateful bastard never asks for my support. He doesn't invite me to anything. Not anything! No inaugurations, no political dinners, no visits to the mansion. Not even a goddamn fish fry or barbecue. Hell! I hate that bastard McDevitt!

"Ever since college he's been a prick, always doing everything his way. Everything had to be perfect, above board. He was always too good to have any fun. I don't think he ever got smashed or laid. No, Saint Henry was in the library helping some blind gimp do his homework or working at some soup kitchen dishing out hash to the street trash. What a goddamn loser."

"Right, what a loser," Melinda agreed, thinking to herself that McDevitt the Loser apparently had done all right by himself. Her husband's enemy was governor of the most controversial state in the country, had appeared on the cover of all of the national news magazines and had nearly been elected President of the United States in 2004. *Hell,* she thought to herself, *Craig would cut off more than his left arm to be in McDevitt's position.*

"Why couldn't he just send me a goddamn invitation?" Craig asked, his voice a drunken whine.

"I don't know, Sugar. Maybe there wasn't enough room, you know that place looked pretty . . ."

"Are you as stupid as you look?" Craig shouted, jumping up from the couch and kicking a wooden chair.

Melinda stiffened and lowered her eyes. There was no stopping him now.

"That bastard had every two-bit asshole politician from Cape Charles to the White House inside that shithouse of a chapel, and he couldn't even send me a goddamn invitation to one of his receptions! I swear, I'm going to get even with his ass. Who does that farmer think he is embarrassing me like this? My own useless chief of police was invited to the Ocean City reception, and I didn't even get that! I have had it with that asshole. The next time I see him, I'm going to kick his royal ass."

Melinda resumed massaging her husband's neck as he fell back into his spot on the couch.

"You're right, Baby Sweets. I don't blame you, neither. You deserve better. Forget McDevitt and the dumb bitch he married. We've got more important things to think about—like Halloween."

Craig paused and slowly began to smile at the thought of his special day.

As he shifted his focus, within moments the snub at being left off McDevitt's wedding list began to fade.

"We've got lots and lots of things to do, Sugar," Melinda cooed. "It won't be long until we'll start hanging decorations, get our new cast together and start having rehearsals in the tobacco barn," Melinda reminded him.

Even though Halloween was nearly two months away, Craig Dire could get stimulated about it with little encouragement. Soon after Labor Day, planning, construction, casting and selecting new special effects consumed his time. More than anyone, Craig knew how much was involved in the creation of Halloween House. His production involved details far beyond what visitors touring the annual project could imagine—so much work, so little time and the season was already pressing upon him.

Craig firmly believed that it was no coincidence that he was born on October 31, the most horrifying day of the year. It was fate. With two thirds of his life behind him, he loved autumn more than ever. To him, it was a time when nature displayed its mortality and began to die. He said it was a reminder to all humans that they were one year closer to their ultimate appointment with death.

Certainly, some people would live longer than others, but luck played the major role in that area. Craig Dire believed there were three things that determined a person's destiny—luck, one's position or status and how hard he played the game of life.

Most would agree that Craig Marshall Dire V had received more than his fair share of luck. His father and grandfather, and the long line of Dires before them, had paved his way. More than 250 years earlier, the quaint water town was settled by Craig's ancestors.

He and Melinda were the richest residents of all who lived in the neighboring three counties. They ruled their subjects from Dire's Mill Mansion, a massive, 18th-century plantation home surrounded by 800 acres of the finest farmland on DelMarVa's Western Shore.

The original section of their brick home had been built before the Revolutionary War. Like most grand estates with a distinguished lineage, the structure had been visited by George Washington, John Adams and several of Maryland's governors. It also was believed to have been a regular stop on the Underground Railway.

With no children, Melinda polished the 28-room homestead with care, turning it into a DelMarVa show-place that she displayed with pride. To be invited into Dire's Mill Mansion at Christmastime was at the top of every status-seeking, county resident's wish list.

During the fall, however, access was no problem. Everyone in the region lined up to experience "Halloween House"—as the grounds were called during the last two weeks of October. It had been that way ever since Craig and Melinda took over the estate nine years earlier.

In addition to the plantation, the couple owned another large parcel of woodland and fields that boasted nine miles of Chesapeake Bay coastline. One of its other assets was a deep channel harbor that could accommodate mini-yachts and other large pleasure craft.

The Dire estate's virgin land was coveted by both predatory land agents and idealistic environmentalists. Its eventual sale would add many millions to Craig and Melinda's bulging coffers and securities portfolio.

The couple had inherited the estate and the majority of the family's businesses several years ago, when Jasper Dire, Craig's domineering father, departed DelMarVa unexpectedly in a drunken state heading for the big ginmill in the clouds. For a still unknown reason, Jasper's Ford pickup's headlights kissed the fast moving metal grill of a megaton freight train engine a mile north of the Dire's Mill town limits. Emergency personnel were bagging pieces of Jasper and his pickup from an acre of adjacent cornfield for the next two months. But that was all ancient history. Now, area residents and business people had to deal with Jasper's sole legal heir—Craig Dire V.

The commercial headquarters and origin of the Dire family fortune was located in Dire's Mill, about midway between Easton to the north and Cambridge to the south. The small water town was built on the banks of Dire's Creek, which flowed directly into the Chesapeake Bay.

Visitors to the village immediately noticed the frequency of the family name, which appeared above storefronts and on road signs. Dire Hardware, Butchery and Dry Goods was two doors down from the Dire Theater and directly across from Dire Shellfish, Coal and Ice Company. News in the town was provided through the *Dire's Mill Ledger*.

Among these enterprises on Water Street stood the Town of Dire's Mill Court House; U.S. Postal Office, Dire's Mill, DMV; and the brick building housing the Dire's Mill Sheriff's Office and Volunteer Fire Co.

Craig's office was located in Dire Federated Equity Savings and Loan, at the intersection of Dire Boulevard and Dire Way. It was an impressive, three-story, red brick structure supported by a quartet of tall, white entry columns. From a second-floor, glass-walled office, Craig lorded over his tellers—making sure they didn't get sticky fingers or take extra long breaks. Spending much of the day in the bank lobby, he mingled with the populace, pressed the flesh, listened to gossip, agreed with his constituents and ran herd over his kingdom.

Of course there was a mayor, town commission and board of licensing and taxation. But most offices were held by Dires or their close relatives with different surnames.

There were a few shops privately owned by newcomers—such as Shirley's Morning Glory Restaurant, Konnie's Krab Kitchen and the Sunrise News and Smoke Stop—but they were exceptions, and often didn't last too long.

Several years ago, a new development opened on the outskirts of town. It was named, appropriately— Dire Estates.

One local wondered aloud why the family had not named the nearby waterway Dire Straits—instead of "creek." A few of the poorer Dires laughed, but more affluent clan members were very annoyed at the comment.

To no one's surprise, all was not perfect in Diredom, since the rich Dires and the poor Dires didn't get along. A few black families used the Dire surname, despite an earnest effort by Craig Dire to legally force "those folks down there in Blacktown" to change their names.

"What would you have these people call themselves, Mister Dire?" Judge Malcolm Lowe Dire asked Craig during a petition process in Dire's Mill Court House.

"I don't really care, Malcolm, I mean, Your Honor," Craig replied. "They can become Washingtons or Lincolns or Carvers, or even name themselves after the Very Reverend Martin Luther King. But I don't want them running around using my name any more. It's embarrassing and annoying, and I aim to put a stop to it!"

To the surprise of many, Judge Dire—Craig's third or fourth cousin, no one was exactly sure which—ruled that members of the black community of Blacktown and adjoining locales had as much a right to the Dire name as the town's owner—and the case was closed. After unfavorable publicity in both the Salisbury and Baltimore newspapers, Craig decided not to file an appeal. But, he instructed all his business and shop managers to refuse credit to any black citizen who bore and used the Dire surname.

Since Blacktown residents were poor farmers and struggling watermen, they depended upon store advances and credit to get through the tough months. If they couldn't get their provisions in Dire's Mill, they would just have to travel 12 miles to Chippers Corner. The embarrassed storekeepers explained that they had their orders and, while it wasn't decent, it was legal. No one was entitled to credit, and they certainly would sell them goods or services if they had the cash in hand—or became Washingtons.

Most went to Chippers Corners.

But money makes short memories of problems, and Craig and Melinda believed very strongly if they tossed enough green around they could pretty much do whatever they wanted. When the church needed money for the orphans and homeless, the Dires were there.

If the hospital needed a new roof, the Dires presented a check.

When the school needed computers, Craig Dire was on the front page of the *Dire's Mill Ledger,* smiling as he donated the needed monitors, printers and paper.

The year the high school marching band had a uniform fund drive, Craig and Melinda delivered 60 complete tailored outfits to the school principal during half-time of the Thanksgiving Day game in Dire Field. With television cameras rolling, the benefactor grabbed the leader's baton and directed the musicians in a chorus of "He's a Jolly Good Fellow"—dedicated appropriately to himself.

If it was tax deductible and generated publicity, Craig and Melinda were standing tall and smiling at the front of the line.

But private citizens and businesses in trouble knew better than to approach Dire Federated Equity Savings and Loan for help. Since Dire Real Estate owned 90 percent of the town's commercial property, if a business owner missed one payment, shutters and a going-out-of-business sale were certain to follow in short order. Others who argued against town council projects or the old ways seemed to have a run of bad luck, a quick change of heart or packed up and moved on.

Most longtime residents believed the town operated better with the ungrateful troublemakers gone.

In Dire's Mill there were parades on the Fourth of July, ceremonies to honor veterans on Memorial Day, the Summer Seafood Festival and safe streets for carolers to stroll along during Christmastime.

In Dire's Mill crime was low, utilities were cheap, the churches were full on Sundays and life was good. Main Street was a replica of Walt Disney's Small Town America and, on every block, Ozzie and Harriet lived next to Ward and June Cleaver.

Washington County, Maine

Sheriff Darryll Potters looked up at the two-story, white frame Cape Cod for the last time. It was just after 1 o'clock in the afternoon on the first Saturday in September. He had hoped to avoid the weekend tourist traffic, but he had been unable to finish packing on Friday, so his departure was delayed a day.

The century-old, weathered structure had been his home for 22 years. Now it was time to leave, load up and head south.

He leaned his beefy, 54-year-old body against the dark green, four-door Pontiac Bonneville. Streaks of gray were beginning to take over his once jet black curly hair. Throughout his life, women found Darryll attractive. But there had been no romantic interest in his life for at least three years.

Potters had lived on the rocky hillside in the wooded mountains of Washington County, Maine, since 1987, when he moved to the area and joined the police force.

Considered a foreigner from the South at the time, he had adjusted well over the years. He learned patience and how to handle the glut of summer tourists. He had adjusted his lifestyle to weather the bitter winters and developed a few hobbies—particularly reading and music—to beat the accompanying boredom that seemed to last longer each year.

Originally, he had come to Maine to escape from his family and his past. Now, he was returning to both. His stepfather's death had come only a week after his retirement from the Washington County Police Force. A letter from a Salisbury, DelMarVa, attorney informed him that what was left of Gobbler's

Knoll, the Potters' rural homestead, now belonged to Darryll, the sole survivor of the family name.

Maine had served Potters well for two decades, but now it was time to return home. With his retirement pension, he could start over. He planned to work the DelMarVa flatlands as an on-site farmer—do some fishing and crabbing—enjoy life for a change and totally forget about the cases he hadn't been able to solve. Maybe even write a book about his experiences. That's what a lot of cops did, he had heard.

Hell, he'd read enough mysteries and murder novels, and, in his mind, it was obvious most of the writers had never held a loaded gun or been slammed against the wall by a drunken slob twice their size. He'd been beaten, kicked, stabbed, cursed out and run over, so he figured he'd be able to write better than someone whose only credentials were an overactive imagination and free time. Darryll had that and more, much more.

If he decided to give writing a try, the battered, tan box crammed in the back seat of his '99 Pontiac would come in handy. It contained all of the documents of six runaways he never found—a half-dozen missing teenage girls who would probably never be discovered. Potters knew that. No one else cared. No one else was looking for them, or ever would. So, when he relieved the Washington County Property Records Office of the files, he knew they would be missed about as much as Cheri Harris, Gail Pillster, Mary Jane Hampill, Sarah S. Small, Joy Gwinty and Debbie Lou Simpson—all young, aged 16 to 19, all attractive, all missing . . . all gone.

Six disappearances in the last eight years, and each one during the summer. Every girl had last been seen near the First Avenue bus stop, directly in front of Chamber's Variety and Hardware, with a one-way ticket out of town. And not one was ever heard from again.

But, they're not my problem any longer, Potters told himself as he shook his head and lowered his massive body into the front seat of his car.

After about three weeks of sightseeing in Canada, Chicago and the small towns, mountains and forests of the Northeast, he'd arrive in Gobbler's Knoll. But he wasn't rushing to get back to the house that he hadn't stepped foot in for more than 20 years, located two miles north of the town limits—or town line, as they called it in Maine—of Dire's Mill, DelMarVa.

Blacktown, DelMarVa

Ol' Mose liked digging graves at night, especially in the spring and fall. It was quiet, and no one was around to interrupt his singing or thinking.

The smell of the woods—seeping from dozens of scents ranging from rambling honeysuckle to wild rose hedgerows—was particularly enjoyable. They were easy to recognize if you'd spent a lot of time in the woods.

Mose liked carving the ground under lantern light. He had been working the cemeteries so long that he knew he could set up a grave even if he went blind. But everything had a price. He knew that when he had made special arrangements with Old Man Dire two generations before. That deal would continue until Ol' Mose died. After that, he didn't know who would carry on. Probably nobody.

But then it wouldn't be his responsibility. Until then, it was all up to him.

His proper given name was Moses Abraham Neigel Jefferson—but nobody ever called him anything but "Mose" or "Ol' Mose." He was born in the early morning darkness of Nov. 3, 1929, the year of the first Great Stock Market Crash. While rich men were jumping off buildings because they had lost everything, a poor black baby, whose family owned next to nothing, was yanked into the world in Miss Hattie's three-room shanty on Razor Strap Lane in Blacktown.

Today, only a few moss-covered planks remained of her small, rundown shack, and they were overgrown by weeds that had survived enough seasons to turn into full-grown trees. It hadn't been occupied since Miss Hattie passed away, back in 1962, the year Ol' Mose placed her next to her kin, into the sandy Eastern Shore ground.

Mose still called it the "Eastern Shore," even though newcomers considered the former Maryland counties to be the "Western Shore" of the new State of DelMarVa. But, just like old folks are set in their personal habits, they feel the same way about names of places, too.

But that's how it works, thought Mose, looking down at the hole he was digging to send another one home. "In ya come, and on ya go. Some'll go fast and some'll go slow," he said aloud to himself, almost in a sing-song tone. "But, in the end, they all end up in the same place. My place."

Now, in 2009, Ol' Mose was almost 80 years old, but he looked to be a healthy 60, and he was the last gravedigger in the region who still cut the earth by hand.

"No fancy backhoe and jackhammers for Ol' Mose. No sir!" he'd say. "Just let me use human muscle and a well-worn prybar, pick an' shovel. An' don't go an' forgit the lantern."

It was the same way gravediggers had done the work from the beginning of time, and he was proud to carry the craft on in the old way.

He had started working when he was 9 years old, taking after his father, Big Ben Jefferson, and his uncle, Little John Tilghman Jefferson. Big Ben had forearms as thick as grown men's thighs. Little John was smaller, but that came in handy for jumping in and out of the graves to get tools and bring down the lunch bags, so they could eat in the shade of the cool earth on humid, Eastern Shore summer days.

Mose paused and recalled his first solo grave. It was the first week in October, real early in the fall. He was told to open one up so it would be ready at sunrise for the box. His father gave young Moses a lantern, hunting knife and shovel, then walked him to the site to be sure he didn't accidentally "dig one up that was 'posed to stay planted."

The young boy spent that crisp autumn night alone—in the boneyard.

Mose smiled, remembering how every sound scared him half to death. He must have paused a hundred times, bothered by every hoot owl, wind gust and swaying tree limb. Eventually, he realized that the quicker he dug, the faster he would get home. It took him six hours, but he got the job done. He counted the amount of dirt he moved, and learned the hard way that it takes 26 wheelbarrows of earth to carve out a regulation grave—four-and-a-half feet deep, eight feet long and three-and-a-half feet wide.

But, that was hundreds, no thousands, of holes ago, and this was now. He wondered who would plant the folks from Blacktown after he was gone. His people couldn't afford an undertaker or buy plots in a real graveyard. They had to come here, to the Old Place—a spot only Mose and his folks and the Dires knew about. Hell, he thought, he'd planted plenty of bodies for the Dires, too. Too many, probably. Whenever they dropped off a bundle in them dark green plastic bags, all zipped up tight. He usually got a few in early November, and others arrived at any old odd times during the rest of the year. He'd bury them, real fast and with no questions asked. That was the arrangement.

He wasn't stupid like they thought.

Mose knew that some of the people that had disappeared from the area were inside the dark plastic sacks that Dire's men left out behind his cabin. But, he learned a long time ago that it didn't pay to ask too many questions—especially when it involved the Dires—and he rarely peeked inside the bags.

Old Man Jasper Dire and Craig, his lazy, good-for-nothing boy, had gotten real hot under the collar that one time when he asked about what happened to Miss Charlotte Ann, Craig's first wife. That was one good woman, Mose thought. Everybody, black and white, liked Miss Charlotte Ann.

But Mose never got an answer and he never spoke up again, and he never complained.

Compared to his father and grandfather, Ol' Mose knew he had the good life. Outlived them by a lot of years, and had himself an electric ice box and combination freezer and a 19-inch color television set. Owned a kerosene heater for winter and two fans for

hot summer nights. Had enough money to buy cold
beer and play a little cards once or twice a week.
What more could a poor man from Blacktown want?

Ol' Mose paused, leaned on his shovel and stared
at the homemade, worn, wooden grave markers,
spread out in an irregular pattern across the flat
ground of Ol' Place.

His people were poor, and only a few could
afford stones to mark the final home of their loved
ones. *But*, he thought, *people still come, leave ribbons,
plant flowers. That's what's important, not the size of
the rock and fancy carvings.*

The other graves, the ones he did for the Dires,
weren't marked. They were off to the side, hidden
and separate and away from his folks. Only Mose
knew where they were.

But, enough relaxin', he thought. Then, lifting his
shovel, he aimed, stabbed at the earth, pulled back a
scoop of yellow-brown dirt, and heaved it to his right,
adding to the growing pile of sand, clay and soil.
Repeating the motion, Mose fell into a rhythm that he
had developed over three quarters of a century. All
over the world, they've been doing it this way, he
thought, since long before him, before his father and
before his grandfather.

But after Ol' Mose, who knows? Who cares?

When his time is up, he won't care neither. But,
until then, he'd just dig more holes in the Old Place.
Put down the poor folks, and the few others that got
dropped off—send them off to dark sleep and not tell
nobody nothing.

Since nobody ever asked, why stir up any interest?

As long as they left Blacktown and Old Place
alone, Mose would die happy.

Mid-October 2009

Joe Don Huckelby and Bobby Lee Groves turned off the headlights and slowed the rusted Ford pickup to a easy, silent stop. They had ended up right where they wanted to be—at the edge of an old fire road, in a thicket of pine scrubs and overgrowth, only about 200 feet from the rear of NoTel Motel.

That wasn't the roadside reststop's real name. The paint-chipped sign that originally declared "Northside Motel" had long ago suffered the effects of broken glass and burned out bulbs. The result was a hodge-podge of remaining pink and blue neon initials that telegraphed the two-word message: "No . . . . tel." To passersby and locals on the old route heading out of Dire's Mill, the name stuck. No one had bothered to correct the damaged marquee. In fact, it became a regional joke, and the colorful name was perpetuated by every subsequent owner.

The 1940s-era overnight lodging site would never see anything close to its original glory days, but its small, 20-foot-square bedrooms—with orange shag carpeting and flamingo pink wallpaper—still served a steady and select clientele. NoTel's patrons fell into three categories: those needing a site for a hasty version of afternoon delight, passing truckers looking for a cheap place to flop and down-on-their-luck locals who needed a spot to call home—temporarily or long term.

It also hosted a steady stream of "passing ladies" who stayed there until they were picked up and moved on. That's what Snarky Jack, the one-eyed manager, called them. Since he had taken the job, he was under orders from someone—a nameless bigshot that Snarky had no interest in knowing or ever meeting—to have four rooms reserved and ready at all times.

That simple order was no problem, except that he couldn't rent them out—not even for a one-hour quickie in the middle of the day.

Unless Snarky Jack got a personal call from someone named Louis, the rooms were never to be used. But, when the never-seen, "Lou the Mysterious" (as Snarky called him) initiated contact, the manager knew that some of the most beautiful women he would ever see were on their way to his humble establishment.

When the women were delivered, all of them—from four to six knockouts—would stay in their rooms and never leave. Cars with stern looking, iron-pumping-type guys would stop by and drop off food and magazines. But the women had no other visitors. Snarky Jack "never saw nothin'," and he and Hazel, his maid, were forbidden to go near the rooms until the "passing ladies" were gone.

The beautiful women usually would wait there from one to three nights, four at the most. Eventually, they were picked up by other colorful characters that Snarky Jack "never saw, didn't know and would never be able to identify."

The rooms were always paid for in advance. Never a problem with that.

A shoebox filled with cash arrived every month on the third, like clockwork. Four rooms at $32 bucks a night, times 30 days was nearly four grand a month, guaranteed. It was good for the owner, whoever he was, and Snarky Jack, too. Since the squinty-eyed manager got a cut of all the rooms he booked, the passing ladies' rooms were like money in the bank.

There was no way he would ask questions, rent out the four rooms or mess with the arrangement. Where the broads came from, what they were doing there and where they went were of no concern to him.

Snarky Jack never had anyone sign in and there was no record in his official registration log. If anything ever happened and the cops checked his books, that could be a problem. But, in his four years on the job, there was never an incident and that's the way he liked it.

So why should there be a problem now?

To get through his days, Snarky Jack maintained a positive outlook on life. Why shouldn't he—he had one glass eye, a bottom of the line job, had struck out with five wives, couldn't afford false teeth, had serious drinking and gambling problems and drove an orange Pinto hatchback.

But, Snarky Jack's luck couldn't hold out forever.

On this fall Sunday night at close to 11 o'clock, Snarky sat in his cramped office home watching a black-and-white video of an old western on a minia-ture TV. In the woods behind his roadside landmark, two men crept through the brush and headed for the rear window of Room #6.

Joe Don and Bobby had been responsible for picking up the women in Rooms 4 through 7 for about a year, until they were fired for getting wasted and arriving at the dropoff point 20 minutes late.

It had been easy work, with good tax-free pay that supplemented their erratic lawncare business. After one bad night, when they showed up late and smashed, the short, young prick of a boss had canned them, saying they were lucky he didn't slit their throats and toss them into the bay.

Joe Don started to argue, but six bodyguards with boxer-like bodies—who were looking for a chance to practice gut punches on out-of-shape flesh—con-vinced the two men to drive off and not look back.

That was two months ago. But now—after weeks of planning—the luckless pair knelt beneath the cracked glass in the loose window frame and count-ed softly to 10. Their bravery was fortified by a half case of National Bo and unbridled expectations of a free night of sexual amusement.

As the countdown reached 1, the pair shot up and grabbed at the loose frame, ripping the entire window out of the crumbling cinderblock walls. As Joe Don tossed the metal and glass to the ground, Bobby Lee jumped into the dark room, shined his flashlight on the woman in the bed and covered her head with a pillow.

Using small searchlights, the two men tied the woman's wrists with duct tape and pressed a smaller strip of the all-purpose gray adhesive across her mouth.

Laughing and excited, but nervous and charged with a mixture of fear and sexual anticipation, Bobby Lee, the larger of the two men, hoisted the girl over his shoulder and ran behind his partner into the dark woods.

Reaching the truck, they tossed their kicking prize into the middle of the front seat and sped off quickly, leaving a spray of wet orange earth and a pair of deep tire ruts behind.

Their destination was about an hour away, a small tenant farmhouse located between Harrington and Denton.

Once there, they untied their living treasure and chained her to a brown, metal bedpost in a second-floor bedroom. Over the next three days, the two kidnappers took turns enjoying the girl's body in all the ways they had described in disgusting detail on their escape trip from NoTel Motel.

Bobby Lee propped a video camera on some clothes atop an old dresser to record their conquests during the sexual orgy. Since their victim resisted, by Wednesday night her face had been bruised and battered by Joe Don's crass attempts to coerce her into submission.

Her name was Judith—only Judith. Before her recent interlude of terror, her model-like, perfect body would have enabled her to enter any world-class beauty contest and most certainly be named a finalist. She had been waiting at the old motel for the pickup car that never arrived in time. Instead, she became the toy of two boy-adults who thought they could mix perverse pleasure with raunchy revenge.

Exhausted from squeezing too much drink, too little food and too many sexual episodes into 72 hours, the landscapers turned kidnappers fell into a deep, deadly sleep.

Sprawled across two beds in an adjoining room, the duo snored so loudly they didn't hear the black, military-style vehicle pull up into the narrow farm lane.

Three of the night visitors went directly to the landscaping truck and examined the distinctive orange mud behind the rear wheels. One rubbed some of the earthen residue off the black rubber mud-flap. As the trio nodded, showing agreement and approval, several other figures appeared.

A short man, who went by the monosyllabic identification of Rolph, pointed toward the run-down building with missing yellow shingles and a tattered gray roof.

The pair of resting rapists never heard the strangers with automatic weapons, their safetys off. Moving swiftly, like dark shapes blown by the wind, the intruders crossed the front yard, passing the broken brick walkway and untended, trash-filled flower garden.

The two drunken kidnappers didn't awaken as the soft-soled footsteps of a half-dozen men dressed in dark green and black glided over the porch steps, jimmied the doorlock and entered the dark, quiet home.

No one was conscious to see the red pin lights of the laser sights that searched every corner of each first-floor room. Then, silently—using familiar hand signals and head movements—the trained killers focused their aim on the hall at the top of the front stairs.

Neither occupant stopped snoring as the first sniper entered the large, trash-filled bedroom that overlooked the waving yellow stalks of the sprawling, dead DelMarVa cornfield.

They never had a chance, as the cold metal muzzles were pressed against their necks and other killing tubes were inserted into their ears.

Joe Don and Bobby Lee didn't have an opportunity to utter a sound as leather-gloved fingers jammed thick wads of white cotton in their mouths.

From behind, muscular, clawlike hands, also covered in gloves, squeezed the victims' heads to the crushing point. As the stunned, hungover captives tried to suck breath through restricted openings, another unseen intruder jammed fingertips above their eyes and pressed flesh-colored, surgical, adhesive tape against their foreheads—this designed to keep their eyelids open.

They were not going to be able to shut out the final visual moments of their earthly existence.

Moving swiftly, others in the rescue team released the girl. One man in black and green tossed a blanket across her naked body and carried her in his arms onto the front porch. Carefully, he placed her beaten body in an old wooden yellow rocker that had seen many seasons without a coat of paint.

Judith watched in silence as her two tormentors were shoved out the front door, fell over the rotted porch steps, and landed face down on the red, dirt-covered driveway.

There were eight men, all dressed the same. They remained silent, their heads covered by skull caps, the details of their faces obscured by uneven globs of camouflage paint. Initially, no one moved.

Suddenly, Rolph, who obviously was in charge, walked toward the kidnappers.

The other men moved back a half pace or more as he passed, apparently a sign of respect, waiting for his next silent command.

The small man looked down on Joe Don and Bobby Lee, who were trying to cry for mercy, attempting to beg for a chance to explain. But the wads of cotton in their mouths made speaking impossible. Animal-like moans were the only sounds able to escape their writhing, naked bodies. When there was no response to their efforts, Joe Don and Bobby Lee began shaking and waving their hands.

Their freaked and feeble minds had given up hoping for the best. Instead, they reached the point of trying not to think at all.

Judith thought she heard a few words from the distance, but wasn't sure. She was still in her own state of shock, but also relieved that the worst for her was over.

Her mind snapped back long enough to focus on the curious, unfolding scene. *These aren't police officers!* she thought, watching one of her rescuers nod, walk a few paces, take a commercial weed cutter off the kidnappers' truck then return and give it to the short man.

Silently she watched as the two kidnappers who had violated her for three full days were stretched out in the small grassy circle in front of the house. Their legs and arms were extended as far as possible, crucifixion style. Their wrists and ankles were tied with thick, plastic cord to metal stakes that had been driven into the ground.

"Whr . . . Whr . . . Whrill! WHRILL!!!"

The sound of the 4-horsepower motor against the damp early morning air drowned out the sounds of passing birds and the families of crickets nesting safely under the front porch.

Rolph aimed the spinning metal wheel that rotated the blue plastic line toward his two, spread-eagled targets. With their mouths jammed shut, only their bulging eyeballs and writhing bodies relayed the fear that consumed their senses.

Two of the attack party turned away, but the others watched, obviously fascinated with Rolph's selection of a unique form of mental and physical torture.

The executioner started at the ankles.

As the cutting edge of the whipping blue plastic connected with Joe Don's skin, a thin line of pink and brown flesh disappeared. Hoarse, whispered groans were heard behind the noise of the whirling weapon.

Bright red blood started to ooze from the wound and immediately scattered through the air—like mini droplets of dark red rain. Some specks hit a few of the nearby audience, other flecks were sucked up the moment they landed on the dry earthen lane.

Bobby Lee watched the scene, then turned away, praying his heart would give out before the torturer disposed of Joe Don and focused his attention on him—Victim Number Two.

About 10 minutes passed before Joe Don reached the blessed unconscious level, but not before he had endured the ravaged ripping of his ankles, legs and chest. His last conscious vision was that his body resembled a rack of raw beef that had fallen off a meat hook and landed on the highway.

As Rolph turned toward Bobby, the pathetic man's cringing body shuddered one final time, giving an abrupt, final jerking motion. The sharp reaction was from the bullet that had entered his chest and transformed Bobby's breathing being into a lifeless heap.

The short man turned, ready to use the weed cutter on his fun-spoiler. But, seeing the scowling face of Craig Dire, Rolph shut off the spinning wheel and tossed the machine onto the ground. His cold blue eyes telegraphed his annoyance.

"You seemed to be having a bit too much fun, Rolph," Craig said, smiling at his assistant.

"I wasn't through," Rolph replied, looking up, obviously bothered at being stopped in mid-murder.

"I don't care about you," Craig said. "I want this wrapped up fast. And your grotesque little game was taking too long."

No one spoke. The rest of the hunting party knew better. Craig was more crazy than he was rich—and he was very rich. It was a dangerous, unsettling combination. He also was their meal ticket and they all knew it.

"Stuff them into bags and drop them off in Blacktown," Craig said, nodding to the dead, butchered man and the one whose lifeblood was seeping into the ground from the bullet wound. "And make sure this area is sanitized. I don't want any traces that we were here."

"What about her?" Rolph asked, pointing to the frightened woman they had rescued.

Craig didn't answer, turned and walked directly toward the porch. Gently, he lifted Judith's chin and studied her face intently. With equal care, he gazed on her body, then turned her head from side to side, inspecting her face and neck very carefully. Smiling, he touched her cheek gently, stroking it with his smooth, black-gloved hand. As she looked at him, with his face less than six inches from her eyes, she noticed a faint scar that started beside his left eye, became wider as it traveled down his face and disappeared into his gray-black beard.

She smiled at his soothing, tender, caring touch. After the last three days, she appreciated his attention, the interest he was giving her.

"These bruises are deep," he whispered to her. "They must hurt," he added.

Nodding, she smiled, looking up.

Turning, he shouted across the yard to Rolph and the others, "The scars across her neck and back will take quite a while to mend. Unfortunately, we don't have that much time," he added, and he turned away abruptly and walked off the porch.

"Kill her, too!" he shouted, gesturing with the back of his hand toward the direction he had just left. "Then bag her up with the others. She's damaged goods and not worth anything now. And I can't wait. I'm not running a hospital. This is a business. I'll get a replacement. Besides, thanks to you she's seen too much."

Hearing the gist of the conversation, Judith jumped from the rocker. The frayed blanket fell onto the floor of the porch. Naked, she started to run toward Craig Dire, who had reached the other side of the gravel lane.

Shouting, she pleaded, "Please! PLEASE! DON'T! I'LL DO ANYTHING! ANYTH . . . ."

This time Rolph's killing tool was a .45 caliber Colt automatic. Within three seconds he had raised his gun and pulled the trigger. In the space of a short breath, the smooth, metal, death slug left the barrel and entered Judith's young forehead. A clean round hole, the size of a quarter, marked the front of her skull, but the force of the bullet tore off the back of Judith's head as it exited and lodged in the base of the porch. The woman's running body continued to take four more steps after she was already dead. Finally, the fresh corpse sprawled in a heap, a lifeless ragdoll of naked flesh.

"Such a pity," Craig said, shaking his head. "Yesterday, a perfect young flower. Today, a soiled, wilted weed, ready for nature's hungry compost."

Mid-October

The courthouse meeting room contained 36 chairs, and all were occupied by young, idealistic tigers who were ready to break out from the cage of education and become major players in the jungle of justice. Their future would include courts, appeals and, even sometimes, punishment and justice. With notepads opened and pencils in hand, the three dozen new employees prepared to take notes as the State of DelMarVa Governor Henry McDevitt started to address the newest group of deputy state prosecutors.

"Law is not justice, and justice is not blind. If law equaled justice—and she couldn't peek through her blindfold—we could get by with our complex, incomprehensible and contradictory legal system," McDevitt said. "Unfortunately, in our enlightened society, justice has been handcuffed. She worries too much about money, influential clients and public opinion. Worst of all, she has developed an unsavory tendency to exhibit prejudicial tolerance toward the criminal and a sense of cold, impersonal interest in the serious plight of the victim.

"To sum it up, we have a screwed up legal system that makes us work very hard to help the criminal and forces us to screw the victim and his or her family."

No one breathed.

"Years ago," he continued, "I sat where you are now. I possessed a seriousness of purpose and held very lofty goals. I was going to work as hard as I could to put criminals away for a long, long time—forever, if necessary." Pausing, the governor laughed at the thought. "I knew I would send them into a cramped, 6 by 8 foot sterile box, where they would be confined and miserable and never get out and harm anyone again. But, we know that isn't true, that it only happens that way in books and movies. Don't we?"

There was a pause, but the audience remained silent. Each of the young hires was trying to avoid being noticed the first day on the job by the chief executive.

Suddenly, McDevitt raised his hand and focused on a man in the back of the room.

"You, Mr. Cagnoni, of Patchouge, New York," McDevitt pointed directly at the tall, dark-haired man with the red and black bowtie in the rear row. "Tell your new colleagues about yourself. The highlights—age, interests, schooling and any background that you think they might find interesting."

The 27-year-old bachelor began. "I'm a graduate of City University of New York and New England Law, studied there at nights for four years, while working as a security guard and auxiliary police officer. I'm a crossword puzzle freak, and that's about it."

"Not quite," McDevitt added. "Your mother, Leonetta Puella Cagnoni, was raped and brutally murdered in her beauty salon she operated in the basement of your home. You were in high school at the time, and came home and discovered the body. You and your father, Mario, attended the trial of the 'alleged' murderer. He had been caught with her jewelry and a carving knife from your home in his car. Tell them the verdict, Mr. Cagnoni," McDevitt ordered.

"Not guilty . . . first due to a technicality in the auto search. During the second trial, he—the murderer—was declared insane," the new prosecutor said, stiffly, exhibiting his unease. "Henry Knotts—that was his . . . the bastard's name—was sent to a state asylum in upstate New York. He was there seven months when he escaped and killed another woman and her son, using the same MO as in my mother's murder. At that trial, he was sentenced to life, but . . ."

"But," McDevitt interjected, "he was killed in an escape attempt, but only after he murdered the prison psychiatrist and a 65-year-old, volunteer librarian during his effort to exit the prison."

Silence.

"Next, Ms. Gilbert, our Yale Law School representative."

"I'm Cathy Gilbert, originally from Arlington, Virginia. A graduate of Old Dominion and Yale. In light of the governor's comments and those of Mr. Cagnoni, I'll add that my sister, Janice, was delivering pizzas when she was run over by a drunk driver. She was crossing the street in a development. His car was going close to 60. It dragged her nearly 100 feet. She was 17, only four days before her 18th birthday. Her killer had been picked up seven times on DUI, three were thrown out because of technicalities. The judges allowed him to keep driving his car to work. He lost his license *again* after my sister's death. Manslaughter, they ruled. He was out on the road, illegally, again within six months. I followed his criminal career and found out he died in a head-on with a cement truck. That made me feel good, but my sister will never come back to me."

"Mister Hollis! Your turn," McDevitt announced.

Everyone in the room turned toward the deep voice coming from the left side of the conference room, near the tall, heavily draped windows. "My name is Avery J. Hollis. I'm from Montgomery, Alabama. I played high school basketball. Was All-State, earned a full scholarship. My father and older brother, Henry, were victims of a robbery. They stopped at a 7-11, on the way home from one of my games. My father was gunned down inside the store—because he only had $15. A witness said my father could see they were going to take a hit and jumped for the gun, to save my brother. But it didn't work.

"The guy who shot my father in the gut wasn't satisfied. He tied my brother to the back of a pickup and dragged him down the highway until he died. They caught the shooting on the store security camera. You could see the killer's face, see him laughing as he shot my father. The defense lawyer used an 'under the influence of drugs' argument, and they gave him 10 years. He should have gotten the chair. But the prosecutor didn't want to fight it, and they brokered a deal. He'll be out in four years, unless they spring him sooner for good behavior. I keep in touch on the case, but there's nothing more that can be done."

McDevitt took a few steps and the heads turned back to the front of the room.

"I can go on. Mr. Bielinski of Chicago, over here in the first row, whose best friend was shot outside a dance club the night before his wedding. Mr. Chance of Price, Ohio, near the door in the back, whose father was the victim of an assassin for hire so his second wife could cash in on his life insurance policy. Ms. Kopec from Polar Bridge, Wisconsin. Her father was killed by a falling tree. His employer, the lumber company, wouldn't pay. The company lawyer said Mr. Kopec was negligent because he wasn't wearing his hard hat. The tree crushed his chest.

"Mr. Wheeler of nearby Philadelphia, whose cousin was the victim of a freeway driveby shooting. Ms. Leokunm, of Clinton, Iowa, whose fiancee told five drunken cretins to stop shoving a retarded high school student at a football game. He was kicked to death."

McDevitt paused, looked at the new hires, making eye contact with each of them, even if only for a second or two.

"There are 36 new prosecutors here today," he said, "and 21 of you were related to or were close in some significant way to victims of serious crimes. It's not by accident that you were hired as DelMarVa state prosecutors; it's by design. I need your zeal, your intelligence and your commitment to fight like hell to even the score, to speak for the dead and for the abused victims and their families. We need you to insure that criminals will not get away with murder, or white collar corporate crime in DelMarVa.

"Any questions?"

Nothing.

"Each of you was interviewed by our chief state prosecutor Matthew Gordon and a committee of law enforcement personnel and members of our state's Victims' Rights Coalition." All of the newcomers looked at the side of the room where Gordon, the top state prosecutor, was standing.

"Matt explained how we operate," McDevitt continued. "He told you of our high expectations. And each of you, for your own personal reasons, agreed and signed a contract of commitment. You are the best and brightest. For your hard work and studies— and for your potential—you will be the highest-paid state prosecutors in the country. In return, we expect much.

"We cannot bring back your parents, your siblings, your friends who have died—in some cases, in your arms. But, you can make damn sure no criminal will walk away from a serious crime in DelMarVa. By doing so, we will deter future serious crime in our state. Frankly, I don't particularly care if criminals are afraid to come here and commit their crimes elsewhere. Eventually, other states will follow our lead and murderers will have nowhere to go. Until then, we'll make the punishment here certain and severe— and that should keep a majority of them away.

"Our conviction rate on serious crime is 86 percent. We have the best tools, the best police force, sympathetic judges and a supportive populace. In addition, you all have been recruited and each of you was in the top 10 percent of your graduating class. We sought you out. You were referred. You would not have gotten this far if we did not believe you have the talent and common sense to do your job better than the best defense attorney that money can buy. And,"

McDevitt paused, smiled and added, "they are bought and paid for very well to get their guilty clients off."

A brief response of laughter broke the stiffness in the air.

"If there are any questions, now is the time to ask them."

"Sir," a hand rose from a man in the middle of the last row. McDevitt nodded, and the young man identified himself, "Jerome Stahtley, Jessup, Maryland, sir. Is it true that if we lose a certain number of cases we are fired? I heard that rumor and wanted to get a clarification from you."

"It's not that harsh," Matthew Gordon said, stepping to McDevitt's side. "If you lose three capital cases, you will be counseled and your entire team, not only you, will be reviewed. We analyze every case that we lose—looking at police procedures, evidence handling, courtroom testimony and case preparation. We want to see how we can improve our efforts the next time. We will not fire you, but you will receive remedial training until we decide you are able to carry a satisfactory caseload and move back to an active courtroom role.

"We are paying you $75,000 to start—double the compensation of the average, graduating attorney. We expect results. Let's be honest. You are here to put criminals away. Your high salary is not a government giveaway program, and, I would like to add that we look very favorably upon convictions that send defendants to death row in Gumwood."

McDevitt added, "We want them to have a very short stay and move them into their next and, hopefully, better life rather quickly."

There was nervous laughter in the room.

McDevitt interjected, "That's your job! If you can't do it, we don't want you taking up space. If we don't get solid convictions, we will act accordingly. We received more than 1,800 applicants for your positions. There are plenty of bright, eager and, most importantly, resourceful lawyers hoping you lose a lot of cases. They are waiting for your offices. We've even received applications from some of the best defense attorneys that we have beaten in court. Does that answer your question?"

Stahtley nodded.

"Anything else?" Gordon asked the group.

"I assume," said Nathan Dorset, a black lawyer from San Antonio, Texas, "there might be a tendency to break the rules to remain on the job?"

McDevitt spoke up. "Yes, Mr. Dorset, that's been considered. Let me clarify this for all of you. We are not running around ripping up the laws of DelMarVa and the Constitution of the United States. However, for decades the law has been slanted in favor of criminals. I'd like you to pause a moment and consider what is wrong with the following picture:

"In this grand, wonderful country of ours, the most *civilized* on earth, criminals follow no rules, have access to the deadliest weapons, can travel at will and, if convicted, enjoy free legal assistance, medical care and education while in jail.

"Hard working citizens, on the other hand, are supposed to live by the rules, register their firearms and pay their own way for all services. If they are victimized, they are subjected to the insulting antics of *enlightened* and *caring* and *loving* members of an unlimited number of federally funded, bleeding-heart organizations. These misguided dimwits fight to grab the microphone and pose in front of TV cameras to defend scum—whether they be rapists, serial murderers, drug dealers, child molesters or white collar criminals.

"These people—who live in security-protected estates far away from street crime—say they want to make sure the criminal is treated fairly. Well, I don't give a tinker's damn about the criminal, or his family, or his needs, opinions or rights. In my mind, and in this state, he or she gave up any rights when they pulled the trigger or crossed over to the bad side.

"We are fighting back. One dramatic change is by hiring the best talent we can find to level the playing field. In this state we own the field and the ballpark and, as a result, we've adjusted the rules. Also, if we have to tilt the field to our advantage, we damn well will. Hopefully, each of you accredited, *summa cum laude* brainiacs should be able to win these cases with your intelligence and legal skill. We do not want our people breaking the law. But, if we can creatively pool our wisdom to make sure a killer doesn't get off to strike again, we most certainly will do so."

McDevitt paused, then added, "Now is the time for anyone uncomfortable with this arrangement to leave. I'm very serious. We will not think less of you, and we will help you find a position doing some meaningless corporate or business law work that will pay your bills, get you a big house, a new car and membership into the elite country clubs—and most certainly leave you unfulfilled and devoid of principle. But, if that's your choice, say so, now.

"We live in a screwed up world, ladies and gentlemen, and the working people out there, who are trying to bring up their kids and play by the rules, need our help. It's up to us to keep them safe."

McDevitt was finished. No one spoke or moved. He thanked the new prosecutors for their time and walked over to Matthew Gordon. The two men shook hands.

As Gordon moved to the front of the room, McDevitt stood in the doorway, just about to leave, when he turned and said, "I'm sorry, Matt. But, I have to say just one more thing."

Everyone turned to face the governor, whose face was somber and thoughtful. He spoke softly, but each word was delivered in a measured, deliberate tone. "Never forget this, ladies and gentlemen. Evil does truly exist. There are some people whose bodies do not contain the slightest shred of humanity. Their souls are as rotten as the stench of roadkill in the August sun. They are beyond rehabilitation or redemption in this life or the next. To think that we can transform them into functioning members of society is ludicrous and a disservice to law abiding citizens."

His audience was still.

McDevitt paused, looked up and then concluded, by saying. "I have seen genuine evil in my lifetime more than once. And I have vowed that it will be destroyed."

Wednesday

It was the middle of the week in the middle of October by the time Darryll Potters finally drove up the gravel lane and stopped his car in the front of the Gobbler's Knoll farmhouse. His scheduled three-week excursion easily turned into four. Several planned one-hour visits with other cop retirees along the way became overnights, and most of them magically extended into weekends—all adding more time to his original trip. Finally, he realized if he continued to visit old friends and take spur-of-the-moment excursions off the main roads, he wouldn't make it to his family farm until Christmas.

His mother's property was four miles north of downtown Dire's Mill. It was nearly 120 acres with close to three miles of road frontage. The terrain was flat, like most of the lower end of the peninsula. About 60 percent of the Knoll was tillable, 25 percent was in woods and the remaining 15 percent wetlands and marsh.

The attorney who had handled his mother's estate had mailed Darryll the keys. Slowly, he approached the front door of a home he hadn't seen in more than two decades. He had made a return trip a few years ago for his mother's funeral, but couldn't bring himself to visit the property—only going to Dire's Funeral Parlor and then heading back to Maine.

So many memories, so many tears.

Too few moments of laughter, he thought.

Pausing, he recalled the darkness under the front porch, where he and his friends would hide to keep out of the summer rain. The "Boy's Club" they had called it at the time.

In the distance, he saw the fat limb of the ancient oak where his father—his real father, Darryll Sr.—had rigged up a swing, right beside the smokehouse. That pleasant memory was overshadowed as he recalled the dark, dirty smokehouse outbuilding where Lenny Shamp, Darryll's stepfather, had given him "whoopin's" more times than he wanted to remember.

Back to the present. The front door needed painting. The walls needed painting. "Hell!" Darryll said, aloud, "the whole damn place needs painting, in and out. And not just the house. The barn, stable. I'm a goddamn fool!"

Then he entered, surveyed the living room and fell into a chair. Covering his eyes with his hands, silence and a swift concentration of more childhood memory flashes turned into sobs, then tears. To have been away for so long. To not have seen his mother before she died. What a waste. Darryll shook his head, blaming himself and his stubbornness.

Gobbler's Knoll had been her family's land, and Gertrude Merrille Potters (later Shamp) had saved the legacy for her only child—Darryll. After the funeral, his mother's lawyer told Darryll that she had arranged to allow Lenny Shamp to live in the house until he died, but she had willed her entire estate to Darryll, and he would be notified when Lenny kicked off.

The good news came at the right time, at the very end of his career path. But, being back, he realized there were too many wasted years in between, so much he had wanted to tell her.

Still, Darryll thought, *what was I supposed to do? Lenny would beat the hell outta me, and she would just watch for a few seconds and walk upstairs and lock her door. Lie on the bed with a pillow over her ears so she didn't hear her own son's screams. She was afraid of Lenny leaving, and I was afraid of him staying.*

When he was in his last year of high school, Darryll told his mother it was either him or his step-father. Without hesitation, she told Darryll he had to leave. The day after graduation, he went straight over to Salisbury and joined the Army. He spent six years in the MPs and came out with a lot of investigative experience that he figured someone would find attractive.

He was turned down for the first three law enforcement positions that he had applied for. But, number four, a small sheriff's department in a rural county, offered him an assignment as a deputy.

When Darryll looked at the county's location in a book-type world atlas, he had difficulty finding his new home. With magnifying glass in hand, he realized that Washington County, Maine, was not far from the Canadian border. With a minimum of personal possessions and a heart filled with hope he headed north to start a new life—planning never to look back. He didn't need or want to remember his past. At that time in his life it wasn't important, only a bag of troubles that would drag him down.

For years, he didn't write to his mother, never even called. He hated her almost as much as he hated his real father for dying when Darryll was so young and needed him so much. But he intensely despised that no good bastard Lenny for the abuse, the broken nose, the crushed fingers, the cigarette burns on his stomach, where his stepfather said the teachers would never see them.

God, thought Darryll, *I'm glad that no good heathen bastard is dead, and he can rot in hell forever.*

Looking across the room at a photograph of his mother kneeling with Duke, his long-gone Chesapeake Bay retriever, Darryll shouted, "But you had to be such an idiot! You had to make me go. If you would have just told him to leave, I would have come right back."

"But, we were both stupid*,"* Darryll answered himself. His tone was quieter, weaker.

He got up, shook his head and stopped regretting the missing moments, lost years, unspoken words. *Nothing could be done about it. This was now, he was here. Just got to move on. Clean the place up. Hell, in my job, I've seen families deal with a hellava lot worse than this.*

He walked out of the parlor. But, as he headed for the kitchen, he noticed a picture of his mother, near the back kitchen door, holding a pie.

He held it up, paused for one more memory. About 10 years after he left home, she started to keep in touch. He sent her a letter, and then she started to mail him cards and photographs twice a year—but she had him reply through a local lady friend. She didn't want Darryll's letters coming to the house. Against Lenny's wishes, she had even traveled by bus to Maine, eight years ago, to attend the promotion ceremony when Darryll made detective.

That was it. No more memories today, Darryll thought. He got busy, emptied his car, cleaned out the kitchen and his bedroom, prepared his old home for his new life.

While getting a glass of water from the kitchen sink, he looked at the table and noticed a stack of unopened mail—dozens of circulars, credit card offers, catalogs, bank statements. The vast majority were addressed to his deceased parents. The rest were advertisements and junk. Most went directly into the trash.

A personally typed envelope in the middle of the pile caught his eye—it was one of the few letters addressed to him: Darryll Potters. The return address indicated it was from Dire Real Estate. He moved toward the kitchen table, took a seat and ripped the white envelope with his fingers.

As he leaned back into the wooden chair, his eyes scanned the letter, dated only three days earlier.

Dear Mr. Potters:

We are sorry to hear of the death of your wonderful father. He was a pillar of the community and he will surely be missed by his family and friends. However, during your grief, we suggest that you look upon his passing as a blessed event that may result in a financial opportunity for you and your kin.

Dire Real Estate is prepared to offer you $150,000 cash for your property. Based on market comparisons of *similar estates that have sold during the last 18 months, our price is well above the market value of your acreage and structures, which are in a state of disrepair and may face possible county condemnation. In addition, as a free service to you, our appraisers have taken the liberty to conduct perk tests throughout your acreage for your benefit. These independent surveyors have determined that your ground, while visually appealing, is unable to support residential or industrial development.*

Also, the commissioner's council of Dire's Mill hundred has reviewed the parcel and has ruled that it cannot be used for any commercial purpose other than its present agricultural use.

However, inspectors from the Dire's Mill Building Inspection Division have told us that their colleagues in the county will soon cite you for a number of structural defects existing on your property, and you will have 30 days to correct these violations. After that date, members of the Dire's Mill Sheriff's Department will be authorized to present you with substantial fines levied by the council.

To help you at this confusing and difficult time, I, personally, or one of my representatives, would be glad to meet with you and arrange to sign the documents necessary to take this derelict property off your hands.

The legal papers have been prepared and are currently in my office. There is no need for you to secure the services of an attorney. We have had our corporate counsel prepare all of the documents and we have assumed these costs—which, I add, have cost us several thousand dollars—as a sign of our good will and interest in your welfare.

Feel free to call my office, in the Dire Federated Equity Savings and Loan and schedule an appointment at your earliest convenience.

Once again, my sympathy for your personal loss, but a wise man like yourself should possess a realistic attitude that sees this as an opportunity to turn tragedy into profit.

Sincerely,
Craig Dire V
President, Dire's Mill Real Estate
President, Dire Federated Equity Savings and Loan

Darryll shook his head and controlled his initial urge to rip up the letter into shreds. The offer might come in handy at a later time. But, he thought, it sure didn't take long for the Dires to start meddling in his life. From the content of the letter it was obvious that the Dire family's influence had not diminished in the last 25 years. And, he guessed that the present patriarch was at least as bad as his predecessors.

Shoving the offer into his back pocket, Darryll walked outside, got in his car and headed toward town.

He might as well get the meeting over with. It was 2:30. He could make it into town and get to the bank before it closed at 3 o'clock.

4

lthough Dire's Mill was only a five-minute ride from Gobbler's Knoll, Darryll slammed down on the gas pedal of his Pontiac and watched the speedometer quickly move beyond 70. October still had about two weeks left, but the corn was brown, or plowed under, and the geese that hadn't decided to winter in the DelMarVa marshes were flying in large V-shaped formations, heading a bit further south.

Just as he released the pressure of his right foot to level his speed at 65, Darryll stared at the long stretch of flat road ahead, preparing for the hairpin turn across Blood Gut Creek that would be coming up within the next mile.

As he glanced in his rearview mirror, he noticed the flashing lights of a blue gray DelMarVa State Police cruiser 10 feet off his back bumper.

"Damn!" he swore aloud, easing off the gas and pulling onto the shoulder.

Rolling down the window, he grabbed his license and registration, preparing for the conversation with the officer who would soon approach his driver's door. He knew the routine and decided to accept the citation.

He remembered when he worked highway speed traps, the worst pains in the ass were cops passing— no, flying—through Washington County from other states. Because they had a Fraternal Order of Police sticker and flashed him their badge—even if it was from Kansas or Arizona—they expected to get a free pass. He never gave one, and he never asked for one in return.

"Good afternoon, Mr. Potters," the tall, dark-haired officer said, as he leaned down and looked inside the window.

"Afternoon," Darryll replied, suddenly realizing that there was no way that his name should be known by the unfamiliar cop.

"Hey! How did you know my name?"

"I'll have to ask you to step out of the car, Mr. Potters, and then place your hands on the roof of your car. Turn around very slowly, please."

Darryll started to protest, but then decided to let it go. This would be over in a few minutes. He was surprised at the caution the troopers took with such a minor traffic stop, but, maybe this was how it was done by the book in the law and order capital of the world.

As he turned to face his car, a second police officer appeared, approached Darryll from the right and said, "Please understand that this is all for your bene-fit, Mr. Potters. In two seconds after I stop talking, I am going to shove you toward the ground, and then my partner and I are going to subdue you and place handcuffs on your wrists, behind your back. Then we will place you into the back of our patrol car. You can resist if you desire, but, if that happens, it could get a little rough."

"What the hell are . . . ."

Before Darryll could get further into his sentence, Trooper B, whose nameplate said L. Higgins, yanked on Darryll's right shoulder and pulled him toward the back of the car. At the same time, Trooper A, named T. Merrick, swept Darryll's feet off the ground. The recently retired Maine detective hit the highway hard, scraping his face and injuring his right shoulder. It took only seconds for the two troopers to cuff the speeder and pull him back onto his feet.

"Cut out the shit!" Darryll shouted as the arresting officers gripped him by his elbows, pulled him up and moved him forward. Suddenly, as they reached the rear of the Pontiac, they slammed Darryll's back onto the curved trunk. Taking a hunk of Darryll's hair, Higgins pulled their victim forward as Merrick punched Darryll swiftly in the gut.

After the air escaped his chest and Darryll bent over to try to suck in the smallest sliver of oxygen, he whispered, "There's got to be a mistake." His voice was hardly heard, a nearly silent hiss is all that escaped his throat and lips.

"No mistake, Mr. Potters," Trooper Higgins said, as he pointed toward the marked highway sedan. With T. Merrick's assistance, he dragged Darryll's still bent body toward their cruiser. His shoe tips stumbled as he tried to regain his footing and make his legs move forward.

Quickly depositing their catch in the rear seat, L. Higgins got on the radio and checked in. "This is DMV 108, speeding suspect in custody. On our way to the house. Charges will include speeding, reckless driving, resisting arrest and assault on arresting officers. That's it, 10-4."

Hearing the transmission, Darryll opened his eyes and began to lean his head toward the black mesh grill that separated the arresting officers from their prisoner. "You assholes! That's a crock of bullshit. I'll have your goddamn badges and shove your asses in a wringer as soon as . . ."

Darryll's voice stopped suddenly as he felt a hand grab his right arm.

Previously unnoticed in the rear of the car was a man dressed in a dark sport jacket. He pulled Darryll's arm toward him and started to speak.

"Who the hell are you?" Darryll snapped. He could feel the heat from the raw open wound on the right of his face.

"Please, give me a minute and I'll explain," the man said. He was calm, smiled and held up a key, indicating that it was to open the locked handcuffs.

Darryll paused, looked up and saw Trooper Merrick in the passenger seat nodding and heard him say, "Sorry. We didn't mean to get rough out there, but you gave us no choice."

"Yeah! Well, I'd watch my back, asshole! 'Cause I aim to get even."

"I can understand your anger and confusion, Mr. Potters, but, if you'll be patient, I'm sure I can explain to your satisfaction."

"Who the hell are you?" Darryll asked as the stranger unlocked the metal cuffs and let them fall onto the floor of the car.

"My name's Mike Pentak, police commissioner of DelMarVa. We're going to go for a little ride, meet a few people. Then, when we're done, I think you'll understand completely."

As DMV 108 headed away from the road leading to Dire's Mill, Sheriff's Deputy Wallace J. Smythe put in a call to headquarters. "You can tell Mr. Dire that our boy ain't comin' in. He got hisself picked up by the state boys and they look like they're takin' him to the barracks over in Salisbury, as far as I can tell."

The dispatcher asked for more of an explanation before he called over to the bank and reported to Mr. Dire.

"All I can tell is, our boy never made it past Blood Gut. Got pulled over for speedin' and tried to make tough with the two biggest troopers I ever saw. Hell! They gave him a goin' over, I tell ya. That Maine detective ain't gonna be walkin' upright for a week, at least, far as I can see. Figure they got 'im for 35 miles over, resistin' and assault of a police officer. He'll have to do some good talkin' to be out before tomorrow. I say we shut down for now and maybe wait 'til we get word from our boy inside the state office."

The Dire's Mill Sheriff's Office dispatcher ordered Wallace Smythe to stay put for an answer.

The reply came less than a minute later. "Mr. Dire says fine, Wallace. Wrap it up. We'll catch Mr. Potters when he comes into town next time."

"A-OK. I'm headin' in."

⌇   ⌇   ⌇   ⌇

Moving at high speed with flashers blazing, DMV 108 was out of the jurisdiction of Dire's Mill and heading down a deserted two-lane straight-away. There was no conversation inside the car.

In slightly more than a half hour since he had been slammed against the highway blacktop, Darryll Potters, uncuffed and the recipient of several apologies, exited the troopers' sedan. Bent forward, he and Michael Pentak headed for a black helicopter that had been waiting across a barren soybean field and surrounded by scattered unused chicken buildings and warehouses.

They were airborne in less than a minute.

Pointing down to the landing field, Darryll shouted to Pentak, "What's this place?"

"It used to be called Fort Augustine. Was a German POW camp in World War II. They used Nazi prisoners as farm workers and road crews in the last few years of the war. Had about 700 housed here. The airfield's been upgraded and we use it from time to time. The buildings have been left alone. Helps keep tourists out of the area and makes the place look more undesirable and threatening. Every now and then, we place a few migrant workers out here for show, so nobody gets suspicious."

"Where are we going?"

"To Liberty Manor, a safe house complex on Slaughter Island, at Deep Creek Refuge. We've got someone we want you to meet, Detective."

"So, you seem to know who I am. When do I find out about you?"

"In about 20 minutes," Pentak said, closing his eyes and leaning his head back against the padded headrest of his seat inside the chopper.

Darryll looked forward, at the pilot, and then turned to his left and stared down at the marshes and flatlands. He'd been home less than an hour and already was involved in something he hadn't looked for. But that was nothing new, except he thought it would have stopped when he quit the force. Darryll wasn't looking for complications and tension, just a fresh start and a simple life—growing some tomatoes, selling produce, steaming a bushel of crabs and getting a dog to sit on the porch with.

Something in the back of his mind was telling him those simple plans would have to wait.

Stephanie and Henry McDevitt had just completed dinner in the dining room of Woodburn. The couple asked the two state police officers—who had been in the small security room that housed the mansion's video monitors and alarms—to join them for coffee in the first floor living room.

The two men were hesitant to accept. The governor and his wife were newlyweds and the officers did not want to intrude, especially in the early days of the new romance. Before the wedding, they would sit with Governor McDevitt and Commissioner Pentak, discussing crime, punishment, women and sports, but the officers knew that circumstances had changed.

Seeing their hesitation, Stephanie insisted and the four sat and talked. For more than a half-hour the two men, State Police Corporal Tom White, who had worked in the Salisbury Barracks, and Mitch Gutterpaus, formerly of the Claymont Barracks, talked and joked about life in general—kids, work, hobbies and sports. Eventually, the topic turned to crime.

"So you were with Chief Tom Brennan in Claymont?" McDevitt asked Gutterpaus.

"Right, sir. I served there about three years."

"Did Brennan complain to you about the lack of crime? Commissioner Pentak says that at about every fourth chief's meeting, your former commander will voice his concern that the men in his command don't have enough criminals to chase down. How do you feel about that?"

Feeling awkward, the trooper began to formulate a careful response.

Seeing his predicament, Stephanie cut in, "Hank, it isn't fair to ask Officer Gutterpaus to comment on his commander. You're making him feel like a snitch. Right?" She turned to look at the trooper she had rescued.

"Well, begging the governor's pardon," Gutterpaus said haltingly, "it's a bit awkward for me to reply, sir. So I tend to agree to a large degree with the First Lady's observation, sir."

The officer was sweating. He had just told his ultimate boss that the question was inappropriate and he may have instigated a lover's quarrel.

"Relax, trooper," McDevitt said. "You're correct to agree with my wife. Hell," McDevitt said, laughing, "I always do. And," he said, smiling and looking directly at Stephanie, "not for the sake of agreeing, but because she always seems to be right."

The quartet laughed, and Stephanie raised her coffee cup to toast her husband.

Throughout the brief conversation, Trooper Tom White remained silent, doing his best to continue to exist unnoticed by any of the others. He did not want to find himself in the same situation as Gutterpaus. But luck doesn't last forever.

"So, what about you, White?" McDevitt said, "What do you think about the crime rate around Salisbury.

Were you busy down there, or were you able to read magazines like they seem to do up in Claymont?"

"We were plenty busy, sir. Just because we're starting to get more control over serious crimes like murder and assault, there still are a number of other areas that need serious attention."

"Like what?" Stephanie asked.

"Drugs, Mrs. McDevitt," he replied. "You can't believe the amount of coke and hash and new experimental stuff that comes in. We find it near the campus in Salisbury. But it's in the summer when it gets really bad. I've pulled details in Ocean City and outside Pirate's Cove, down in Accomack County. We're always finding the stuff, and in large quantities."

"So you won't work yourself out of a job?" Stephanie asked, smiling.

"That's not our worry," White replied. "Even with the high tech gear, increased manpower and better legislation, drugs still seem to be getting in."

"Same thing up our way, sir," Gutterpaus interjected. "Loads of it fly down I-95, hour after hour. God knows how much just rides right by us—in tractor trailers, false car panels and trunks, inside spare tires and even in plastic bags inside drivers and passengers. They swallow the stuff and then pass it out the other end of their system at delivery."

"That's sickening," Stephanie said, shaking her head.

"And dangerous," McDevitt added. "If that bag rips while it's inside the courier's body, it's certain death as the dope hits the poor bastard's system at full force."

"I've seen it happen," White said, "and it's not pretty. But, I've learned one thing in this job: You can never be surprised by what people will do for money. Aren't I right about that, Gutts?" White looked over at his partner.

"Absolutely," Gutterpaus replied. "People will sell their bodies, their family heirlooms, even their kids, for just enough money to buy a single dose of coke to get them through the next hour. Then, they'll go out and do it again. We may have problems, but they're nothing like what goes on in Philly and in the big cities. It's blatant up there. I don't know how those officers can stand working those streets. They get no support. They catch a dealer or a user or a pimp, and they're out in an hour, giving the officer the finger right in front of the police station. I've seen it happen."

Gutterpaus shook his head, amazed and thankful at the same time.

"You must have been talking to Commissioner Pentak. You know he was a detective in the City of Brotherly Love?" McDevitt asked.

"Yes, sir. We've heard he was their top homicide case closer," Gutterpaus said.

"He was," McDevitt said, "and we were very fortunate to get him here, working with us. But," the governor said, pausing a moment, "getting back to what you said before, it sounds like your job is similar to the story of the little boy in the dike. When you close one hole up, or resolve one emergency, another opens up, and then another, and then another."

The two officers nodded, agreeing with the assessment.

"So why do you do it?" Stephanie asked, joining the conversation. "If it's an occupation where you can never finish what you've started, where you can never solve the problem, why do you do it? Why risk your life to do a thankless, impossible job for people who don't seem to care?"

Neither man responded at first, then White looked at the governor and toward the First Lady. Proudly, but softly, he replied, "Somebody has to catch the bad guys, ma'am."

Immediately, Gutterpaus nodded, showing his agreement. "That's right. If we don't get them, who else will? It's what we do, and we do it well."

❧   ❧   ❧   ❧

Pentak led Darryll into the entry hall of Liberty Manor. The three-story-high foyer impressed every visitor and Darryll's reaction was no different than those who had stood in the same spot on previous occasions.

At least three dozen animal heads, stuffed and staring, looked down on the two intruders. His eyes went quickly from North American bison to African elephant, from a pair of Bengal tigers to a mammoth snarling black bear that hung beside a Canadian moose. Assorted smaller trophies—including ducks, fish and fowl—were interspersed among the big prizes.

The Victorian-style lodge had been built by a ship builder and import dealer in the late 19th century. The stock market crash of 1929 ruined his business and caused him to hang himself from the third floor railing. The interior was totally built of wood and subsequent residents said the builder's ghost had been seen walking the balconies, carrying a lantern and seeking the eternal peace that had not yet arrived.

Hearing the bell announce the arrival of the elevator door, Darryll Potters turned and stared at the bookshelf from where the ringing sound had come. As the 8-foot-square bookcase moved to the side, a pair of sliding doors opened to allow entry into the traveling chamber that transported visitors to the hidden rooms on the lower levels of the lodge.

Darryll expected to see Ernest Hemingway appear as the dull silver doors moved aside. Instead, DelMarVa Governor Henry McDevitt walked into the entry hall and extended his hand.

"Detective Potters, I'm Hank McDevitt. Thanks for coming." McDevitt had gotten Pentak's message, boarded a chopper at the State Police Headquarters in Dover and had arrived only 15 minutes earlier.

Still annoyed and confused, Darryll responded, "It wasn't like I had much of a choice."

"I understand," McDevitt said. "My apologies, but we had to get to you before you headed into town. And," he glanced at Michael Pentak, "we wanted to make sure that anyone watching would believe that you were taken away against your will."

"Well, I can tell you, your two goons accomplished that part of their mission. They cracked me pretty good. Now I'd like to know what the hell's going on and why I'm here and when I get to leave."

McDevitt smiled. "Of course," he said, indicating that Darryll should enter the elevator. "We'll explain all of this downstairs."

Pentak and McDevitt led him into the chamber. As the door closed, Pentak pushed the letter D. As the elevator descended, McDevitt explained that the lower floors of the lodge were added during World War II, as a center to monitor sea traffic in the Chesapeake Bay. Radar and surveillance technology at the time were concerned with German submarine infiltration, which could cripple domestic and military shipping, especially cargo bound in and out of Baltimore and through the C & D Canal.

Although never publicized, the "Eastern Shore Underground Network," with several complexes on both sides of the Chesapeake Bay shoreline, was responsible for identifying and directing U.S. Coast Guard sub chasers to more than 68 unpublicized "kills" of Nazi subs.

By the mid-1950s, the secret sites were abandoned and tuned over to the state of Maryland. Most were sealed up with concrete. A few were used for storage of munitions and disaster relief supplies and communications equipment. The one on Slaughter Island became Maryland's Emergency Communications Control Center, renovated to operate as the state government's headquarters during a natural or military disaster—particularly in the event Annapolis, Maryland's capital city, ever had to be evacuated.

"About two years ago," Pentak interjected, "we did some extensive remodeling. We use the A floor, the first beneath the surface, for training. The next two—B and C—house high tech interrogation chambers, all climate controlled, with the very latest audio and video technology. They've come in handy for serious interrogations of some prisoners who were a little more reluctant, or uncooperative, than others.

"There are several medical staff who live on the grounds. We're surrounded by 600 acres of Deep Creek Refuge and only accessible by water or air. We don't take kindly to unannounced visitors," Pentak added, smiling.

McDevitt interrupted,. "Here were are, gentlemen, Level D. Please, come this way into my office."

The men walked past four civilian-clothed guards who nodded, moving only their chins and eyes, at DelMarVa's governor as he passed.

McDevitt pressed his hand against a square gray leather pad affixed at waist-level to the wall on the right side of the door. A green pulsing light blinked softly about the entryway and the three men entered.

They took seats, all made of dark padded leather, directly in front of a massive desk that was dwarfed below the State of DelMarVa official seal that hung on the large wall.

The room was impressive, thought Darryll, his eyes darting from the colonial style furniture—including the desk, chairs, secretary, bookshelves and computer table. The hardwood floors led to a private restroom and an alcove that accommodated a large conference table that could seat 20. At the far end was a blank wall that served as a screen for the recessed projection equipment that was built into the ceiling.

On the desk were photographs of McDevitt and his wife. There also was a photo of an elderly couple with two young boys, about 15 and 10. Darryll assumed the older one was his host. The younger one had to be Georgie, the youngster that was beaten to death by the same two drunks who had killed McDevitt's fiancee many years ago.

Darryll recalled the details from the stories about the former Delaware governor when he ran for President of the United States and almost won the whole damn election. It was all over the news and in every major newspaper and magazine. You had to be dead, blind or totally illiterate to be unaware of Henry McDevitt.

He and then-Maryland Governor Lydia Chase—who currently served as vice governor of DelMarVa—

had run on the Victims Rights Coalition. To the surprise of many and fear of some, the VRC attracted so many votes that the presidential election of 2004 almost ended up in the House of Representatives.

A last minute pullout by McDevitt insured the election of Scott Woodyard. Within the next two years, the Congress approved the formation of the new state of DelMarVa, describing it as an experiment in regional government. The legislation stated that the peninsula's jurisdiction and effectiveness would be examined to see if it would apply to other unusually-shaped geographic locations—such as areas in north-western Florida, the northern tip of West Virginia and the Panhandle of Oklahoma. In all these areas, governance and delivery of services was difficult and might be more efficient if new state lines were drawn.

A strict, no nonsense approach to crime, with fewer appeals and swifter executions of convicted murderers, had resulted in a dramatic reduction in killings and serious crime. Relocation of major manufacturing plants, plus five new casinos and a popular theme park created minimal unemployment and a bulging state treasury. Within a year of his inauguration, DelMarVa state income taxes were eliminated.

As an added bonus, the state police force was consolidated—to incorporate the former officers in the affected counties of the three states—and the starting salary for law enforcement officers was $65,000 a year. It was said that a number of CIA, FBI and Military Intelligence retirees were serving as McDevitt's investigators and in special anti-terrorist and anti-white-collar crime divisions.

So, Darryll wondered, why was he here, and why was he roughed up on his way into Dire's Mill?

Pentak began by thanking Darryll for his patience, then he started to explain the background on the formation of DelMarVa and the pro-victim, anti-criminal philosophy.

"You can cut the history lesson, Mr. Pentak," snapped Darryll. "My mother lived here and she was in love with the governor," he nodded toward McDevitt. "She would send me clippings in the mail. She especially liked the execution of a few years back when you threw the switch on Sugar Daddy Looney yourself. That was a big hit with her, and with all the cops up my way, too. Anyway, I know about your state. I moved down here. No, make that *tried* to move back down here. Have gotten jumped, beaten, kidnapped and received a letter from this asshole, who owns the county, telling me if I don't take his offer my land is going to be condemned. And all this in four hours of getting in the door. God only knows what's going to happen tomorrow. Other than that, I've had a great welcome home. So, if you've got something interesting to say, make if fast, 'cause I'm about to my limit with guess what's behind door number 3."

Pentak leaned forward and began to talk quickly. "We have a problem, Mr. Potters."

"Cut the 'mister' crap. Darryll's fine. Go on."

"Fine. Darryll. We have an investigation concerning Craig Dire. The . . ."

"The royal asshole who owns just about everything in the whole town and county and who wants to run me out of my house. So, what's new? His father was an asshole. His grandfather and all the greats were assholes. Why should he be any different?"

"We don't expect him to be different, Darryll. Our purpose is to arrest him and convict him of at least one murder and perhaps up to more than a dozen disappearances. In addition, there are numerous less serious charges—like gambling, loan sharking, intimidation of witnesses, fraud, money laundering. The list is a long one."

"So, why don't you just go into town and shoot the bastard in the head, hook him to a bumper and drag him down Main Street of Dire's Mill? We heard how you people do things down here. Quick, dirty and permanent."

McDevitt jumped in, annoyed at the sarcastic comment. "Okay, Potters, let's cut the crap. First, we don't run around assassinating criminals with our secret DelMarVa version of the old CIA hit squads. If you heard that, you've heard wrong. We do make sure those who are convicted get punished, and punished hard. But anything else is the result of the overactive imagination of the writers of the supermarket tabloids. We're here to seek your help to solve a serious problem. If you're interested, fine. If not, you'll be taken back to your home. But, we need you to have an open mind and hear us out."

"Also," Pentak added, "we might have saved your neck today. There was a sheriff's vehicle waiting for you near Blood Gut Creek. He was there expecting you to go flying into town. It would have been real convenient for Craig Dire's sake to have you show up in a car wreck off the edge of that narrow bridge. Then he could legally steal your property and no one would be around to care."

"All right," Darryll said, leaning back in his chair. "What's the story? I'm calm now and I'm listening."

Pentak explained about the accidental disappearance at sea of Craig Dire's first wife. Shortly afterwards, the accidental deaths of her three relatives who had spoken of serious trouble in Dire's Mill Mansion raised a red flag and investigators opened a file—one that was still pending and unsolved.

"There's a link there somewhere," McDevitt added. "We just haven't found it yet. Also, there is Craig Dire's gambling and outside business interests."

"Craig and his second wife," Pentak added, "who he met in an Atlantic City cocktail lounge, have a condo in A.C. They visit there at least three or four times a month and drop big bucks. I'm talking 10 grand a weekend, and sometimes up to 50 Gs. All cash, and obviously not coming from his legitimate businesses. Real estate, farming, hardware, crabbing and the family funeral parlor activity can only bring in so much. Plus, that all has to be accounted for. This is coming from somewhere else, and we want to find out the source."

"Does he gamble in DelMarVa?"

"Rarely," McDevitt replied. "We have a strict limit on the amount of money DelMarVa citizens can spend in our five casinos. It's tied to their annual income and each person has to place a special card in the slot machine or give it to the pit boss. Anyone outside the state can spend as much as they want, but not our citizens. Dire went through his monthly limit on his first visit and we had to escort him and his wife out of our Chesapeake Casino in Cambridge. He swore he would never come back. No loss. But our people have tailed him to A.C. and kept a tally of his spending and losses. He's definitely got a deep pocket source. We want to know who it is and what he's doing to get it."

"So you want me to do you a favor and snoop around?" Darryll asked his hosts.

"Not quite. We would like to hire you as a consultant. There will be $1,000 a month, to be placed in an account in the bank of your choice. We'd strongly recommend Dover or Salisbury. You decide. You'll use your own judgment regarding your dealings with Craig Dire over your property. However, we are particularly interested in anything you can find out about his first wife's disappearance, the deaths of her relatives and his current business operations."

"Look," Darryll cut in, "I was a resort cop and part-time homicide and missing persons detective up in Maine. I'm sorry to disappoint you, but we only had a killing once every few years, not like down here. Don't expect too much."

"We know what to expect," Pentak said. "We have a copy of your military personnel file and your Washington County Police Department records. We're aware of every case you solved and those that you didn't."

Darryll turned, immediately thinking of the six runaways that still bothered him after so many years.

"If you agree, you can take these folders," Pentak said, pointing to three thick manila packets stacked on the nearby desk. "The top one contains biographical information and photos of Craig Dire, his present wife and their closest business associates. The second holds information on his first wife, very little on her disappearance, and material about her dead relatives. In the third are newspaper articles and historical information about Dire's Mill and the whole Dire clan.

"It goes back to the family's slave trading days when they made their big money, plus a bit on their smuggling, plus family poisonings, a few duels and the varied businesses they've owned. They adapted their business interests through the years, modifying with the changing economy. It should all prove helpful and be good reading."

"There's no guarantee I'll find anything out," Darryll said.

"There's never a guarantee," Pentak answered, "but there's always a chance. What we're seeking is a break. You'll look at this with a fresh eye. You know the area, know some of the people. You'll live there and be one of them. Anything you can find out might be the one special part of this puzzle that will lead to the start of the solution."

"How long do I have?"

"There's no time limit. You'll be paid for a full year, even if you bail out after two days or change your mind," Pentak explained. "You go into it and decide. The money is yours no matter what. But, from what I've read in your file, you'll come on board, and you won't stay on this for the money. You'll be eager to help us put this guy away."

"You have your little meeting with Craig Dire," McDevitt interjected. "After that, there's absolutely no doubt in my mind that you will be more than happy to help us fry his no good, rotten ass."

"Sounds like you know him pretty well," Darryll said.

"Oh, I do," McDevitt said. "I've seen him kill a man and get away with it, more than 35 years ago. If he's totally innocent and as pure as the virgin birth, he still has to pay for that crime. And I am going to get him into a Death Row cell in Gumwood. That's one of my campaign promises to myself."

Although they both wanted to hear more, neither Pentak nor Darryll pursued the rest of McDevitt's story.

"So, are you in?" Pentak asked.

"Sure," Darryll said. "Of course, there are about a hundred details that I need to know. How to get in touch with you, if you need recordings, should I keep notes, how often you need a report, how I respond if I get into a jam? Little incidentals like that. I'll also assume that your people in the area will know I'm back on the job."

"We'll take care of all of that. Very few people are involved in this operation," Pentak said. "The two troopers who brought you in, of course."

"Of course," Darryll said, rubbing his sore shoulder. "Lurch and his uglier brother Igor."

Ignoring the comment, Pentak said, "Your contact in town is a guy named Mo the Know."

"Mo the Know? You've got to be kidding," Darryll said, rolling his eyes.

"No. He's undercover. Good man. He's been living the role in Dire's Mill for two years. Retired from Military Intelligence after 20, ran spies in Southeast Asia and the Middle East. Hates the Dires. His real name's so far hidden that I don't think he even remembers it. Currently, the records have him down as Maurice Knowles, but everyone calls him Mo the Know. You'll find out why.

"He makes a living taking tourists out for daytrips on his boat—*Little Mo*—crabbing, fishing. You can hook up with him in the Bay Wolf Saloon, just outside town, close to where Blood Gut Creek meets the bay. It's a rough place, but you've probably been in worse. Get him to take you out, and he'll fill you in, provide plenty of background. He'll be your contact to us.

"Also," Pentak passed Darryll a small piece of paper, "take this and memorize it. The number will get you in touch with me anytime. You call it and I'll know where you are. It has an immediate trace capability. If you're in a jam, use it. Don't wait too long. These people are bad news. Any questions?"

"Yeah. What about my car and how the hell do I get home?"

"We've entered your highway incident, complete with a resisting arrest citation, into the Salisbury Barracks. They also have you in the overnight lockup roster. Your name will appear in our computer records. Anyone from another police agency looking you up in the criminal division will see your name as an overnight. Tomorrow morning, we'll fly you to the jail, get you in the back door and have a cab waiting to take you back to your vehicle. You can meet Dire, then head to the Bay Wolf and bitch about the rough treatment. They'll love it."

"I assume the Dire's Mill Sheriff's Office is on the take."

"Good thinking," Pentak said, smiling. "So don't go there seeking any information."

The three men exchanged handshakes and an orderly, with no neck who looked like a professional wrestler, escorted Darryll Potters out of the sublevel chambers and into a comfortable guest room on the second floor.

Alone, McDevitt turned to Pentak and asked, "What do you think?"

"He's as good as any we've used before," Pentak replied.

"Right, but if that's the case, he could end up the same way. For his sake, I hope he's better than they were. Then maybe he'll stay alive."

5

Friday afternoon

After leaving the Salisbury jail, Darryll drove home, changed, then headed into Dire's Mill. With a new attitude and sense of purpose, he entered Dire Federated Equity Savings and Loan. Dressed in new jeans, an open collar white shirt and a dark blue sports jacket, he asked to see Craig Dire.

Unfortunately, the attractive receptionist explained that Mr. Dire was out for the day and would not return until Monday. Darryll said he'd stop back and headed for the Bay Wolf.

Three sad sack pickups, a rusted, refrigerated crab truck and a splintered stakebody were parked outside the rectangular wooden fortress. On the roof, a weathered sign proclaimed visitors had arrived at the Bay Wolf Saloon. Beside the brown block letters was the carved outline of a wolf, its head lifted, its mouth open, apparently howling toward the sky.

As Darryll entered the bar, late afternoon yellow and blue turned into midnight jet black. In the moments it took his eyes to adjust to night vision, seven regulars and a greasy headed bartender turned their heads and stood motionless facing the stranger.

Responding to their looks, Darryll snapped, "What's the problem, never seen a paying customer?"

Two guys feeling no pain and hugging the top of the bar laughed. The one sitting alone, a heavy guy two stools over, nodded and toasted his longneck bottle in Darryll's direction. The other four shooting pool stayed glued in place, cue sticks in their hands.

"Okay," Darryll said, speaking very slowly and looking at the pool shooters, "I'm . . going . . to . . walk . . over . . to . . the . . bar . . and . . buy . . me . . a . . nice . . cold . . beer." Turning to the bartender, he added, "Can you translate that sentence to the four morons in the pool parlor?"

Without speaking, the one nearest Darryll approached. As he got within striking distance, the boy raised his cue stick, aiming to hit the stranger across the head.

Darryll bent low and avoided the boy's swing that connected with the stale smoky air of the bar. Grabbing his attacker from behind and below, Darryll pulled out a 9 millimeter automatic and shoved the barrel hard into the soft front muscles of the boy's neck.

Watching, the other three heard Darryll say, at a very slow pace, "I . . said . . I . . am . . going . . to . . have . . a . . beer . . . . Then . . I . . may . . want . . to . . relax . . and . . unwind . . . . I . . am . . not . . looking . . for . . trouble . . . . Do . . you . . inbred . . idiots . . understand?"

The boy tried to speak, but the metal of the gun barrel restricted his ability to even squeak out sound.

Even in the darkness, from across the room the others could see their friend was turning an unsightly color, caused by his inability to get fresh breath into his lungs.

"Let him go!" someone shouted.

"All right!" Darryll replied, pulling the gun away from the boy's neck and suddenly smashing the side of the metal grip against his captive's head.

As the unconscious boy fell to the filthy floor, the trio started to move forward.

"Not so fast, boys," Darryll said, walking toward them with his weapon—held at eye level—and pointing and waving at the three frightened men. "If you are coming to pick up your friend and leave, fine. But, if you want a piece of me, I'm sure as hell going to take all three of you with me. Now, what is it?"

No one answered.

The sound of the round going off in the Bay Wolf caused the two sleeping drunks to stir. All eyes looked at the thin stream of sunlight shooting in through the fresh hole that Darryll had put in the ceiling and roof.

"The next one is lower and straighter. Understand dipshits?" Darryll shouted, his right foot on top of the first boy's face, his heel grinding into the boy's cheek and nose.

"You better get him out of here soon. I'm getting real nervous," Darryll said. "I might aim at the floor next. Then who do you think I'll hit first, this stupid kid or a Chinaman?"

"We don't want no trouble, man," one of the pool sharks said, tossing his stick onto the table and heading toward the boy on the floor. "Just let us get him and we're outta here. Okay?"

"Fine," Darryll said. "At least one of you can speak in full sentences."

As he backed up toward the bar, the three boys carried out their friend. A moment later, he heard two trucks drive off.

"Okay. Now how about that beer?" Darryll said to the man behind the bar.

"Allow me, friend," a heavy set man, sitting alone on the barstool, said. He had a thick crop of shiny black hair, an infectious smile and a wide girth that was held in place by two wide, red suspenders. "Have the first one on me," the jolly man said. "My name's Maurice Knowles, but everyone around here calls me Mo the Know."

Darryll took the big man's paw and returned a firm handshake, as Ape the Bartender set him up.

Side by side, passing nearly an hour in enjoyable conversation, the two men seemed to hit it off well—discussing sports, old television programs, the status of fishing and the poor crabbing season on the bay, plus prospects for the Oriole's upcoming season. Mo, obviously, was in the know, for the man was able to discuss any topic and knew a large number of facts and figures.

Eventually, by some phrase or comment, Darryll mentioned his interest in local history and his recent return to the region after two decades working in Maine.

"You know," Mo said, smiling, "You been away such a short time, isn't nothing much that could have happened while you were gone."

"What do you mean by that?" Darryll asked.

"Hell, boy!" Mo said, laughing, "they say things change quite a bit on the Eastern Shore . . . of course, that's if you count every hundred years or so." Then, laughing at his version of the well-known saying, Mo hit the bar with his hand and shouted for another round.

Laughing, Ape returned, grabbed some slightly stained bar glasses and delivered two more drafts.

"Now, you want to hear local history?" Mo asked. "Take the Dires. Been here since the 1600s or close to that time. Ran the Indians off, stole as much property as they could, killed more of their slaves than they bought. Hell, that is some family. Am I right, Ape?"

"Right you are, Mo. Right as rain as always."

"Here's a little fact for the attic in the top of your head," Mo said to Darryll. "Back in the 1700s, the early Dires—I forget the first names, Crosby Dire or Morris or Craig the Second. It doesn't really matter. The story's the thing. They say he would get up in the morning and on a sunny day, call for his ship to take him into town. Now, town is only two miles away. He could have been there in 10 minutes on horseback, but, no, he wanted to go by water in his own little 18th century version of a yacht.

"That meant, they would have to gather up 50 slaves, pull them out of the fields, and march them poor suckers over to the dock of Dire's Mill Mansion. Then, these poor, sad bastards would be locked in leg irons and have to row . . . . Yes, I said ROW, the little powder-puffed dandy into town to the wharf.

"It was like the movie *Ben Hur*, with Charlton Heston chained down there in the galley, rowing back and forth, except these slaves were doing it about 1,600 years later, and right here on the Eastern Shore. Then, to make sure everyone in town knew that Morris or Craig the Second was arriving at the wharf, he would fire his cannon in the harbor to announce his entrance into the town. What a prince!

"Of course," Mo continued, "after walking around in silk stockings and buckled shoes and waving his silk hankie and doing a little snuff, the clown prince would have the slaves row him back to his estate. Then, it was straight out into the hot fields. And the poor bastards had to make up for the time they lost, because the field bosses and overseers were on their asses for being off on the boat. But, that's the Dires."

"And things haven't changed, I hear," Darryll said.

Looking straight at the detective, Mo replied, "Sure they have, they've gotten worse." Then, smiling slowly at his quip, Mo ordered more beer.

During the next hour, Darryll received an overload of little known regional trivia.

Trying to look interested, enjoy his beer and stay awake, the detective caught segments of Mo's local history lesson, which included stories about Caesar Rodney's ride in 1776 to cast the deciding vote for the Declaration of Independence; how in colonial days difficulties in transportation caused the colony of Maryland to have two capitals, one in Annapolis and one in Easton; that the skull of Patty Cannon, the peninsula's first serial killer, still sits in a red hatbox in the Dover Public Library; that Betsy Ross' Stars and Stripes flag was first unfurled in conflict during the Battle of Cooch's Bridge, south of Newark; and that a hexagonal church, south of Easton, was built with six sides to stop the Devil from finding a deep corner to sit in and "hatch up evil doin's."

Just as Darryll thought Mo had run out of steam, the smiling, beer-drinking regional encyclopedia started on one of his favorite subjects—marriage.

"Did you know," Mo asked, "that in 1936, in Elkton alone, they performed nearly 12,000 marriages, and 95 percent of those couples were from outside of the state?

"No," Darryll said, shaking his head.

"And today, that single town issues more licenses per year—close to 22,000—than any of DelMarVa's other 14 counties."

"Who cares?" Darryll replied.

"Hell, the county treasurer cares. Those licenses bring in big bucks."

"Look, I've got to get go . . . ." Darryll tried to say, moving up from his stool and heading toward the door.

"Hear me out," Mo said, ordering another round and pulling Darryll back onto his seat. "Speaking of marriage," Mo continued, "can you tell me what the luckiest color is to be married in, for a woman?"

Giving up the fight, Darryll realized there was nothing to be gained by resisting. He was trapped and escape was hours away. "White, I guess," he said, tossing out the most obvious color in a weary tone.

"Right!" Mo said, excitedly, while nodding and sucking a quick sip of suds. "But, do you know what is unlucky at wedding time?"

"No, but I have a feeling you're going to tell me."

"Listen up," Mo said, spinning his barstool to face Darryll. "Rain on the wedding day will bring tears within the first year. Every heard that?"

"Nope. And I really don't give a damn!"

"Listen. There's more," Mo said, cutting him off. "If, on the way to the church, the bride happens to see a funeral, a crow or a black cat, that's bad news. Also, it's bad luck if the wedding party meets a monkey, cat, dog, lizard, rabbit or snake along the way. What do you think about that?"

"I'd say they better not pass a zoo on the way to the freakin' church," Darryll replied, laughing.

Ape, who had been listening from behind the bar, didn't follow Darryll's reaction immediately, but the barkeep sported a grin when Mo responded with a burst of drunken laughter.

"I think I've had my fill of useless information for one day," Darryll said as he finished his third beer and again started to leave. Grabbing his new friend by the arm, Mo the Know asked Darryll a final question. "What government building has twice as many bathrooms as it needs?"

Taking a last sip of his draft, the cop shook his head, indicating he had no idea in the world.

Smiling, Mo replied, "Gotcha again! The Pentagon, because it was built during the 1940s when the state of Virginia still had segregation laws, which required separate toilet facilities for whites and blacks."

"How do I know that's correct?" Darryll asked.

"Because a man in my position is supposed to know such things." Mo replied, his response was reinforced by approving laughter from Ape the Bartender, who nodded, adding, "Mo, he knows."

And that was only the beginning.

〜　　〜　　〜　　〜

The black Lincoln Mark IX limousine cruised over the narrow streets of South Philly. It was Friday afternoon when the driver drove through an industrial area and stopped. The nose of the limo was pointed at a tall, chainlink-fenced compound with barbed wire strung across the top of the metal mesh barrier. The driver hit a button on the console and waited for the gates and wide garage door to open. Slowly, the sleek, $100,000 state-of-the-art luxury vehicle entered the empty warehouse and prowled through the nearly empty building. Gently, the driver stopped at the metal stairway that led up to the second-floor office.

A short, muscular man, dressed in dark gray formal attire, walked swiftly to the middle of the Lincoln and opened the double doors. Reaching inside, he respectfully offered the woman his hand. Slowly, he helped her alight from the plush, dark interior.

Her long dark hair matched the slinky black velvet dress and her glistening curls draping over thin, tanned shoulders. The twin slits in her long black gown revealed a pair of attractive legs.

Following behind without assistance, a bearded gentleman stepped out, surveyed the building, then straightened his vest and tuxedo jacket.

He checked his watch, making a mental note that he had plenty of time. But, he didn't want to arrive late for the evening gala in Wilmington.

Ignoring the metal steps, the couple and driver walked to the rear of the three-story, block-like tower in the center of the empty warehouse. On the other side, a glass elevator carried the guests to the second level.

An opening in the rear led into a large, attractive carpeted office where three young women were answering telephone calls and another was inputting information into a computer.

From an elevated set of steps that lead to a rear room, Theo, the Austrian-born manager of Chez Cheveux, came down and greeted his distinguished guests.

"Mr. and Mrs. Dire. Such a pleasant surprise. You should have called ahead. We would have prepared some refreshments. Please, come up into my office."

Nodding for Rolph to follow, Craig Dire raised his hand indicating that Melinda should go first. Soon the Dires were seated in comfortable chairs facing Theo, who looked at his guests from behind his desk. Rolph stood in the back of the room at a discrete distance, serving as bodyguard and an all-around annoyance.

"Here's a little bonus, Theo," Craig said, tossing a envelope on the manager's desk. "Open it, please," Craig added.

Inside were five $1,000 bills. "Thank you so much, Mr. Dire. You didn't . . ."

"I don't ever have to do anything for anyone, Theo! Don't ever presume to tell me what I can or should do," he snapped. "I received a substantial bonus from our overseas friends, and I decided to pass a small portion along to the man at the beginning of the chain. You've kept our supply coming, and I take it there's no problem with the flow in the coming months?"

"Of course not, Mr. Dire. Everything is fine. Ten to 15 a month is quite manageable."

"Very good. Remember, Theo, always take care of your people. Loyalty isn't dead, it can still be bought." Laughing loudly at his wit, Craig looked at Melinda then over to Rolph, who both smiled and joined in, cheerily agreeing with their master.

"But," Craig added, "this isn't just a social call. We're here on serious business. It's that time of year again," he added, clapping his hands together. "Time for you to recommend three fresh, young beauties for our little Halloween extravaganza at Dire's Mill Mansion."

Theo forced a smile, for he hated sending his girls to Dire's cursed Halloween show. In spite of assurances to the contrary, they never returned, and, over the years, he had heard rumors about their misuse and abuse. But, he had no choice in the matter. Craig and Melinda owned 100 percent of Chez Cheveux. Whatever they wanted had to be done. Otherwise, he would be gone and someone else would take his place.

He planned to leave their employ within a few years. Until then, the six-figure salary, plus generous tips, helped him ignore frequent thoughts wondering what happened to his girls after they left his care. After all, he couldn't be responsible for them forever.

"I have three very young beauties—all only 17—prepared for you, Mr. Dire," Theo said, smiling as he opened a trio of folders that displayed full color photographs and pages of biographical information on each of the young women.

Craig passed the material toward Melinda, who grabbed them eagerly. "They are my bride's playthings," Craig said, nodding at his wife. "She can decide if they're suitable. If so, when can we expect shipment?"

"Whenever you want them, of course," Theo said. "That's the way it's always been in previous years. If Mrs. Dire desires, she can take them home with her today, I hope you find that satisfactory?" Theo looked at the beautiful woman, expecting an affirmative response.

"No. That's not necessary," Melinda said, looking up from the files. "I'd like them delivered on Sunday afternoon. But," she added, stopping in mid-sentence.

"Is there something wrong?" Theo asked with a trace of nervousness in his voice.

"Not really," Melinda replied. "It was just that I thought this year I might want one older playmate. These two are fine," she said, returning the files on the redhead and blonde to Theo. "But, I don't want to cause you a problem, Theo."

"It is my honor to fulfill your every wish, Mrs. Dire. What do you want?"

"I don't know," Melinda said, troubled. "I'm just a bit tired of the same thing each year. This year," she continued, rising from her seat and heading to the curtained window. "I think I'd like," her hand moved the drapery aside and she looked down into the empty warehouse. "I'd like to have someone who, someone a little bit older, a woman who looks more like me. Someone," she paused, suddenly pointing down toward the parked limousine. "Someone just like HER!"

At that moment, Angeleen was walking away from the office building, moving across the cement floor of the warehouse. She reminded Melinda of an attractive prowling tigress. Also, the girl's dark hair and curls were very similar to Melinda's own.

Looking down from behind his wife, Craig snapped his fingers and summoned Rolph to his side. "Get her up here, NOW!"

Masking his concern and annoyance, Theo knew that Angeleen would be leaving by the end of the week, never to return. As the Dires watched Rolph tip his hat and request her presence in the top of the tower, Theo composed himself, closed the three files and pasted a false smile across his face.

When Angeleen entered the room, both Dires greeted her warmly. They were introduced to her only as very special clients and personal friends who were eager to have Angeleen spend three weeks at their private estate and play a leading role in a small stage production.

It was the same tale Theo told all of the women each year. For performing each night, during two full weeks, each of the women would receive $15,000 tax free. However, there would be a few days of intense rehearsals. The girls also would have ample free time to travel around the area during the day, with a car provided, of course.

All meals and personal needs were covered, and there was a $200 a day inconvenience bonus that would be paid at the end of the job.

Theo added, "This is a very special opportunity, and, if I may be frank," he looked at the Dires, "my friends are very connected with Hollywood and New York modeling and theatrical agents. Who knows what worthwhile acquaintances you will make? What do you think?"

Craig interrupted, "Please, Theo, don't press this beautiful lady. She may want to think it over."

"I've thought it over," Angeleen said, quickly, realizing the job could substantially reduce the length of her five-year plan, "and my answer is yes. I'd be delighted. When do I leave?"

"This Sunday, in two days," Theo said. "But, you can tell no one. There's a lot of prying ears where this assignment is concerned. Let's just keep it to ourselves, and we'll meet and work out the details in a few days."

"Fine," Angeleen said. "Anything else?"

"No," Theo said, his eyes heavy, but his smile still in place.

Craig Dire rose and took Angeleen's hand. Slowly, he bent forward as he raised her left wrist toward his lips. As he gently kissed her skin, she smiled and lowered her eyes.

Melinda was beside him and her eyes locked on something that intrigued her immensely. Taking Angeleen's left hand, she turned it over and pointed to the pentagram.

"This is interesting," Melinda said. "How did you come to receive this?"

"My mother did it, many years ago. Is it a problem?"

Smiling, Melinda's eyes sparkled as she looked at Theo, Rolph and Craig. "Quite the contrary, my dear. You are going to be just perfect for the part."

6

Governor Henry McDevitt, his wife, Dr. Stephanie Litera-McDevitt, Vice Governor Lydia Chase and her husband, Professor Ronald Chase, exited DMV 6, the state limousine used for formal occasions. McDevitt's bodyguard, Sgt. Randy Poplos, stood near the open rear door as the two couples headed toward the steps of Wilmington's Hotel du Pont.

Each year during the third Friday evening in October, the state's Double Rainbow Foundation, committed to fulfilling the special wishes for children in the region with terminal illnesses, held a black-tie reception and fashion show. With tickets at $300 each, the event was the organization's major annual fund raiser. This year, McDevitt's wife, 2009 honorary chairperson, would welcome the audience and make brief remarks before the program.

Senior and graduate fashion design students from the University of DelMarVa's six campuses—located in Wilmington, Newark, Salisbury, Dover, Easton and Parksley—modeled traditional and contemporary

designs. The event gave them an opportunity to
exhibit their classwork and gain practical design and
marketing experience.

A sellout crowd of more than 500 shared muted
conversation while consuming drinks and unpro-
nounceable appetizers in two reception areas—in the
DuBarry Room and in the lounge immediately below.
A runway was constructed in the Gold Ballroom and
theater-style seating was arranged to accommodate
the attendees.

A large number of plastic people displayed ornate
jewelry, expensive gowns and uncomfortable black
bowties as they offered stiff smiles, tossed air kisses,
raised champagne glasses and shared forced laughter.
For $300 a head, DelMarVa's affluent and pretentious
came so they were sure to be seen. That was the way
it worked and they all knew it. Many of the men came
because their wives or their bosses had made them.
At least they could spend the evening downing free
drinks and scanning the crowd to glimpse women
who would be displaying their best appearance.

The ladies, on the other hand, came to see how
severely their counterparts had aged. Catty to the
extreme, those who were better preserved, or cosmeti-
cally enhanced, made an effort to stand beside their
"friends" who were on the downward slope.

In one corner, drinking a glass of scotch and
water, McDevitt whispered to Ron Chase, "Maybe
someone will accidentally fall into the fire alarm and
we can get out of this."

Ron laughed and raised his drink toward the governor. "Hell, Hank. Lydia has been browbeating me
all week about how I had better be smiling all night
and how *I will* enjoy myself. I bet if the bell went off,

the women would all stay inside and the guys would trample each other to death heading for the doors."

McDevitt smiled back, then abruptly became stiff. "Bandits at 10 o'clock," he said, indicating the return from the ladies room of his wife and Vice Governor Lydia Chase.

"Having a good time, dear?" Stephanie asked her husband, her mocking tone noticed by the others.

"Better than the Rock Hall Fish Fry," McDevitt said, smiling.

"Go ahead, be sarcastic, but tonight you're my guest and on the way home I bet you $10 you will be telling me how it was one of the most interesting nights of your life."

Ron laughed as Lydia nodded in agreement.

The two couples mingled through the crowd, speaking briefly with several local politicians and friends they hadn't seen for some time. About 7:40 p.m., twenty minutes before the start of the program, Stephanie began to walk away.

Suddenly, forcefully pushing several people aside, a man and woman approached McDevitt's party.

"Hank McDevitt! How the hell are you?"

The governor turned and looked directly at Craig and Melinda Dire.

Stephanie, who had stopped and turned in reaction to the strange voice, was surprised as Craig grabbed her hand, bent his head forward and gently kissed the tips of her fingers.

There was an awkward silence, for McDevitt was obviously not excited to see his old college classmate.

"Hello, Craig. Melinda," the governor said, forcing a smile.

"Hang anybody this week, Hank?" Craig asked, laughing at his own joke.

"Not today," McDevitt replied, "but it's still early, I usually make my kills just after midnight. So, I suggest you leave before then, Craig."

Dire forced a smile, but his face turned bright red. Melinda started to pull on her husband's arm, signaling it was time to leave.

Shrugging forcefully and standing his ground, Dire ignored both his wife and McDevitt's insult. Turning to Stephanie, he said, "You must be the new bride. I'm Hank's old college classmate, but I didn't get an invitation to the wedding."

"It was a small affair," Stephanie said, a bit confused and not sure how to respond. "It certainly must have been an oversight. I'm sorry."

"Not an issue," Craig said. "We had other plans. Ask your husband sometime about how I helped him get through his courses."

"Pleased to meet you," Stephanie said, shaking Craig's hand and smiling at Melinda. McDevitt's wife was trying to cover up her husband's coldness. "Maybe you can visit us at Woodburn?"

Grinning at McDevitt, Craig answered, "Thank you, so much, Stephanie. We've never been invited there either. We would love to. Wouldn't we, Melinda dear?."

Craig's wife nodded, smiling.

"And you and Hank, and of course Vice Governor Lydia Chase and her husband, must come to Halloween House at the end of the month. Well, we must run. Nice meeting all of you. We'll call, so we can get together soon."

As Stephanie and the Chases waved goodbye,

McDevitt downed his glass, lowered it and whispered, "Asshole."

"What's wrong with you, Hank?" Stephanie asked, a bit annoyed at her husband.

"Nothing."

"You were rude! They seem like a fascinating and charming couple. Why haven't you ever mentioned them? I think you made them uncomfortable, and you should apologize to them after tonight's program. Let's have them over for a visit."

"We'll talk about it later. You had better get ready. Don't you have to speak in about 10 minutes?"

"All right, but we'll pursue this later. Don't think you'll put me off on this one," Stephanie said, as she kissed him on the lips.

After Stephanie left and headed to the podium, Hank, Lydia and Ron walked toward their reserved seats right next to the runway.

Lydia whispered to the governor. "What's his story, Hank?"

"Tell you later. Just believe me, after five minutes alone with Craig Dire, the Pope would be looking for a pair of scissors to shove into his throat."

"That bad?"

"Worse. The guy forces himself into the spotlight, whether he's invited or not. And if he steps on people on the way, so much the better. He's a low-life, sleaze-ball who should have been put to sleep at birth."

By 8 o'clock, the majority of the audience was seated, and McDevitt looked toward the stage and smiled at his wife.

This was her night and he was happy for her. She and the working committee had agreed that the lack of long speeches or meaningless awards was the primary reason that the turnout for the annual show was so overwhelming.

One short welcome, lasting no more than six minutes, was it. It was the rule and it had never been broken.

"Welcome. My name is Stephanie Litera-McDevitt," she said into the microphone. Immediately, a large round of applause filled the room. "Thank you. Thank you very much. On behalf of the children and families who are beneficiaries of the work of the Double Rainbow Foundation, I'd like to express our sincere appreciation to all of you, and we are very pleased that so many of you are with us tonight.

"Because of your moral commitment and financial support, the dreams of children of all ages, races and backgrounds are coming true. There are so many people who have worked extremely hard, the staff, volunteers and, most importantly, the parents. But, if you want to learn who they are, look in your program."

The audience laughed.

"Counting tonight's reception, plus generous contributions from corporate sponsors and individual anonymous donors, this year we have raised more than $1 million for the Double Rainbow Foundation. And this is only the beginning."

More loud applause.

"Once again. Thank you. Now, as we start our program, I would like to turn the podium over to Dr. Carol Webster, associate professor of textiles, design and consumer economics at the University of DelMarVa's Salisbury campus, who will introduce our student models."

Before the professor reached the podium, Craig Dire popped up from his front row seat like a piece of crisp toast. With two smooth leaps he mounted the stage and grabbed hold of the microphone. His abrupt grasp caused a loud piercing screech of uncomfortable feedback. Unaffected and sporting a smile, Craig turned on his thickest downstate drawl and said, "By, God! This is just wonderful, ain't it?"

No one responded as 500 immobile faces stared at the stage. Among those, gritting his teeth, was Gov. Henry McDevitt.

"Hell, I mean, helping little feeble, dyin' kids is just the kinda thing that makes you wanna dig down deep, you know? So, me and Melinda, my beautiful wife, who herself was a beauty queen and model . . . ."

Waving to the front row of chairs, Craig motioned for his wife to join him on stage. "Get up here, darlin'. Good. Good. Let's hear it for the little lady!" he shouted into the mike. A few hands clapped. Very few.

"We were sittin' there listenin' to the governor's, my old classmate's, wife. And me and Melinda said, we should kick in some of our own money for this here beneficial cause. So, on behalf of Dire Real Estate, in Dire's Mill—one sweet growing community downstate, that you all should come and see—we are presenting the Dying Rainbow Kids, or whatever they're called, a check for $150. How's that?"

As the vast majority of the audience sought some guidance on how to react, Stephanie returned to the podium and said, "On behalf of the board of directors, we all would like to thank Mr. and Mrs. Dire for their generous gift, which will be the start, the pacesetter donation, of our second million-dollar fundraising goal."

As she moved aside and began applauding, the audience joined in. While the clapping continued, Craig and Melinda shook Stephanie's hand. Then Craig whispered into Stephanie's ear and she nodded.

When the applause died down, the chairperson waved for the photographer to take a picture of herself and the Dires holding the company check. Awkward silence turned into murmurs of disapproval, as the Dire couple waved to the assembly and took a few bows as they left the stage.

"Now," Stephanie announced, "Dr. Webster, I believe you're on."

As Stephanie sat down between her husband and Lydia Chase, the vice governor said, "Well done, Stephanie."

While trying to control her rage through a stiff smile, the First Lady nodded to a few photographers. Waiting for just the right moment to make his move, McDevitt leaned over and whispered to his wife with a lilt in his voice, "They seem like such a charming couple, my dove. Let's have them over to Woodburn for a visit."

〰️　　〰️　　〰️　　〰️

The ride home in DMV 6 was spirited. Stephanie was thrilled with the program's success, Lydia was happy to have spent a rare night out with her husband, and McDevitt and Ron Chase were relieved the event was over.

After undoing their black bowties, the two men opened cold beers they had pulled from the limo refrigerator. At the wheel, with the glass partition down so he could participate in conversation, Sgt. Randy Poplos drove the vehicle along Route 13, heading for home—Woodburn, the governor's mansion in Dover.

"It was nice being at the Hotel tonight," Stephanie said. "Did you know that was the site of our first date?" she asked the others.

"Really!" Lydia said. "Let's hear all the details," she added, smiling as Hank rolled his eyes.

"There's more than one version," the governor interjected, "probably because of differing perspectives. You see, Stephanie didn't want to go out with me. In fact, it took me a full day to track her down just to return my phone calls."

"Let's get this straight," Stephanie said, quickly, "they weren't your phone calls. You had Grace, your assistant call me. You didn't even do it yourself."

"Well, dear, I couldn't really sit near the phone for six hours while your office tried to find you. From what I hear, you came in with a horrible hangover because you got sloshed the night before at the reception at Buena Vista."

"Right!" Lydia shouted excitedly. "That was when you two first met, when Stephanie was telling her boss that the governor needed psychiatric counseling."

The limo howled with delight hearing Lydia's recollection.

"Then," McDevitt added, "she demanded I sign a bill, right there at the reception—which I did—and then she got so drunk that Marty, her boss drove her home, carried her to her couch. The next day she was missing in action and crawled into work about 2 in the afternoon, wearing sunglasses to cover her bloodshot eyes."

"Fine!" Stephanie replied, opening a wine cooler, and taking a sip, "but I did agree to go out with you, and I did have a nice time, and I thought I made a good impression, and then you and Randy take off and leave me in the Brandywine Room to finish dinner alone and get home on my own."

Ron and Lydia clapped with delight as Randy yelled to his riders from the driver's seat, "I told him, 'That's no way to treat a lady, Hank.' I also predicted that you would never go out with him again, and you shouldn't have! But, who listens to me?"

A hearty laugh filled the rear of the car. Then, gently McDevitt reached across the back seat, took his wife's hand and kissed it gently. "I love you," he said. "And I'm proud of you tonight. Your event was a terrific success."

"Thank you, darling," Stephanie replied, kissing her husband on the lips.

After a few moments of silence, Ron asked McDevitt, "Can you tell us the story of that guy Dire? What a strange case he is."

"Strange is an understatement," Lydia added, agreeing.

While he was gathering his thoughts, Stephanie said, "He said you went to school, college, together, Hank. Were you friends at one time?"

"No," he replied, looking at his friends. "We were in the same class, at Salisbury State in the late '60s. If you start talking about the Dires, and Craig, you could spend the entire evening and just scratch the surface.

"The family's rich—very rich. Arrived here in the 1600s. The first Dires were criminals, sent from England to work on the farms. The Eastern Shore was a penal colony, much like Australia. They needed workers here, so they came as indentured servants, who would pay back their passage in five years; and convicts, who would work off their sentences in 15 years. Later came the slaves.

"But the Dires were bad news even in Colonial times. Eventually, through a murder or two, their descendants got enough money to get into smuggling and piracy. Later, they were big landowners and slaveholders.

"A good number of slaveowners took care of their human property, for two reasons—to get the most work out of them and for humanitarian reasons. They say the Dires were among the worst when it came to treatment. Dire's Mill had auctions in the square every week and it was the site of some very bad incidents. One Dire particularly enjoyed breaking up slave families. He would sell some children to traders from Louisiana and Mississippi, send others to the Carolinas and sell the parents to buyers from Virginia. They've always been evil, unfeeling people.

"One day, in the midst of an auction, Jebediah Winslow Dire whipped a male slave to death—on the auction platform in front of 200 buyers and spectators— because the man dared ask for a cup of water. It was insane. Even the buyers—slaveowners themselves— couldn't believe it. The slave was in good condition, and he could have brought Dire nearly $1,500.

"Strangely, during the Civil War, the family sided with the North, although there were many Southern sympathizers on the Eastern Shore. But the Dires saw the might of the Union and ended up 'selling off' their slaves to the government and got a bundle of money.

"Then they turned in their Confederate neighbors and led a group of Union volunteers, burning out a number of local homesteads. Word was, the Dires still stayed in the slave trade, even during and after the war, selling and transporting free blacks back to the Caribbean.

"Anyway, closer to the present, the family was into all types of business and bought every local politician they could, and had state delegates in their pockets, as well. This enabled them to get privileged information on state and federal projects and plans, make appropriate land deals and sell the property back to the government at a very large profit.

"At present, Dire's Mill is a world unto its own, governed much like a feudal estate. Dire's land companies are involved in expanding its holdings around the town limits with hopes of controlling a large segment of the state economy."

No one spoke for a moment, then Stephanie asked, "What about your classmate?"

"Yes," McDevitt said, "Craig Dire the Fifth, as he told everyone he met when we arrived at college. He had the name, the looks—for a while anyway—the connections and the money. But he lacked the will to study or apply himself. Craig and a group of other guys who wanted to party until the sun came up lived in a Victorian home on the edge of campus.

"The cops were always getting complaints about Craig's place, but nothing ever happened to him or his dopehead roommates. Seems Papa Dire had influential friends in Salisbury, too. Craig was involved in buying exams. In one case, he supplied a professor who had a drinking problem with an unlimited supply of joy juice in return for grade inflation. But, one event will illustrate Craig's idea of a good time on the town."

McDevitt explained that every town and campus has its share of characters. One of downtown Salisbury's local legends was Bobby Bottles, a sort of slow witted, unemployed young man who lived with his mother in a ramshackle hut near the railroad tracks.

From his earliest days, people could find Bobby and Ma searching under bushes and rummaging through trash cans, seeking bottles they could return to get the deposit money or aluminum cans they could crush and take to the recycling center.

Pushing a rusted grocery store shopping cart, Bobby and Ma would guide their cart on the street, in the imaginary lane between parked cars and moving traffic. When Ma got up in years, Bobby became the breadwinner—or canfinder—and supported the family from his daily search-and-find missions. This small amount of money, added to a monthly Social Security allowance, kept mother and son off the welfare roles. They were doing the best they could, and, while they were mocked by many, their presence and activities added to the character of the city and campus.

Sometimes, well-meaning campus clubs would try to adopt Bobby and Ma as a special Christmas project, but their efforts were turned down. A shy person, Bobby didn't like to get into conversations with strangers. Therefore, any attempt by students to explain their charitable purpose was fruitless. The most they could do was leave a box of food outside the shack and hope it was found by the intended recipients before a passing bum stole it.

One day, Craig and his boys had consumed a fair amount of liquor and were hanging on the corner of a small deli/grocery store. Even when they had no plans to raise hell, fate never failed to deliver them an opportunity that they rarely passed up.

"Bobby was shoving his cart," McDevitt said. "He was about a block away when they saw him. Craig got the idea to put five empty bottles on a boarded-up window ledge that was about 10 feet off the ground. Standing on one of the guy's shoulders, they got the beer bottles in place. As Bobby passed, they planned to point out the longneck treasures and watch him try to jump up and get them down.

"When he was about 20 feet away, they started chanting, 'Bobby Bottles! Bobby Bottles! Bobby Bottles!' Waving to Craig and the boys, Bobby parked his cart and walked over. When they pointed to the bottles, someone suggested that Bobby jump up and get them. After a half-dozen unsuccessful attempts on Bobby's part, Craig and the boys were laughing so hard that they had to lean against the wall to keep from falling to the sidewalk.

"Getting upset, Bobby pushed one of the boys, who hit Bobby in the arm. Holding the aching spot, Bobby started cursing and spitting at Craig's gang. Laughing, Craig told Bobby that if he stood underneath the window, Craig would use a stone to knock the bottles down and Bobby could catch them.

"As Bobby waited, looking up at his haul, Craig stood back and tossed a rock at the first bottle. When Bobby missed the catch, everyone on the sidewalk erupted in laughter and applause. Craig told Bobby he'd get the next one. Again, Bobby missed. Only three bottles were left, but Bobby missed the next two.

"Very frustrated, Bobby stood below, hoping to catch the last bottle. As he looked up, the group started chanting, 'Bobby Bottles! Bobby Bottles! Bobby Bottles!' They were screaming and the poor guy was really nervous. Craig tossed the rock and the brown bottle fell, landing right into Bobby's cradled arms. Thrilled, he raised his glass trophy. While Bobby was smiling proudly at the applause, Craig went over and patted the boy on the back, offering congratulations.

"As Craig put out his right hand, Bobby stared, uncertain of what to do. Craig opened his left hand and took the bottle from Bobby, saying he would hold it as they shook hands. Shaking hands, Craig shouted, 'Let's hear it for Bobby Bottles!' Everyone cheered. Then, releasing the grip, Bobby said, 'Gimme my bottle.'

"But Craig said, 'This bottle? This one here? No, this is my bottle, Bobby,' and held the glass container up in the air, over his head.

"Bobby jumped and clawed for the bottle, but Craig kept shoving him away. Finally, Craig said, 'Okay, Bobby Bottles, here's your toy. Take it home and show it to your ugly, smelly mama.' And he dropped the bottle to the sidewalk, laughing as it broke into a half-dozen pieces.

"Bobby went crazy, and grabbed a shard of the broken glass. Before anyone could stop him, he threw the brown, jagged projectile at Craig, hitting him in the face. Blood immediately flowed from the good-sized head wound. Never expecting to be hurt by Bobby Bottles, Craig went wild. Within seconds he was on Bobby, beating his head against the sidewalk.

"After about six slams against the sidewalk, one of the group pulled Craig off and suggested they drag Bobby into the alley behind the shop. There was a trail of blood leading to the blacktop drive. Once there, and out of the sight of any passing witnesses, the five drunken and enraged students took turns kicking Bobby Bottles to death.

"At that moment, when they were finishing up their murder, I was walking down the street and passed the driveway entrance into the alley. I heard someone shout, 'Eat shit, asshole!'

"Looking to my right, I saw Craig Dire, holding the side of his face. Immediately, the group ran off, but I recognized Craig. We stared at each other for a few seconds, then he was gone.

"I went back and turned the body over. Bobby wasn't breathing. His face was kicked to a pulp. It looked like raw meat. I gave the police a statement. Unfortunately, no one was ever arrested or tried for the crime. Craig already had a lawyer at his side when the cops arrived at his house. They all had disposed of the bloody clothing. There was no evidence. The facial cut was explained by the broken glass in the apartment's kitchen sink.

"I told you the Dires had connections every-where. I pieced together the story over the years, from neighbors near the deli and from one of the guys who was there, but no one was going to testify against Craig Dire. No doubt, there were some pay-offs, too. In my mind, he's guilty as sin. All of them are, but he's the one responsible."

7

On Sunday afternoon, two days after the Dires' visit with Theo, a white stretch limousine stopped at the residences of Tina, Nannette and Angeleen in Philadelphia and delivered the actresses to the manicured grounds of Dire's Mill Mansion.

The three ladies of the night passed through the tall iron gates with their faces pressed against the darkened glass. They all pointed to the oversized, black sculptured bats—with wings extended, mouths snarling and teeth bared—stiff silent sentries atop the brick pillars on either side of the entryway.

Always the amicable host, Craig Dire was waiting to greet his special guests, ordering three servants to take suitcases and dress bags to the guest quarters—a converted Victorian carriage house situated a comfortable distance from the main estate house.

"Welcome to Dire's Mill Mansion," he announced, bowing low and kissing the hand of each of the lovelies.

Impressed with such a formal welcome, Tina and Nannette—the two younger girls—giggled and shifted nervously. Angeleen was a bit more reserved, thinking the reception was a bit overdone.

"We'll have a welcome dinner tonight," Craig said, turning to introduce the women to his wife. "My dear Melinda—the Mistress of Dire's Mill Mansion—will make sure you are comfortable. She will be available to answer any questions. We will do all we can during the next three weeks to make your stay with us absolutely unforgettable."

The ladies would find Craig Dire was true to his word.

On Sunday night, at the welcome dinner, they were treated to a feast, Chesapeake Bay style—featuring snapper soup, roast turkey, crab imperial, fresh pastries and breads and flaming desserts.

Craig mentioned that there was nothing much to see in the area. Everything one would ever need was on the mansion grounds—boating, swimming and water skiing (Indian Summer weather permitting), hiking, fishing and crabbing, tennis courts, a private theater, bowling alley, exercise and weight room and gaming parlor with a video arcade, billiards and darts. An extensive library was in the mansion and, with notice, they would be escorted into the main building.

All meals would be served in their carriage house guest parlor. The large room was off the main hallway that led to the private bedrooms. They were able to select from a menu the chef would provide at the end of each previous meal—just like the finest resorts or hospitals. Their building also contained a full-size kitchen on the first floor. The refrigerator was stocked with microwave meals, fruits, vegetables and beverages—including sodas, wine and beer. A full pantry contained canned goods, breads and snacks.

The first evening, the three women got acquainted. Even though they worked through Chez Cheveux, they had never met before the limo ride.

Dressed in sweatsuits, they agreed it was wonderful to relax and enjoy a quiet evening. There was no need to be dressed to the hilt, no pressure to perform bed tricks for strange clients, and no question about when they would get to bed. Apparently, while at Dire's Mill they could get a good rest every night.

Polite introductory conversation quickly shifted to a more specific direction, particularly, how each of them got into the business and hooked up with Chez Cheveux.

Tina, the young blond from Galesburg, Illinois, ran away from home at 14 because her stepfather started attacking her as soon as she turned 13. He had plenty of opportunities, since her mother was a night-shift nurse.

"After a few months, I told my mother about it," Tina said, "and she told me I was a little, jealous liar. Then, she said that even if it was true, it was *my* fault for teasing him, by walking around in tight shorts and my nightgown. She didn't give a damn about me. I had to get away and decided that if I was going to get screwed I should get paid for it. After a year on my own, making out okay, I met a black guy at a bus terminal in Chicago, where I'd run off to. We had coffee, got to talking. He was dressed real good, looked like a businessman. I thought he sold computers. After a while, I told him what I did. He had this way of listening that made you want to share things with him. He was the real trustworthy type. He told me he could help, said I was a 'real good looker' and 'smart.' I liked that. No one ever told me that before. He said he just knew if I went to Philly,

I could make a lot more money there, and that they were looking for clean, white girls with the baby doll look. He said he'd pay my fare if I promised to call the number on the card, and give his name—Orleans—as a reference. It sounded good to me. I called as soon as I got off the bus and went over to the warehouse. Theo hired me on sight. That was two years ago. It's the best life I've ever had. I've got no complaints."

Finished, Tina paused and looked over at Nannette. "How about you?"

"I met this guy in Richmond," she said. "He sounds a lot like your guy, except this one was white. He was hanging out at a diner on the strip where I stood, trying to flag down business. I 'member wonderin' what a good lookin', clean dressed fella like that was doin' on the strip. He looked sorta outta place.

"He came up to me. I thought he was lookin' for a date, but he said he just wanted to talk. I told him talk was time, you know the rules. He laughed and nodded, gave me a $50 bill and I followed him into a booth. He asked me how much I made a night. It was about $50 after room expenses and payin' off Ernest, my pimp. The man told me I was sellin' myself for about $10 an hour. Made me think about how he was right.

"He told me I was young and hot, and didn't have that many years left before it started to show. I was just 16, about 18 months ago, and he gave me a card with a number. Said the same as the black guy did to you. Philly was the place. He paid a train fare for me, Amtrak coach. I got in, called Theo and haven't had to worry about a thing for the last year. I'm even taking classes to get a GED. I figure that meeting was good luck for me."

Tina and Nannette looked at Angeleen.

"How about you?" Tina asked.

"Pretty much the same," she said. "I met my messenger angel in my hometown, when I was working as a morning shift waitress in Kaptain's Kitchen, a little family restaurant. He sweet talked me, said with my looks I could make a lot more money as a professional escort and model, going out to fancy dinners with rich guys, and I'd get to wear beautiful gowns and expensive clothes. What did I know, except I needed a way to get out of a small town, away from my foster parents and start over? I had nothing but bad memories and was going nowhere fast. So I gave it a shot. He paid for my bus ticket to Boston and from there he gave me enough money for a one-way fare to Philadelphia.

"Later, I figured he got a finder's fee from the agency for girls like me he sent down. The guys who sent you to Theo are probably part of the same network. But, what did I care if he made a few bucks? I consider him, and the other ones who found you two, sort of like hooker talent scouts. They pick us from the pack and send us up to the pros.

"Things have worked out pretty good," Angeleen said, "considering I had nothing and was going nowhere. But I've been on the street a lot longer than you two, and I can tell you this: You'd better plan ahead, because when your body's gone, baby, they aren't going to want you any more. You've got to stash a lot away, because there are a lot of rainy days ahead. This little gig down here in Green Acres is an exception. And, frankly, I don't care to talk about the good times, because there are damn few."

Changing the subject, Tina got up from her chair and walked between Nannette and Angeleen and said, "Okay, how about this? Tell me your strangest, craziest or most embarrassing moment on the job."

The other two women groaned and waved at Tina, telling her to forget the idea, but she wouldn't be put off.

"Come on," she continued pressing them to speak. "I'll start. I've got a good one, then you can try to top it. Please? It's still early, and I don't want to go to bed yet. It'll be fun. All right?"

Nannette agreed and Angeleen said she'd listen and then decide after the other two were through.

"This is so bad," Tina said. "I was working a main drag near Michigan Avenue. It was my first month out there, and I was still really nervous. This old guy, about 55 pulled up in a station wagon. I'll never forget, it had his kids' toys and car seat in the back. We agreed on a price and I got in.

"The cheap bastard wouldn't even spring for a hotel. Drove to a park in the middle of town, straight across the grass and parked behind a bunch of trees. Then he said we're going to do it here. And I said, 'Where?' And he pointed to the back of the station wagon.

"When I told him no, he said he'd pay me twice my price. I still argued and he tossed in another $50. I was up to $150 for action in the wagon in the park. It didn't make sense. I told him I knew a cheap clean hotel two blocks away, but he said we had to do it in the car."

The other two hookers were listening intently, interested in what was behind Tina's guy's hangup.

"While he's dropping the rear seat down and tossing the car seat and toys in the front seat, I asked him why we had to do it in the wagon. And he said he wanted to be able to drive his frigid wife and screaming kids around and know that he had a good time right there, where the family was sitting. He said thinking about me and him back there would keep him from killing them one day when they were all driving him nuts and screaming.

"I agreed to do it. He tossed down a blanket and gave me a kid's Winnie the Pooh pillow to rest my head on. After we were done, which took all of about a minute and a half, I started to grab for my clothes. But the nut said no. He wanted to keep them as souvenirs. I got upset, said, 'No way, pal!' He laughed, because he had already gathered everything up except my bra, panties and spikes.

"I didn't have anything on other than that. So I started grabbing for the rest of my stuff. I had gotten the money in advance, but it was inside my jacket pocket—$150 and it was disappearing before my naked eyes."

Angeleen and Nannette were laughing now, slapping their thighs and bending over with delight.

"See, I told you this would be fun. But, not then," Tina said. Picking up the story, she said, "So I have no money, Mister Family Man has grabbed up most of my clothes and he's holding them in his arms. I have no idea of what to do next. So, smart me, Miss High School Dropout, with hardly anything to wear—and not wanting to play hide and seek all the way to my apartment—tries to reason with him, bargaining for any clothes he'll toss my way.

"He's not budging. Says he needed to have them all, for his collection. Then I ask for the money, and he acts like he gave it to me and I lost it. That really pissed me off, and I started screaming at the bastard. Told him he was a ugly pervert who could never get a kiss without paying for it."

"Real smart move," Angeleen said, laughing.

"Right, anyway, the bastard takes his foot and kicks me out the tailgate, jumps in his driver's seat and takes off—tooting his horn, like he's announcing to anyone around to have a look at the half naked idiot. I had no money, hardly any clothes."

"What in the world did you do?" Nannette asked, nearly choking, she was laughing so hard.

"Well, it was about two in the morning, thankfully not lunch hour. I took off my stockings and shoes and carried them in my hands. I figured I could use them to cover more of my most strategic parts if necessary. Then I just looked and ran, looked and ran, over and over for the next half hour, from bushes and trees all across the park. God must have been watching down on me—and I know he had a good laugh that night. Anyway, I got to the edge of the park, near a coffee shop, where there was a fair amount of traffic. And, parked across the street was a police car."

"Oh no!" Nannette said. "You didn't!"

"Hell, I didn't! I waited until I saw the cops coming out and I yelled at the top of my freaking lungs: 'RAPE! HELP ME! RAPE! RAPE!'

"Those two cops dropped their coffee and came running, with guns drawn. I was huddled behind some ferns and held my shoes and stockings between my legs. When they got there, they couldn't find me. Since they were close, I started going, 'Psst! Psst!'

"They turned around and saw me. It was humiliating. When they figured out my situation, they started laughing and wouldn't move, just kept focusing in on what they could see. They weren't even mad about dropping their coffee. Then they started arguing about who should get the car and who should stay with me.

Finally, I said I'd let them look at everything I had all the way back to the station, if they would just get me in the car. It was getting cold out there.

"They were so nice. They didn't even run me in and drove me all the way home. They had an eyeful that night. All I know is they finished that shift smiling. One of them even asked for my phone number. I guess he thought he could get me religion or something. So, how was that?"

Tina stood and bowed at the end of her tale.

"Fan-tas-tic!" Angeleen said, clapping along with Nannette.

"Okay, I'm next," Nannette said, now eager to share her story.

"This was about six months after I was on the street on the edge of Richmond, and Randy, my pimp, drops me off at this here motel room, and then he says he'll be comin' on back to get me in one hour, exactly. As I'm walkin' to the door of the room, he's yellin' at me to be sure to finish up with the guy by then, or else he'll be a comin' in a swingin' with both fists."

"Haven't we heard that one before," Tina said, nodding to Angeleen.

"I went inside," Nannette said, "and I'm only 16 and a half, so I haven't done a lot of kinky stuff yet. This guy is about 35 . . . 40, and not bad lookin'. He points to about eight cans of shavin' cream an' says he's Father Frost an' I'm his Winter Princess."

The other two women dropped their jaws.

"No way!" Tina screamed.

"I swear to God!" Nannette replied. "He said I should put on the white teddy, made outta stiff lace and all starched up like a ballerina costume. And he said he was gonna go into the bathroom and come out like the Ice Man or some shit, in 10 minutes."

"So I said, all right. Then he said, while he's in there, I should take the shavin' cream—in these red-white-and-blue, tall aerosol cans—and decorate the room like it's a winter storm."

A burst of laughter filled the carriage house parlor.

"Well, I didn't know what the hell he was talkin' about, but I was new in the game, so I said, 'Okay, you want me to decorate anythin' special.' And real polite like, he says, 'No, Miss. You all decide.' Then he turned and went on in the bathroom and shut the door.

"At that moment, I'm thinkin' of runnin' off, but Randy would get real pissed about that, me comin' back with no money. So I take off my clothes, put on the Little Snow Queen tutu, that's about three sizes too big and fallin' off my chest and thighs. And I start runnin' around the room, shooting white foam on the walls, puttin' dots like snow clumps on the furniture, the lampshades, the mirrors and even the drapes and rug.

"I'm emptyin' these cans like crazy, and I don't know how much time I got left. Then I get a good idea to make a snow path from the bathroom door to the bed, so Father Frost can follow it right to his Snow Bunny."

Angeleen was shaking her head while Tina was staring, wide-eyed in amazement.

"When I finished with all the cans, I sat on the bed, in red spike heels, to match my red hair, wearin' a dancin' school recital costume, complete with a sparklin' white and silver crown. Suddenly, he opens the bathroom door. He's got on a red thong with a cute little gold bell that's just a dinglin' and a jinglin' away. His chest is bare, except for a red tuxedo tie, and atop his head is a real, honest-to-God toy crown, made out of plastic with sparklin' glass jewels. And he shouts, 'Father Frost is ready and eager to come. Is Winter Princess ardent and cheerful?'

"And I wave at him from the bed and shout, 'Come and get it, Snowman!' My Lord, he took off like a race car that hadn't been on the track in a year and was all lubed up and ready to get his spark plugs goin'. But, when he hit my little snow path, poor Father Frost's feet went way up in the air, flyin' in front of him higher than his head. I think they call it a pratfall. Anyway, when he landed on his back, right on the creamy white runway, it sounded like a refrigerator fell over. It shook the walls of the room."

Nannette started laughing, thinking back to the scene. "I'm sorry," she said, "but I can still see him there, flat on his back, his head to one side, still smilin' in anticipation. Just hardly breathin', and that little gold bell not doin' a nothin' like he had hoped, just a leanin' so sad beside his bare thigh.

"He was out cold. Of course, I made sure he was alive. Then I looked at my watch. I had 30 minutes to wait for Randy. I got dressed and cleaned up good, and there was still 15 minutes to go. Father Frost was out so bad, I wasn't worried about him coming to. I emptied his wallet. Got over $400—$100 for Randy and the rest for me—and I even left the guy $20 to use to get home or go to wherever.

"Took his watch, beeper and camera, too. Shoved them in my little ol' travelin' bag. But I left his princess outfit and crowns. Just couldn't take his *special* things. Didn't feel that woulda been right. When it was only two minutes before Randy was to pull up, I picked up the phone with a towel and ordered a pizza delivery. Made it a small plain, since I didn't know what he liked. You know, you just can't go wrong with a small plain. Plus, I figured he'd need something to eat when he came to. I also made a call to 911. Told the lady the motel name and room number. Said I was the maid and that a poor man just fell over and couldn't get back up. I left the door ajar, so they could get in quick, in case he was still in that gone-to-the-beyond condition where he couldn't here them knocking."

"So that's my little tale. Now," Nannette said, "how about you Angeleen? Tell us your craziest time."

The oldest of the group decided to tell them a silly little experience to keep them satisfied. She didn't want to tell them where she came from—in northern Maine. The simple reasons she left—bad memories and boredom.

Tina and Nannette were immediately interested in Angeleen's story about the night she was scheduled to escort a visiting congressman, who—unknown to her—was in town to meet with the archbishop of Philadelphia and important community leaders. They were hosting a formal dinner to discuss the school voucher program and how important it was for parents of children in parochial schools. She was to wait for his call and would be picked up at a center city hotel lobby.

On the way back from a reception and dinner meeting at the palatial residence on the Main Line, the congressman was pretty well wasted, having drunk too much and eaten too little. Also, his mind was more focused on what delights he was going to experience after the horribly boring dinner meeting with blue haired ladies and old men in black suits with stiff

white collars. Not totally in control, he asked the limousine chauffeur to take him to pick up his granddaughter on the way back to his hotel. The congressman gave his priest driver Angeleen's phone number.

"When he called for directions, I told the driver,
who I thought was just some schmuck from a rental
agency, the address where I would be waiting.
Seriously, when's the last time you ever heard of a
priest driving a limo? I didn't know where the old
congressman was coming from, and I didn't know he
was making believe I was his grandchild."

Nannette and Tina waited impatiently for more.

"Oh, it gets better, believe me," Angeleen said.
"Before I hung up with the driver, I asked him if the 'old
boy was primed and ready to go?' And he stuttered,
and said that it seemed that the congressman was a bit
'happy and maybe had consumed one too many.'

"When they pulled up, I came down in a red
strapless gown with a slit up to my waist and enough
Shalimar to choke a camel. The priest driver, who
Theo later said was wearing a collar—but I didn't see
it—held the door open. I jumped into the back and
started smothering my date-for-the-evening congressmen with kisses that most men have never gotten
from their wives, let alone a granddaughter. And then
I notice that the driver hasn't shut the door and he's
staring at me as I'm proceeding to jump start
Congressman Over the Hill."

Angeleen even had to pause and laugh, recalling
the Kodak moment.

"That's when I turned around and shouted, 'Shut
the sonovabitchin' door you little goddamn pervert!'
The priest and part-time chauffeur jumped about six
feet, then slammed the door and got in the front.

"Well, I'll tell you what, all the way back to the congressman's hotel, he was moaning with delight and that little pervert driver was dividing his time about 20/80 between the road in front of him and the show in the back. It's lucky he was a man of God, because it was a definite miracle we made it alive to our destination.

"When we got to his hotel, which was only 10 minutes away, my date was so exhausted I had to get two bellhops to carry him up to his room. I was through with him for the night and went home early, took a hot bath and had one of those rare early quiet nights at home. The next day, Theo was on the phone, shouting and asking if I realized that I did a guy in the back of the freakin' archbishop of Philadelphia's private, holy, blessed limousine.

" 'Hey,' I said. 'How was I supposed to know it was a holy car. Besides, it serves them right. Why does an archbishop need a stretch limo like that anyway?' I told Theo none of that would have happened if the church bigshot had practiced his vow of poverty and owned a Chevy or a Yugo."

A round of applause greeted the last story of the evening.

It was late. The three women, strangers who had bridged a gap through the brief story sharing session, headed to their rooms for a good night's rest.

In her bed, with the lights out and blinds open, Angeleen looked up at the stars. Drifting toward dreamland, she thought: *There was no way I would tell two total strangers my most bizarre experience. If I did, they'd be afraid to sleep in the same house.*

Then, in little frames—fuzzy and black-and-white and distant—she recalled the times she had hidden, quietly in motel room closets, clutching her dirty, gray, stuffed rabbit in her arms. There she sat, in the dark with her face pressed into the rabbit's back as her mother—Mammo Marguariete—earned money for their next meal. Whenever Angeleen tried to recall pleasant childhood images, her secret road down Memory Lane begins and ends with lonely nights, listening to her mother in heated moments of false passion in the rented beds of passing strangers.

Then the other, more frightening, pictures come. The ones with red blood, lifeless bodies, buckets of sticky water and damp pink washcloths. She's there, rubbing down the room, erasing evidence that she and her mother had been there. Sneaking out with stolen money and riding off in strangers' cars. Hiding in unfamiliar towns. Eating strange food. Not eating at all. Not sleeping. The smell of stale beer, cheap whiskey, dirty clothes . . . fresh blood.

No, those stories would have been too frightening for her new roommates. Better to keep them to herself.

Monday

I t was early on the first day of the work week when
Darryll arrived at the Dire Federated Equity Savings
and Loan. Ushered directly into Craig Dire's office,
the detective returned a wide smile as the banker
greeted the area's recently arrived prodigal son.

"I'm glad you came in, Mr. Potters. May I call you
Darryll?"

"Sure, go ahead."

"Thank you. I'm glad you took no offense at my
letter, but I like to do things directly. Out in the open.
Above board. Understand?"

"Sure."

"Good. Now, what about my offer?"

"Well, Craig, you don't mind if I call you Craig, do
you, Craig?"

"No, of course not."

"Good. Well, it's like this Craig. My mother left me
the property, and it's been in the family for quite a
while."

"Five generations, Darryll," Craig smiled. "I do my homework, as you know. But, please, go on."

"As I was saying, it would be sort of irreverent to my dead kin to sell the old historic estate off within a few days of coming back home. I'd like to think that I would be able to settle in, get the lay of the land. One thing I would sure hate is to think someone was trying to run me off for some other reason. Like the state was putting a highway through the land, or the government was going to build an airport or military base there, and I sold just a might bit too soon. Understand?"

"Yes," Craig said, "of course."

Darryll smiled. "Good. I like to get to the point, myself, not beat around the bush. So, I only been back a few days, but I know that you're the man to see. Hell, I can't pick up the paper without reading about you, or seeing your picture. There you were this morning, right up there with the governor's wife. That's some pretty strong connection, the way I see it."

Craig smiled, pleased that even this newcomer had noticed the *Dire Mill Ledger's* front page shot of him and Melinda with Stephanie McDevitt at last weekend's charity event in Wilmington.

"So, do I hear a proposal of some sort, an offer?"

"Yeah," Darryll responded. "Give me 12 months to get settled, give the farm a go and call off the goons from licenses and inspection. I figure you can do that. If, after the year, I decide to pull up roots, or sell off the property, then you can have first option for the sale—at 800 grand."

Craig's eyes narrowed. He hated being outfoxed, but he also respected a formidable challenge. "You've done your homework. Let's say I give you 6 months."

"Ten!" Darryll countered.

"All right, 10 months, and we settle on $300,000."

"I'll need 500 grand, tax free, and I can live with the 10 months," Darryll replied.

The game was still in play. Craig paused, breathed a heavy sigh and said, "My final offer, Ten months and $450,000."

"Tax free," Darryll completed the sentence.

"Agreed," Craig said.

"It's a deal," Darryll said. "I assume you'll have some papers drawn up for me to sign."

"Come back tomorrow morning, Darryll. We can take care of it then." Craig offered his hand, and Darryll completed the handshake. "Before you go, I hear you had some trouble outside town last Thursday."

"Yeah. Got pulled over for speeding, then the bastards roughed me up, took me to jail in Salisbury. Hell, this place is like a Third World country. We could never get away with that shit in Maine."

"Yes," Craig said. "Our governor's been believing the publicity they write about him. A number of us believe his master plan of law and order at any cost is getting out of hand. Do you want to file a lawsuit? I'd be glad to provide the services of one of my legal team."

"No, but thanks anyway. I think I can handle it. Got the bruises to show the judge at the trial. That ought to be worth something."

"Don't count on it," Craig said. "One other thing. What are you going to do, just work the farm for the next few months? Are you seeking a job?"

"Are you offering?" Darryll asked, smiling.

"Perhaps. We could use a man with your talents. I have a number of interesting enterprises that reach far beyond DelMarVa. A good man with a set of balls like you displayed in the Bay Wolf the other day could come in handy."

Darryll looked up, only slightly surprised. "I guess word gets around."

"Sure does," Craig said. "Well, I'll see you soon. If I'm out, my secretary will have the documents. You can have someone look them over."

"That won't be necessary. I trust you," Darryll said, staring Craig in the eye. "Shouldn't I?"

"Of course, and I appreciate the compliment," Craig said. "If you can't trust me, the town father, who can you trust? Any plans for the rest of the day?"

"Yeah, I'm going crabbing."

"Really!" Craig said. "With anyone in particular?"

"Some guy named Maurice Knowles. I met him in the Bay Wolf. He seems like he knows the water around here, and the season's almost over. I wanted to get out, and he had an open day."

"Yes. Mo the Know is certainly one of our more colorful characters and a good man. Knows the bay. Enjoy the water."

"Thanks."

As Darryll closed the main office door, Rolph walked in from a side entrance.

"What do you think?" Craig asked.

"He stinks."

"Now, Rolph, why do you think that? I find him a bit intriguing."

"Once a cop, always a cop, plus he roughed up one of our boys pretty good at the Bay Wolf, and he's already hooked up with Mo the Know—who's been on our watch list for some time."

"Yes," Craig said, "in town only a few days and he's in the center of a string of coincidences. Interesting."

"I don't believe in coincidences," Rolph said, his eyes hard and cold, "but, you can sign those documents, or you can forget about them. It doesn't matter."

"Why?" Craig asked.

"Because, I have a very strong feeling that your new friend will be dead before you start hanging your Christmas decorations."

❧   ❧   ❧   ❧

As *Little Mo* bobbed in the water, Mo the Know and Darryll tossed over crabpots, followed the trail of white bleach bottles that formed their operating perimeter and headed the boat back to pull up ones they had deposited at the start of their outing an hour earlier. The afternoon wind was calm, making the deep water off Dires Mill Landing as smooth as glass.

The 70-foot, shallow keeled wooden craft was as close to a skipjack as one could find. The single inboard motor insured its movement on windless days, but when she was under sail it was like being one with nature.

"When the sails are up and catching a good wind, you feel just like a flying fish," Mo said. "Now, where do we stand after your little sit down with the big man in town this morning?"

"I think Craig offered me a job, at least he broached the topic. What do you think?"

"I think you should be very careful. This guy is a certifiable nut. He's like a mean ol' jumbo crab. The closer you get to him, the more likely you're going to get hurt—and when he hurts, the injuries seem to be of a fatal nature. Have you met Rolph, his little body-guard-sidekick-toady, yet?"

"No. Who's he?"

"A short Neo Nazi with an inferiority complex that he calms by hurting people very severely. He shows up as Dire's chauffeur, business partner, butler, whatever role he's told to play. He's never far from Craig's side. He also heads up a small commando-style security unit of about 12 other local militia crazies. You met four of them in the Bay Wolf. You're already on their hit list, so you can imagine how they'd react if you became one of their coworkers."

Darryll shook his head, reviewing the information he'd been receiving at a rapid pace.

Mo broke the silence by asking, "Have you always been a shit magnet, 'cause I'd like to know if this is something I'm going to have to get used to on a long-term basis?"

"Hey!" Darryll replied, "in Maine all we had to do was bring in stranded boaters, pick up the town drunks and pass out parking tickets during the tourist season. We didn't have knights in black armor running around killing off their wives or robber barons buying up the countryside and burying the bodies in the town square."

Mo laughed, reached under a tarp and pulled out a gray crock.

"What's that?" Darryll asked.

"A little something to warm us up, take off the chill from the water, 'a little spirits against the cold' the old watermen used to call it. Nowadays, we call it 'whiskey against the wind.' "

With a cup of liquor in a dented metal cup, Mo the Know leaned back against a small pile of canvas and began summarizing the Dire business empire, tossing in the background on his first wife, Charlotte Ann, who conveniently drowned accidentally in the bay.

Darryll listened intently, storing the important facts for later use while sipping on his share of the *Little Mo's* medicinal brew.

Finally, Mo offered Darryll two suggestions—he should drive the territory, get the lay of the land, as any newcomer would.

"And," Mo added, "you've got to go through Halloween House."

"What the hell is that?"

"Craig Dire's passion of all passions," Mo said. "Every year, for 10 days during the last two weeks of October, he opens his tobacco barn for free to everybody in the area. It's filled with the most horrifying stuff you can conceive of. I mean, I imagine there are professional people—shrinks with degrees out the ass—who would pay good money to get a peek into our boy's head."

"So, you want me to waste my time standing in line with a bunch of screaming kids, waiting to get a glimpse of Casper the Friendly Ghost and the Wicked Witch of the West?"

"No," Mo snapped, "give me a little credit, wiseass. First, you'll get an excellent, somewhat restricted, opportunity to get on the property where Dire lives without question, and that could prove to be a great advantage sometime in the near future. The second thing is, you'll get an idea of the sick bastard that you are dealing with. He spends thousands of dollars each year on this little hobby. He hires real actors, has the place filled with high-tech gadgets, live animals in cages, and who knows what the hell else is out there. Plus, our friend Rolph will be lurking around somewhere. So, do what I say and check it out."

"When does it open?"

"Tuesday of this week, tomorrow night, and it runs straight through to the next weekend, if it's like the last few years. It will be easy for you to find out. Come and see me after you get through. I'll be interested in your reaction. Fireworks show the last night. You can see them from here to half way to Easton, they say."

"All right," Darryll replied, still wondering how big a deal it could be. He hated rides and had never had any desire to visit Disneyland or any of the amusement parks. But, he added it to his growing list of chores. "I'll get there and give you my impressions when I get back."

"Good. But you better get there early. You'll be amazed at how fast the lines start forming. Now, you play checkers?"

"Not often. I'm more of a card player. Why?"

"I've got a board here. We might do a game or two after lunch. All right?"

Darryll shrugged his shoulders.

"How old do you think checkers is?" Mo asked, casually.

"I don't know."

"Take a guess," Mo urged.

"God, do we have to do this all the time?"

"Just guess!"

"Two hundred. No! Wait. A thousand years old. How's that?"

"Not bad," said Mo, opening a can of beer from a nearby cooler. "Checkers was played in the early history of Egypt. That mean's it's about 5,000 years old, at least. Plato and Homer mentioned the game in their writings. So the Greeks knew about it, and later the

Romans. In England, checkers was called draughts, and the first book about the game was written in 1756. Interesting, isn't it?"

"Yeah, real nice to know," Darryll said, weakly.

"How about this one?" Mo said, eagerly.

"NO!" Darryll snapped. "I can't stand it. You don't ask anything anybody knows except you."

"This will be an easy one," Mo said, his voice a plea. "Just one more. Okay? And it has to do with boats and water, so its appropriate, with us being out here crabbing."

"Fine," Darryll agreed.

"Why do watermen believe that blue is a bad luck color for a boat? If you look around, you'll never see blue paint on any part of a waterman's boat. In fact, I've heard some watermen will turn their boats around and head back to shore if they discover anything bearing the color blue on their boat. Do you know why?"

Darryll rolled his eye and replied, "Probably has something to do with the god of the sea, Neptune, getting pissed off because that's his favorite color, or some absurd shit like that."

For the first time that day, Mo was speechless.

"Well?" Darryll asked, "Did I win the prize or something?"

"You're very close. In fact you're right!" Mo replied. "The superstition associated with the color blue dates back to the days," Mo said, "when Indians paddled the waters of the Chesapeake Bay in dugout log canoes. Indians who lived near the Choptank River would never paint the color blue on their canoes, because they believed that color belonged to the water gods. The Indians thought if they used blue, it would make the water gods jealous and unhappy. So they avoided the color out of fear and respect. Today, it's avoided out of superstition."

"Great," Darryll said. "Now are we done?"

"Done," Mo said, running a hand through his black oily hair.

"You mean it?" Darryll asked, not believing his new partner.

"I swear," Mo said, holding up a can of beer in his right hand while taking the oath.

"Good," Darryll said, starting to head for the side and pull up a trap.

"Now, you like chicken?" Mo asked.

"Huh?"

"Chicken, you know, yellow beak, white feathers, why did the chicken cross the road—that kind of chicken. You like chicken or not?"

"Yeah, I guess so, why?"

" 'Cause I got some excellent, fresh, DelMarVa fried chicken for us to eat for lunch in this cooler."

"Thanks," Darryll said. "Pass it over."

"Not so fast. Answer this first: What is the length of the longest recorded flight of a chicken?"

"You promised, you no good bastard!" Darryll said, smiling slightly.

"That was for conversational questions," Mo replied. "This is a lunch question. There's a difference. So. What's the longest a chicken can fly, according to the current record?"

"How the hell would I know?" Darryll asked.

"Hey, you knew the last one. But, I don't know how you could possibly know this answer. Just guess," Mo urged him.

"I have no freakin' idea."

"I'll give you a clue. The answer is in seconds."

"Five!" Darryll said, tossing out a figure to get the game over with and eat.

"Nope. Try again."

Darryll shrugged, "Ten. Any better?"

"Better, but wrong again. One more chance."

"What happens if I get it right?"

"You get to eat," Mo said, unwrapping a chicken leg from the aluminum foil and taking a good-size bite.

"What if I get it wrong? Do I sit here and starve?"

"We'll see. Just guess."

"Hell, 25 seconds! I don't know."

"Are you crazy?" Mo said, a bit annoyed at Darryll's pathetic and unenthusiastic response. "Don't you know that chickens can't fly?"

"So what's the damn answer?" Darryll said, getting hungrier and more agitated, as he was quite eager to eat.

"Twelve seconds," Mo said, quite pleased with himself, "but I think they tossed it off a cliff."

"How the hell do you know?" Darryll demanded, reaching in the basket for a piece of fried fowl.

"I just do," Mo said, stiffly, adding, "a man in my position has to know these kinds of things."

9

Tuesday

During her first days at Dire's Mill Mansion, Angeleen and her new friends marveled at the relaxed atmosphere and considered the gig more a vacation than work. It was almost criminal to receive money for doing absolutely nothing but lounging by the pool and enjoying the fresh breezes coming off the bay.

She began to get concerned on Monday, the second day, when she was restricted from leaving the grounds. She had decided to take a drive into town and was forcibly pulled from a sport utility vehicle (SUV). During the scuffle, a security guard threatened her with physical harm if she tried to "escape" again—saying, "I got my orders!"

Storming off, she reported the incident to Melinda, who assured Angeleen that the guard would be reprimanded and it was all a slight misunderstanding. The next day, they all would take a ride and tour the countryside.

The following morning, on Tuesday, blond-haired Tina and Nannette, the redhead, waited in the driveway with Angeleen near the rear of the mansion, expecting to head into town. Melinda called them into the house to talk to Craig, who was pacing across the living room. In the far corner stood Rolph, his arms folded, looking like a rent-a-cop at a rock concert.

"Ladies, come in," Craig cooed. "Take a seat, please."

"We're ready to go," Angeleen said, a bit impatient and asked if there was going to be a delay.

"No. No delay, my sweet," Craig said. "Just a little chat before we get too far along."

"We don't need a chat," Tina said, "we need to get going and see the sights, Sugar. We've been cooped up here for three days and we're ready to spend some of our hard earned money and party!"

As the tiny blond waved her arms in the air, Nannette and Angeleen laughed.

Craig and Rolph were silent. Melinda walked over to the trio, standing by the doorway and led them to the couch, where they sat in a row. It was Wink, Blink and Nod, having no idea of what was going on and too blissful to expect a problem had been ignited and its fuse could not be doused.

"We have to talk," Melinda said, kneeling in front of the girls.

" 'Bout what?" Nannette asked, her face a question mark of confusion.

"About the rules."

"Rules? Who needs rules?" Tina said, laughing. "We're here to play and get paid. That's the only rule I want. Right, Sugar?" She winked at Rolph, who remained a frozen Boy Scout in the distance.

"Look," Angeleen said, "we're a bit antsy to get going, so can we make this quick? What's the story here? Are we going or not?"

"No!" Craig said quickly. The answer was totally unexpected, so the three girls didn't initially comprehend his response.

"What the hell did you say?" Nannette asked, getting off the couch and moving toward Craig.

Melinda watched, shaking her head, knowing that trouble was imminent.

"I said, 'No.' " Craig replied. "No one is going anywhere off these grounds until your jobs are over. There's plenty for you to do here. Swim. Relax. Listen to records. Eat. Read. Watch television. But no one leaves the grounds."

"Do you hear this guy," Nannette said, walking around Craig in a circle, quite angry by this time and taunting him with her imitation of his earlier recommendation. "*Read! Relax!* Listen to *records!* What time warp is this guy from? The 1950s? Go screw yourself grandpa. We're heading out to drink and screw and do whatever the hell we want. So shove it!"

As Nannette turned and started marching toward the door, an armed security guard appeared and blocked the way.

The other two women jumped up from the couch.

"What the hell is this?" Tina shouted.

"Are we goddamn prisoners or something? Angeleen snapped.

"*Or something.* That's a nice term. Yes, *or something* would be a good way to phrase it," Craig said. "You can either sit back down and listen—and obey, or you will be made to sit down and listen—and obey. Understand? Which will it be, dear ladies?"

The two nearest the couch sat down. Nannette, tried to rush past the guard, but was knocked in the stomach with the butt end of his rifle.

She was on her knees and gasping for air. Craig, seeing her pain, walked to her side. Forcefully, he grabbed her hair and dragged her across the floor, tossing her toward the other two women.

"Now. Here are the rules, ladies," Craig snapped. His voice was a snarl, his tone evil and deranged. "You do what I say. You don't ask questions, and you get to live. You screw with me, and you die. Anybody not understand that? I tried to make it very simple, not difficult to memorize. Now, any problems with that?"

No one spoke.

Melinda approached. "Girls, please, we're under a lot of pressure to get the show together. So you will have free movement around the grounds. The pool, the refrigerator, the game room and unlimited refreshments are all yours. Just don't go where the guards tell you not to."

"Why?" Nannette asked from her spot on the floor, her voice filled with anger, as she rubbed her head.

"For your own safety and because . . ."

Melinda's explanation was cut off as Craig's boot connected with Nannette's head. "I SAID NO QUESTIONS! YOU STUPID BITCH!"

Tina and Angeleen cringed as they saw Nannette's body fly forward and hit the floor.

Craig paced over to her and grabbed her hair. "That's two stupid mistakes in less than five minutes for you, bitch. Want to go for number three?"

As he released her head, it fell onto the carpet. Nannette was breathing, but not conscious. No one else had any questions, and no one else made a sound as the two guests who could walk were escorted back to the guest house. They both stayed inside during the rest of the morning. When Nannette returned two hours later, the three women ate a cold meal that was delivered to their door.

~ ~ ~ ~

Later on Tuesday afternoon, all three nervous actresses were shown the stage area where they would perform, beginning that night. They were hopeful when a guard told them they were going to be witches working with Melinda, who they believed was the Good Queen of Halloween House.

After costume measurements and a two-hour rehearsal they knew their parts. Scream at the crowd, take turns banging on the glass and act like they were in pain and trying to get away. The most important rule was to come to Melinda when she commanded them to do so.

The audience would see their facial expressions, but not be able to hear anything they said.

"You can scream, call out for help or curse out the crowd," Melinda said, "but no one will hear one word. This enclosure is totally soundproof, so your body language is very important."

The work wasn't hard, but they still resented their lack of freedom. Most of all they were scared of Craig Dire. They had only seen him a few times but, all three agreed, he was a Grade A, Numero Uno nutcase.

Melinda, they had decided, was going to be their salvation, and they sucked up to her big time. Throughout the rehearsals she was wonderful, and during the off time she was a gracious hostess. More than once they asked each other how she could stand her husband.

Before opening night, in their guest house living room, Tina said, "I'll tell you this, when I get done with this gig, I'm never coming anywhere near this state. I don't want to accidentally meet that asshole Dire, because I'll kill him and be sitting on Death Row."

"Yeah," Nannette agreed. "What a crazy bastard. How did someone like Melinda get hooked up with a nutcake like that?"

Smiling, Angeleen said, "For the same reason all of us are here, baby. Money with a capital 'M.' Did you see her rings, and those cars, and that house? Hell, they've got to be mega rich to pull this shit off. Think what they're paying us for doing next to nothing."

"Except being kept as prisoners for three weeks," Tina said.

"Yeah," Nannette said, "you can pay me $300 a day—plus 15Gs on top of that—to lay on my ass and swim and do nothin'. Hell, I say this is the best gig I ever had. And, before we go, I'm tellin' that Mr. Nutcase that I'll be glad to come back next year. No! Change that. I'll be glad to stay for six more months and just hide my little ass out here. I've got nobody layin' their dirty hands on me, nobody insultin' me. I can sleep all night long. I don't have to get dressed up in anything but a black sheet and wear a pointed hat and scream for a few hours. Hell, I've been fake screamin' for my Johns for years, and that pay isn't anythin' near what I'm gettin' here. If you ask me, this is the next best thing to heaven on earth."

⊗　　⊗　　⊗　　⊗

That evening, on opening night, the witch trio entered the glass chamber and waited for Melinda. Nannette was still bruised from her morning beating. They were alone, the audience hadn't arrived and they looked over the set.

"Right now, with the lights and scary music, this is one eerie place," Tina said, staring through the glass at the high ceiling of the tall tobacco barn.

"Gives me the damn creeps," Nannette said.

"Me too," Angeleen agreed. "Reminds me of the kind of place my mother would have loved to have. She was a witch."

"A real witch?" Nannette asked.

"Yes. Where do you think I got this?" she said, raising her left palm toward Nannette's face. "My mother, Mammo Marguariete, carved it into my hand with a hunting knife and then filled in the gashes with ink. It will never wash away. You'd have to cut it out. Goes nearly down to the bone.

"What's it mean?" Tina said, holding Angeleen's hand to get a better look at the markings.

"It means I'm a child of the devil, and he'll always protect me, especially against any other evils, no matter how powerful, because I belong to him."

"Damn, that's serious stuff," Nannette said.

"Well," Tina said, forcing a weak laugh, "working here, you might get a chance to see if it works."

Just then Melinda entered the room. She was dressed in black, tight-fitting leather. Her face was covered with pale white make-up that was accented with jet black lines and thick, blood-red lips. Her eyes were on fire, like she had been charged by a set of jumper cables.

Her tall spike heels enabled her to look down on her assistants.

Angeleen was the first to notice the change in Melinda's eyes. They were wild, filled with rage. Her right hand grasped the thick handle of a long leather whip whose end separated into six pointed slivers.

She slammed the door tightly, locking it with a key that she shoved in the top pocket of her pants.

"BITCHES!" she shouted. "COME TO ME NOW! RUN!"

As the trio turned and began to walk to Melinda, the sharp end of the whip hit Angeleen's shoulder.

"That hurt!"

"It'll hurt a lot more if you don't do as you're told!" Melinda snapped.

"Screw you!" Angeleen replied.

This time, Melinda's reply was a crack of the whip that cut into Angeleen's cheek.

Tina and Nannette backed off, moving away from their new friend and heading for the far corners.

Enraged, Angeleen charged toward Melinda, who had been expecting the attack. When Angeleen got within striking distance, Melinda easily avoided the woman's advance and jammed the handle of the whip into Angeleen's gut. Falling to the floor, Angeleen gasped for air. While Angeleen was on her knees and unable to breathe, Melinda slapped the girl across her face and knocked to the ground.

Jumping on the dazed girl, Melinda punched Angeleen in the head with savage force. Screaming, Melinda said, "Now, my little disobedient witch, this is what happens when you don't listen to your elders."

The pounding and punches moved down, into Angeleen's midsection and didn't stop until the woman was huddled on the ground, a human ball moaning in pain.

Leaving Angeleen on the dirt floor, Melinda went to a corner and pulled out a lengthy section of heavy chain. As the other two witches watched, their mistress placed a rusted shackle around Angeleen's right ankle and shoved the chain through a loose link. When locked, it gave Angeleen just enough movement to reach the front and side sections of the glass. After she stood and recovered from the beating, there was no way she would get out of the room—unless Melinda unlocked her prisoner.

"Do either of you want the same thing?" she snapped.

They shook their heads.

"Good. When I say scream, you'll scream. When I say bang on the window, you'll do it. If I say bark or meow, you'll do that too. Or it's the whip and the chain. Understand?"

They nodded again.

"Good. Now get ready and lift her up off the ground. The first group is coming and my husband will be watching. We don't want to disappoint him do we?"

"No," Tina said, pulling Angeleen to her feet.

At the end of the first night's performances, Halloween House was a success. In the *Dire's Mill Ledger* article the next day, the reporter wrote that the performance by the Wicked Witches was "the most realistic acting of the evening."

The three women made it through the first night and had kept Craig Dire at bay. However, they knew they couldn't rely on Melinda to save them. She was almost as crazed as her husband. During the following nights, they discovered conditions getting a lot worse. They realized they were definitely going to earn every cent of what first had seemed a very easy gig with generous pay.

10

Thursday night

O l' Mose could hear the sounds of traffic, coming across the meadows. The source was
about four miles in the distance as the geese
fly. The night was black and crisp, but the glow from
several rotating searchlights flared across the sky. It
was Thursday of the third week of October and, like
he did every year, Craig Dire had opened up his
three-story tobacco barn to anyone who wanted to
come up and see the horrifying sights.

Crazy people, Mose thought, as he shook his head
and relit his well worn pipe. Sitting in a cane rocker
on the wooden porch of his small home in
Blacktown, the scent of burnt cherry surrounded his
face. *Only crazy people would stand in line for up to
three hours to see them creatures in wild costumes
screamin' and carryin' on and actin' like they was
being tortured to death.*

Tall, black iron gates with spear-like tips closed off
the 800-foot paved lane leading to the main entrance of

Dire's Mill Mansion. Two of Craig Dire's full-time security guards were assigned to keep unauthorized vehicles from entering that private section of the estate. If the main gates weren't locked, some of the overflow crowd would have tried to head up the driveway and cut across the open fields to get to the front of the line.

For the past eight years during the end of October, Craig and Melinda Dire had turned a portion of their property into a Halloween lover's extravaganza. The inside of their barn was a state-of-the-art chamber of horrors, with mechanical and human figures of vampires rising from coffins, zombies climbing out of open graves, devils appearing behind clouds of red smoke and the highlight of the show—three young witches trying to break through their glass enclosure and attack the passing crowds.

As more than 400 people stood in the slow—but steadily moving—line, puppeteers, musicians, jugglers and mimes walked through the crowd, entertaining those who were awaiting their turn to enter Halloween House.

It was two days before the weekend crowds, and it was a mob scene. Smiling and leading four members of the press on a tour, Craig Dire stopped on the edge of a hill, about 30 feet from the winding line, and pointed with pride.

"Here you are," he said. "The long and winding road of satisfied citizens enjoying good clean fun during the height of the Halloween season, compliments of Craig and Melinda Dire!"

Craig was clothed in a tuxedo, complete with top hat and a black cape lined in red satin. His skin was hidden under heavy make-up, and a pair of $1,000 custom-made fangs protruded from beneath his lips.

"We opened Tuesday, two nights ago. That's helped us get the kinks out of the performances before the larger weekend crowds. But," Dire said, pointing to the long line, "this is both expected and satisfying. Already, this year, we have crowds approaching the weekend numbers in the middle of the week."

"Where's your wife, Mr. Dire?" asked Diane Kramer, on-camera reporter from WDMV-TV, *Your Eye on DelMarVa*.

"Good question, Ms. Kramer. You'll see shortly. All I'll say right now is that this year Melinda decided to take an active role in our little production."

The reporters jotted down a few notes and then looked up, waiting for more. And Craig Dire wasn't one to disappoint the members of the press.

"This successful enterprise was my brainchild, a healthy, entertaining family event where all of DelMarVa could come—for free I stress—and enjoy a horrifying evening of blood-curdling fun. Of course, we have an age limit—no one below the age of 7 is allowed to experience Halloween House. That's because we don't want our little ones up all night screaming and crying from the frightful scenes."

"Could you tell us how expensive this is?" asked Tom Harrison of the *Baltimore Bullet*.

"No problem. I'd estimate that with the professionally designed scenery—which is different each year—plus security patrols, extra police for traffic control and, most importantly, the guild actors from New York City that we hire each year, we spend in excess of $75,000. But, what better way to show the community how much we care than to throw a party and invite everyone to come?"

"I've heard that since you were born on Halloween, this is something like your own private birthday party. Is that right?" The question came from Liz Hardy, a reporter from the *Diamond State Ledger*.

"I won't deny that I enjoy All Hallows Eve more than the Yuletide season. The amount of decorating we do at Christmastime is far less than the effort we expend on Halloween, as you can imagine. So, in a way, I will admit that, for me personally, this is a very special event. We use real coffins delivered from a casket company in the Midwest. We buy the hogs heads, freshly butchered from the slaughter house, so those rotting eyes and bristly snouts you pass on stumps of logs are as real as can be." Smiling with pride, he added, "You should see the reaction when someone touches them and the rotting slime gets all over their hands. It's absolutely delightful to watch the reaction. But," he added with a laugh, "it's their own fault, since we have signs posted that specifically state: 'Do not touch the dead bodies or slaughtered animals.' "

The reporters took more notes and jotted down the pearls that Dire knew he was dispensing.

Seeing his comments were having the desired effect, he continued, "Everything is as close to the real world of horror as we can possibly make it. When Baron Zomdee, our 8-foot-tall zombie, crawls out of his grave and heads for the passing line of gawkers, they are truly glad there is a wire mesh screen keeping him contained. And those who get too close can smell the stench from his rotting flesh and ragged clothing. It's much like the perfume of a mixture of rotten eggs and dead crabs left in the August sun.

"When my gray-haired werewolf swings over the crowd on a rope hanging from the rafters of the barn, the men actually clutch their women for protection. I recall the night we had a fraternity group from Salisbury University. They came with their ladies. We heard the jocks boasting of their bravery as they approached the barn doors. They were complaining that our presentation was a weak show, 'a lame attempt at horror' one boy said.

"Essentially, they came with an attitude," Craig said, pausing and laughing aloud as he recalled that night.

"I instructed my werewolf to drop into the crowd and, literally, pick up the biggest macho jock he could find. That year, Wolfman, who was quite a huge specimen standing well over 6 feet in height and built like an Olympian, fell from his rope and landed in their midst. Immediately, all of the fraternity *men* grabbed their dates and hid behind them. As instructed, Wolfman moved directly toward the group, latched onto the biggest jock and carried the young man out the door. Unfortunately, the student was so scared he began shouting, 'Let me down! Put me down!' It was pathetic and the crowed roared with laughter. When he was released, the boy was so embarrassed that he walked back to his car and waited for his friends to finish the tour. We have it all on film. I forgot to mention that there are 18 security cameras in the barn and we file the tapes every year. Often, we have friends over for a private showing in the mansion theater."

"In light of that incident," Diane Kramer said, "I'm a bit surprised about your age limit. Do you think it's really appropriate to allow children as young as 7 into your private chamber of horrors?"

It was obvious Craig was stung by the comment. "I beg to differ with your terminology, Ms. Kramer," he said, sharply. "This is not *my private chamber of horrors*. It is an entertaining and educational presentation that, I repeat, is presented totally FREE to the community. I also believe that parents can make the best decision as to whether their children should attend or not. If they want to come, they are most welcome. We haven't had any complaints in all these years. And, I might add, if you look down the waiting line, I don't think you will see anyone dragging bodies along and pushing them in the door. Do you?"

"No," she replied, "but my specific question was related to the appro . . ."

"PLEASE!" Craig snapped, holding up his right hand. "Allow me to complete my statement. Besides," Dire continued, "I firmly believe that a good dose of horror is important to one's healthy psychological development. My bedtime stories were filled with threats of Patty Cannon crawling up the side of my house and entering through my bedroom window with the sole purpose of ripping out my liver and eating it in front of me while I died in my bed.

"And my mother told me if I didn't clean my room Bigg Lizz was going to come over, take out her tobacco knife, chop off my head and I'd have to carry it under my arm when I went to school.

"One of my most interesting experiences during my youth, was the evening my uncle—Elrod Dire the town undertaker—locked me overnight in a coffin in his casket warehouse. I had carved my initials in the top of the bronze metal finish, messing it up quite badly, and he grabbed me by the shirt collar and said, 'Craig, you little no good bastard! If you intend to put your name on it, then you better be ready to use it!' and he locked me inside."

"Weren't you scared to death?" Tom Harrison asked.

"Quite the contrary," Craig said. "It was more comfortable than I thought it would be, and I used the time productively, thinking about how he handled the situation, and if I would do the same.

"And, today, I trust you can tell by looking at me that I haven't suffered any ill effects from being scared out of my wits at a tender young age."

Everyone but Diane Kramer laughed. She forced a smile and felt a definite chill as she stared at Craig Dire's cold, dark eyes.

"Enough talk!" he snapped. Turning away from his media guests, Craig commanded, "Now, come. Let's get you inside Halloween House."

〰   〰   〰   〰

Having stood patiently for 90 minutes, Darryll Potters had progressed from the rear of the line, up the rolling hill and was standing about 10 feet from the front of the waiting fun seekers. He could clearly see the group of eager reporters who had formed a small semicircle around Craig Dire.

Only four persons from the front of the line, Darryll watched, using his experienced eyes to record the sound, sights and smells. Craig was too busy to notice the detective's recent arrival to the area, but Darryll wore a Shorebirds baseball cap pulled well down onto his forehead.

Off to the side, Darryll recognized the two security guards. He had met them in the Bay Wolf. One was the boy he had slammed to the floor, the other was a partner who had carried his injured friend out the door. It was a small world indeed.

As Craig directed the reporters toward the Halloween House entrance passing those at the front of the line, several people started to shout complaints about the line butters.

Prepared as always, Craig shouted, "It is I, Craig Dire, the Master of Halloween House, and these people are my special guests! Thank you for your understanding in allowing us to proceed!"

"HELL WITH THAT!" a man in a purple Baltimore Ravens cap and matching sweatshirt shouted. "I'VE BEEN IN LINE FOR TWO HOURS! GET THEM TO THE BACK OF THE LINE!"

Several others standing nearby applauded the man's complaining.

Calling a short, alien-like creature in a gray rubber suit to his side, Craig passed him an envelop and pointed to the crowd.

"There are four of us moving ahead of you," Craig shouted. "My assistant," Craig pointed at the little guy, who was approaching the visitors, "will be handing out $20 bills to the next 20 people standing in line, as compensation for your understanding and patience."

Most applauded, but, as Craig turned to head toward the entrance with the press, the man became more vocal.

"I DON'T WANT YOUR DAMN MONEY, DIPSHIT! I WANT TO GET INTO THE HOUSE RIGHT NOW!"

Enjoying the spectacle, the crowd urged the man on.

Obviously annoyed, Craig called the short man, who Darryll assumed was Rolph in an alien disguise. After a brief whispered conversation, the alien walked to the man in purple. He spoke to him briefly, then nodding, led the loudmouthed Ravens fan and his embarrassed wife alone into Halloween House, ahead of the reporters.

As the crowd clapped, Craig bowed and shouted, "Everyone who comes to Halloween House leaves a satisfied customer."

After a brief conversation with the press, Craig began his guided tour, directing his employees to add 24 more people to the press group. Because Darryll was only 10 feet behind, he ended up with the right crowd and edged up as close as possible, hearing all of the information that Craig shared with the press.

The outside entrance was impressive, with yellow planks affixed to the sides of the old barn. As they approached the door, visitors passed through a cemetery complete with more than 100 real marble headstones of all varieties.

"These were all carved especially for Halloween House," Craig said, laughing, adding, "No. We did not rob any local resting sites, but had craftsmen make reproductions. And, I am proud to add, many bear the names of famous Dires of days past."

Darryll noticed the names of the Craigs I through IV, then there was Jebediah Dire. Near the wrought iron fencing rested markers indicating a relationship to the Johnstons—a 19th century gang of kidnappers whose worst and dumbest apparently somehow had married into the Dire Dynasty.

A winding flagstone path through the graveyard led past hundreds of lit candles, giving the eerie scene the impression that a large number of recent visitors had dropped by to pay their special respects to the well-liked family.

"These candles are replaced three times each evening," Craig said, "and the scent of hundreds of them burning and mixing with the night air is just divine."

Off in a secluded section of the graveyard, where there were no tombstones, Darryll could make out a circle burned in the grass. Within the round black outline was a five-pointed star with a number of scattered lines intersecting each other. Fat, tall black candles were burning at the five points of what Darryll realized was a Satanic "pentagram." He hadn't seen the symbol for many years and was slightly jarred at the sight.

Noticing movement, Darryll had to walk swiftly to catch up with his group, getting inside just as an assistant was closing the main door.

"Keep in mind," Craig said, "each of these seven scary scenes is presented several times during the evening. The actors must keep alert and always be ready for the next group. It's quite a demanding evening for them, But," he laughed, "they all are paid well. Very well."

Turning, he pointed to the cage to his right. "This is the first scene," Craig said. "To maximize enjoyment, we limit each tour group to no more than 50. Ladies and gentlemen, meet Baron Zomdee."

Behind a mesh screen on the left side of the barn, a dozen voodoo women, all black skinned, wearing white loose dresses and tops, sat on the ground in a Haitian graveyard set and beat out a steady, enchanting and repetitive rhythm.

In the distance, beside a small mud and grass hut, six family grave mounds were marked by pieces of burnt and shattered tan and gray wood.

As the chanting and drumming got louder, the women began to dance and jump, eventually throwing down their drums and swirling in circles until they let out a deafening scream and fell to the ground.

The area was about 30 feet square, more than large enough to accommodate the scene.

Suddenly, a light shone on the tallest mound and music, piped in from a speaker, began to fill the area. It was hypnotic and mysterious, a mixture of savage sounds of the jungle and Gregorian chant. The light changed from green to red to yellow to white—again—green to red to yellow to white—again—green to red to yellow to white.

Then a hand bolted through the earth, then another, until a huge human form was shoved up above the ground. It's arms extended upward made the height of the body seem larger.

The moving ragpile looked like it wore the bowels of the earth as clothing. The women in white screamed and ran to the farthest corners of the cubicle. Many of them had their backs pressed against the wire mesh in front of the guests, blocking the view of the smaller visitors.

Snarling, the tall creature from the Netherworld moved forward, looking from side to side with green eyes that glowed like bright stars. Obviously a theatrical gimmick that proved effective.

Soon, he focused on one of the women, who, when she knew she was the chosen one screamed and tried to get away. But the Baron kept advancing, slowly, stomping his dead feet on the ground with each advancing step.

"NO!" she screamed. "NO! HELP ME!" But no one responded. The other women, to save themselves gathered in a circle, closed in and together, as a group, dove upon the Baron's woman of the night.

Up and down, up and down, their clenched fists went, hundreds of blows were inflicted on the woman at the base of the death pile.

"Better to give her up than themselves," Craig shouted. "An elementary lesson in survival," he added, laughing at his comment. "Now watch this."

As if on cue, they all stood up, moved back, blood covering their hands and faces. And, in what was the center of the circle, was a battered, beaten chicken.

Gently, like Frankenstein when he met the little girl by the lake, Baron Zomdee picked up the dead fowl, cradled it in his arms and stumbled back into his grave.

"If that's not true love, I don't know what is," said Craig. "Now, this way, please."

No one spoke as they progressed to Scene II: The Witch Trials.

At the second stop, the group was directed to a small set of bleachers, "to get a better view of the court proceedings," Craig explained, smiling.

On an elevated stage—about 10 feet deep and 30 feet wide—there were two scenes separated by a divider. A small courtroom was on the left and a torture chamber was situated on the right.

The proceedings picked up in mid-session. A scowling, white-wigged judge shouted down at the defendant, a man locked in hand and leg irons that had been erected directly below the judicial bench.

"What dost thou plead, Demon?"

"I'll not respond to that question," the young man answered.

"LASH!" the judge shouted, directing an officer of the court, who appeared from the left to strike the criminal.

"SLASSH!" The whip cracked as it connected with the defendant's back and ripped a section from his brown cloth shirt.

"Will you respond now, Brother of Satan?"

The man shook his head, indicating no.

Again the judge directed the application of the lash, and the action was repeated six times before the weakened accused fell to the courtroom floor.

As blood appeared to flow from the actor's back, two more court guards dragged him off, leaving a trail of red liquid in his wake.

"Amazing what they can do with props and make-up these days," Craig said to his guests.

Suddenly the lights appeared on the right side of the stage, where the accused was lying between two doors, one resting on the floor of the stage and the other pressed atop his chest.

The judge bent over, looked him in the face, and again asked for a response.

The beaten man, now the interior of a door sandwich, shook his head as far as he was able—indicating no response.

Pointing to three hefty assistants, the judge announced, "Crush him to death for his crimes and may the Lord have mercy on his heathen Satanic soul."

Immediately, the stage darkened and a spotlight shone on the face of the accused, which was turned in the direction of the astounded audience.

In the background, one could make out the silhouettes of three executioners, in Pilgrim-style hats, dropping small boulders on the top of the door. With each application of jagged rock, a deadly sound reverberated through the stage and reached the ears of the audience.

Darryll counted at least 30 rocks. If each weighed 25 pounds, there was 750 pounds on top of the actor. But, good acting and well sculpted paper apparently made the scene very realistic.

The victim's initial screams turned into gasps for air, and, throughout his punishment, the spotlight never left the actor's contorted face. Finally, the light's focus became smaller and smaller, until nothing more than the elongated tongue of the dead warlock was seen. Then, a final gasp, and all the lights went out.

This time, a healthy round of applause rose from the bleachers as the crowd showed its approval.

"This was based on an actual incident that occurred in Salem, Massachusetts, the only town in America to legally crush a person to death.

"Better to speak early than to forever hold your peace, eh?" Craig the punster said, pointing to the crushed, oozing dummy jammed under the door. "Next stop, we will see what delights the future has to offer."

In Scene Three, the group was led into a round chamber, similar to the inside of a space ship. Once all were inside, a flashing sign said, "Select A Seat," referring to the several dozen molded silver plastic resting places that were built in a semi-circle into the circular wall.

Darryll was careful to select a spot to Craig's left, just out of the host's line of vision.

A series of pulsating, multicolored lights flashed overhead, and a booming voice announced: "Welcome to Earth—Alien Wasteland."

During the next six minutes, an array of surround-sound audio—plus video display technology projected on the entire circular wall and ceiling—presented a futuristic film of an alien invasion that causes the end of present day life on Earth.

The depressing film included droughts, infestation of insects, major cities in rubble, starving children, the total breakdown of society and humans existing as slaves to bug-eyed aliens. An end-of-the-film insurrection by a secret commando military unit is unsuccessful. Finally, to survive, humans are forced to eat their own dead and bear children who are sent to live on other planets.

"No happy endings here, folks," Craig said. "We have a few moments for questions before we continue. Anyone?"

"Are there any happy endings anywhere on this tour?" Diane Kramer asked, obviously the only one bold enough to be blunt with Dire.

Annoyed, the host replied, "In your case, Ms. Kramer, my happy ending will be getting rid of you the end of the tour."

"I have a question, Mr. Dire," said Tom Harrison of the *Baltimore Bullet*, attempting to deflect Dire's malice. "Who thought these scenes up? Was it like a package deal you bought from a consulting firm, or a group development decision? I mean, some of what we've seen so far is pretty rough and jarring."

Breathing heavily, Craig tried to control his response. "Of all the people who have been through here, this is the only time my creativity has been questioned. To answer your question, I am the one who thought up the scenes, wrote the scripts, hired the actors, supervised the lighting. It's all mine, and I'm proud that it is having the effects I intended."

"And what is that, Mr. Dire?" Liz Hardy of the *Diamond State Ledger* asked, shoving a microphone toward his lips.

Craig was annoyed by now and had lost any sense of control. To hell with them, he thought as he answered, "To scare the living hell out of anyone who comes here and to make all of you stay up all night and worry that you'll be killed in your sleep. That's my intent and, as I can see, it's working.

"Obviously, none of you have the slightest idea of what the public wants and what it needs. This is Halloween, the time of the year when evil is allowed to prevail, and many wish and hope it does. I am delivering—at tremendous cost, Tom, and for free—a wonderful night of horror, and none of you seem to be capable of appreciating my largess or my creativity. I look at you, Ms. Kramer, and wonder if your annual salary is half what I've spent on constructing the shell of this spaceship chamber alone.

"In a most entertaining fashion, I have presented Haitian culture, an actual scene from the Salem Witch Trials, fodder for futuristic thought and more, but," he shook his head, "there's no use attempting to convert the ignorant."

Suddenly, changing his tone, the polite Craig Dire said, "Now, if you'll excuse me, I'm late for an appointment. My assistant, Mister Alien, here, will lead you through the rest of the tour. I'll try to meet you at the end, but, if not, have a horrifying evening."

The new host guided the party through scary scene Four, "Vampire Vengeance"; Five, "Chainsaw in the Cellar"; and Six, "Surviving a Cremation."

Darryll would describe those three scenes as he would all the others, blood, blood and more blood.

Except for the alien invasion, he thought to himself, *there was enough fake blood flowing on those stages to service all the blood banks in New England and half of the hospitals in Canada.*

It was Trouble Among the Wicked Witches, the last scene, that Darryll found most disturbing.

The group stood behind thick velvet theater ropes that kept the spectators about five feet from the edge of a glass enclosure where the show was performed. As the curtain opened, three young witches, all dressed in black, charged for the glass wall and began pounding against the window. Several of the viewers jumped back in fright.

A fourth witch, more beautiful than the rest and obviously in control, held a dark leather whip that she cracked in the air. With each sharp snap, the three underlings screamed and beat upon the glass.

"It looks like they're trying to break out," Tom Harrison said, amazed at what he saw.

From behind, came the voice of Craig Dire, who had rejoined the group. "These are the most realistic actresses I could find," he said, proudly. "Except for one. That beauty in the back, cracking the whip, is my lovely Melinda. As I said earlier, my wife likes to be heavily involved in our little show."

The group stared into the glass chamber, which held a bubbling caldron of greenish liquid, several roaming black cats and the trio of troubled sorceresses who were there to do Melinda's bidding.

For the moment, the whip was still. Melinda was shouting something, but there was no audio. No sounds reached beyond the thick plate glass.

"We've tried to make this last scene the most realistic," Craig said, looking intently into the glass box. "We want our visitors to leave with the crack of the whip imprinted in their minds."

Again, the sound of fists beating against the glass caused the group to turn back to the window. Darryll got the impression that the three slaves of Melinda weren't trying to scare the crowd. *No, they were crying out for help.* He stared into the eyes of the woman with red hair, watching the bottom of her fists beating the glass. Melinda walked forward and pulled the redhead back toward the bubbling pot, chaining her left leg to a ring connected to a metal stake protruding from the ground.

As he surveyed the scene, Darryll looked into the wide, dark eyes of the witch with black hair. The left side of her face was pressed against the inside of the glass tomb. Melinda approached, tried to pull the girl back, but the younger witch resisted, fought off Dire's powerful wife. The girl caught Darryll's eye. She knew it. Then, in one last effort to keep his attention, she pressed the palms of both hands flat against the dirty glass.

That's when Darryll saw the worn outline of the pentagram carved in the black-haired girl's left palm. At that moment, something jarred in his brain. It was the same symbol he noticed in the gravesite, outside the entrance of Halloween House. Perhaps. Maybe there was something else. Just as quickly as it came, the thought faded away.

Grabbing the young witch's long hair, Melinda Dire, looking both evil and powerful, used her strength to pull the reluctant witch away, chaining her next to the redhead. Only the blonde was left. Seeing her two sisters in chains, she lowered her head and walked toward the cauldron.

Silently, the curtain closed, and, for the last time of the evening, the group applauded.

There was absolutely no doubt in Darryll's mind that the three women weren't acting. They were all calling out for help, beating the glass to get out, trying to attract the attention of anyone who would notice their suffering and fear. That was the cruelest joke of all, that Dire and his wife would abuse their human trifles publicly, to the applause of the passing ignorant masses. He could only imagine the utter frustration of the captives, hoping and praying that someone could see the horror that was occurring and do something to free them.

Beaming, Craig thanked the visitors for coming. "Tell your friends. Come again. Everyone is welcome in Halloween House. Also, on your way out, be sure to fill out the free chance forms. We will be giving away a solid bronze adult casket during our grand prize drawing on closing night. It will be stored at Dire's Funeral Parlor for your eventual use. And," he added with pride, "we will gladly exchange it for a child's coffin if that becomes necessary."

On the way to his car, passing several dozen idiots who were busily filling out multiple coffin chance forms, Darryll realized he had a lot to think about, and a lot to share with Mo the Know. He planned to go home, have a cold beer and visit Mo's dock early Friday morning.

       ❦   ❦   ❦   ❦

An hour after the last performance, Rolph entered the kitchen of Dire's Mill Mansion, planning, as he did each night, to make a final report to his superiors. Melinda and Craig were waiting for him at the round table, a cup of coffee in front of each.

"I took care of the loudmouth," Rolph said, "just like you said. But we've got problems." Rolph's face showed traces of concern.

"What are you talking about?" Craig asked. "I'm not in the mood for any problems tonight. I think we'll get some bad reviews in the paper about the Alien Wasteland segment." Craig's voice was weak, indicating his concern about press comments questioning his artistic efforts.

"You're what?" Rolph snapped, astounded at his boss's priorities. "Well, you better concentrate on this, because I caught our friend Mo the Know in a canoe, under the deep dock, down near *The Melinda*. He said he was fishing. That's probably true, but I'll bet it wasn't for bass. I think the bastard was trying to get something on the operation."

When Craig didn't answer, Melinda tried to take control of the conversation. "What does he say?" Melinda snapped, realizing Craig was too depressed to think clearly.

"Nothing! For a guy who has all the answers to everything, he's not willing to talk."

Melinda thought for a moment. "If he's found anything, there hasn't been time for him to relay it to anyone. What was on *The Melinda* for him to find? Anything?"

"Not a damn thing," Rolph said confidently. "We checked it over, plus we went through his canoe and clothing. If he found anything at all, and I say there was nothing to find, it wasn't on him."

After a few seconds of silence, Melinda spoke. "I say let him go. If we make a big deal of it, who knows what attention it will bring. We can have your men keep an eye on him. Did they work him over?"

Rolph smiled, "Oh yes. Very well. I think if he had something he'd have given it up. I took some pictures of their work. Look at these," he said, proudly placing six instant snapshots on the Dire's kitchen table.

One of Mo's eyes was totally closed, the other was half shut. Black and red bruises covered his cheeks and forehead. Blood trickled down his nose and stained his neck and the collar of his sweatshirt. The photos stopped at mid chest.

"They gave him some good gut shots, too. He didn't sing a word, kept saying he didn't do anything wrong. I'm inclined to agree with you, Mrs. Dire."

"Good, then let him go with a warning. Give him a few hundred dollars for his trouble, and tell him to get out of town and not come back until he's cleaned up."

As Rolph nodded and began to head for the door, Craig exploded from his seat. It was as if an electric prod had been jammed into his back. "JUST WHO THE HELL IS IN CHARGE AROUND HERE?" he shouted, making Melinda spill her coffee.

"WHO? DAMMIT, WHO?"

"You, Sugar Doll! Of course," Melinda said, lowering her head.

"Yes, sir! You, as always," Rolph added.

"I've listened to you two pathetic weaklings, ready to let this intruder go. He was on our property, wasn't he?"

No one answered.

"WASN'T HE?"

"Yes," Rolph said, "but . . . ."

"Don't but me you little short piece of shit. I can break you like I can break her," he said, pointing to Melinda. "I won't have anybody snooping around my estate. The next thing you know, I'll have McDevitt and his state police up my ass. Nobody comes on this property and gets off alive. Understand?"

"Yes, sir," Rolph said, nodding.

"Now, come outside with me, my little general, and I'll tell you how you will deal with the problem of Mo the Schmo." As they walked into the yard, Craig laughed at his joke and Rolph forced a smile.

Alone in the kitchen, Melinda remained calm. It was during times like this when she became concerned. She had always known Craig was a bit unstable, but his explosive reactions were becoming more frequent, and his temper was affecting his judgment. She was smart to have hidden away money in her safety deposit box in Salisbury.

In fact, she decided that tomorrow might be a good day to check on the contents and review her false passport, in case things got as hot as she feared they might.

≈   ≈   ≈   ≈

Darryll sat in an overstuffed chair in his living room, a beer in hand and his feet resting on a cardboard box that hadn't been stored away. A single kitchen light cast a dim glow that escaped from its source into the edges of the adjacent room where he tried to relax.

Early Friday morning, just around sunrise, he planned to go talk to Mo the Know. God, Dire was a certifiable schizo—one minute the gracious host, the next a foaming zealot. Darryll couldn't wait to read the reviews of Halloween House in the regional newspapers that Dire didn't control.

The whole tour had bothered him. The security patrol, the guy with the Ravens hat being escorted off,

Dire passing out $20 bills to the crowd, like a king tossing pennies to his pathetic subjects.

Then the scenes inside Halloween House. Was that a walk through Freak City or what?

Sipping his beer, Darryll reviewed the seven scenes in his mind. From Baron Zomdee to the Wicked Witches the entire experience was unnerving. He admitted that Halloween was supposed to be scary, but Dire's message was nothing but troubling. Darryll could only imagine the increase in the crime rate 10 years after the first 7-year-olds passed through Dires' private chamber of horrors.

At 2 in the morning, Darryll couldn't think anymore. He had been on his feet all night. His eyes were tired, his legs were sore and his brain was fried. Taking another swig of his beer, he set the bottle on the edge of the tan box sitting in front of his chair. Standing up, he stretched his arms toward the ceiling.

Whether it was the effects of the brew or the lateness of the night, he began to fall over. Righting himself, his foot hit the cardboard box, causing the bottle to topple. The remaining liquid spilled on the top of the box, ran down the sides and dumped a stream on the wooden floor.

"DAMN!" he shouted to himself. It was too late at night, or too early in the morning, to be up playing Susie Homemaker. Grabbing a towel from the kitchen, he ran back and started wiping up the liquid mess.

As he rubbed the front of the box, the black lettering began to smear. He paused and read the names—Sarah A. Small, Cheri Harris, Gail Pillster, Mary Jane Hampill, Joy Gwinty and Debbie Lou Simpson. Six ghosts who have haunted him for years, now calling out again. But what was he supposed to do. There was no way he could find them or their kidnapp . . . . .

"JESUS H. CHRIST!" he shouted. "It can't be, but it just might. I don't freakin' believe this. If this is true, it's the biggest goddamn coincidence in . . . . No! There's no such thing as a coincidence." He stopped talking aloud to himself.

Silence is what he needed now. Quiet would help him find the file he wanted. It was in the box. He knew it.

Hitting the overhead light, he grabbed the manila folders and spread them all across the living room floor.

He could see the facts of the case just as clearly as if it were four, no six—who the hell cares how many years ago. It was there, in the damn box, and he was going to dig it out, solve the missing person case. Solve them all.

He leafed through Cheri Harris. Six foot, 210 pounds, red hair. No good. He threw it aside.

Debbie Lou Sampson. A blonde—4 foot 11 inches. Forget her.

Joy Twinty. A 5-foot, 6-inch brunette. The right height. Her hair could have been dyed. No. She wasn't the one.

Sarah A. Small.

Darryll ripped open the file and flipped through the sheets of the report. His finger raced down the pages, typed more than a half-dozen years ago by an unknown secretary living a thousand miles away.

His finger stopped.

"BINGO!" he said, aloud. "I knew it! I've got you, you little, beautiful, black-haired bitch! Come to papa. YES!"

Getting up off the floor, he sat at the dining room table and read the entire history of the girl who had disappeared in 2002, at the age of 17, from a street corner bus stop in Maine.

At the time, Sarah A. Small was a ward of the state, and placed in a foster home with an older couple in Washington County. She had been no trouble, but they sensed she was restless and bored with life. She had told them she "wanted some excitement."

Sarah had been taken from her mother—Margaret Small, who went by the gypsy name of Mammo Marguariete. Soon after the forced separation of mother from daughter, Mother Small was tried, convicted and sentenced to life in prison for the murder of three traveling salesmen.

She killed all of them in resort town motel rooms. The news was a real downer for the tourist business. The rooms were in sad shape after Mother Small was done with her prey, even though there had been some effort to tidy them up.

Her M.O. was to meet lonely men—usually traveling salesmen or conventioneers—in a middle class bar, take them to a cheap motel in the next town, and stab them in the throat after they passed out following a romp in the sack.

When Mother Marguariete was captured, her 14-year-old daughter told authorities her own mother had threatened to kill her through the "mobo muja" hex. The child was convinced she was going to die. Sarah never participated in any of the murders. Her mother called on her to do cleanup after the fact. On one occasion, she was involved in the disposition of a body—helping Mammo Marguariete stuff the dead gent in the back of a family tourist van that had been left unlocked in the same motel complex.

When she was 17, Sarah left her foster home for a neighborhood walk and disappeared. She was last sighted getting on a bus heading out of town.

She was described as attractive—weighing 110 pounds, standing 5 foot 4 inches tall—and possessing one distinguishing mark, a black pentagram that her mother had carved into the palm of the girl's left hand.

Closing the folder, Darryll asked aloud, "Sarah A. Small, what the hell are you doing in a Halloween play in Dire's Mill Mansion, and where the hell have you been for all these years?"

Friday at sunrise

I t was cold and a light coating of frost had formed on the windows of Darryll's car. As he used his broken handled scraper to make a rectangular viewing area on his windshield, his warm breath formed small white clouds of smoke as it connected with the chilly air.

The heater hadn't had time to warm up the interior of his car by the time Darryll parked in front of Mo the Know's nautically decorated, single-story, white-shingled residence.

The front yard was small and narrow, only 10 feet from the black-topped roadway, but in that distance between the public street and the steps of Mo's modest seaside castle were at least a hundred ceramic and wooden creatures of the land and sea.

Gnomes stood guard beside fish and crabs. Cats and dogs—frozen in a pose created by a poor Asian, sweatshop worker 10 thousand miles away—looked at Darryll through dull, paint-chipped eyes.

A dozen painted plaques were nailed to the sides of the house. Ranging in size from a foot square—with crudely painted images of crabs and fish—to full size shipboards bearing the names of vessels long gone—*Lord Baltimore, Princess, Mary Jane* and *Treasure Seeker*. Other than the decorative name-plates, the rest of the ships were beneath the bay or had been chopped up as scrap to feed cabin coal stoves or duck blind fires.

Darryll thought about pulling on the thick weathered rope to ring the rusted iron bell affixed to the doorframe. But, it was six in the morning, and he didn't want to announce his arrival to the whole street—even though that would only be the occupants of the other three fishermen's huts in sight. But they probably had been up before sunrise and were already out on the Bay.

Darryll rapped on the front door. No answer.

He waited for what seemed like a minute and hit the door again, this time a bit harder.

No sounds of stirring escaped from the inside of Mo's place.

The third attempt was directed against the window glass that surrounded the long narrow front porch off to the right of the main entrance. Giving it a good half-dozen quick raps, he felt the wobbly glass release a healthy sound that should have reached even a sound sleeper.

When no Mo responded, Darryll walked to the rear of the building and headed for the red-stained, one-story fishing hut where Mo kept his traps.

The *Little Mo* was tied up to the rocking dock, so Dire's Mill's resident philosopher had to be nearby, Darryll thought. Shelly's, the town's early breakfast diner opened at 5, but Darryll, the new squire of Gobbler's Knoll, hadn't see Mo as he had driven past the eatery on his way over to the waterman's house.

An assortment of colorful floats was strung together through thick rope. The chipped paint on the round surfaces was what a perceptive artist would call "primitive beauty," and the painter would probably use the term as the name of a finished oil or print.

As Darryll's eyes followed the string of crabtraps and floats, hanging on the outside of the shed, he walked to the front. A white sheet of paper, its top right edge blowing as the wind got underneath, tried to escape. The other three corners were stapled, to make sure it was there when the first visitor arrived.

The note read: *How many crab traps can one Mo the Know fill?*

Darryll's mind began to spin out of control. Was this a Maurice Knowles joke, a riddle that he pulled on his friends?

Hopefully, yes. Probably not.

Darryll looked near the door handle. The hasp had been broken, the splintered wood fresh, indicating a recent break-in. He looked around to see if Mo was peeking out from behind the kitchen window, enjoying the scene, ready to jump out and shout "Surprise!"

Nothing.

Grabbing the door handle, Darryll hoped it was locked. It flew open too easily.

It was dark inside. At the angle it was situated, the morning sun couldn't reach the interior of Mo's fish hut. Darryll walked back, through traps stacked on either side, high as shoulder level. His foot kicked something. It was metal. It make a clanging sound.

He continued, heading for the thin string that dangled from the low-watt overhead bulb.

A click . . . and dim light filled the center of the shed. Then, to his left, a section of traps was covered with a ripped and frayed, gray-green tarp. Stapled to the front was a sheet of white paper and writing that matched the note affixed to the front door.

Answer! 20 was written in bold, black letters.

His eyes wide, expecting what he hoped would not be, Darryll carefully pulled the coarse covering off the mound of metal traps and stared at the decapitated head of Mo the Know.

It had been hacked off at the neck and arranged at the top of the temple of human fishbait so that the beaten face would greet the finder of the grisly deed.

Scanning the surrounding traps, Darryll saw arms, hands, legs, thighs, a half of a torso, the matching portion probably in another rusted cage.

Racing from the hut, he knelt on the dock, leaned his head over the side and tossed whatever had been left in his stomach into the water. He rested the palm of his hand against the planks. He was dizzy. His face was soaking from beads of perspiration that covered his entire body.

With his hand he wiped a layer of water from his forehead and cheeks. Sitting on Mo's dock he thought of the sick animals that had hacked Mo to death, how they looked at him as he screamed when they removed his hand, his arm, his leg. Maybe they took off the head first. At least then the pain would have ended early.

But Darryll knew that wasn't the way they did it—Dire and Rolph and as many of their followers they had needed to hold the poor bastard down.

They made him suffer, enjoyed his screams. They did it somewhere on the rich bastard's estate and then delivered him here. Darryll knew they were watching him right now, laughing and satisfied with his reaction to their handiwork.

They could have this moment to enjoy, he thought, standing up and stumbling toward the shed. But he had to go back into the death hut and pay his last respects to Mo. He owed him that, and maybe he could find something, figure out some way, to pin the crime on the killers.

A few minutes later, Darryll left the fish hut that was heavy with the scent of rotting flesh. He walked directly toward his car and drove to the Dire's Mill Sheriff's Office to report the murder. He knew the locals would never find the killer—since they already knew who it was. But Darryll was going to play along, make them wonder, not show his hand. Then, in the end, he would give them more grief than they ever could imagine.

∽ ∽ ∽ ∽

Darryll spent the rest of the morning in the police interrogation room and at the crime scene, going over what he saw, when he saw it, what he touched, what he thought, what he had for dinner the night before, where he was all evening, where he was through the night, describing his route into town and why he went to see Mo the Know.

"To go fishing, I told you," Darryll said, annoyed and exhausted.

"Them don't look like no fishin' clothes ya got on, Mr. Potters," Sheriff Saxton Dire said. The main man was in charge of the investigation and didn't want to—or had been told not to—let Darryll Potters off the hook too easily.

"Look, I explained 20 goddamn times," Darryll snapped, "I went down to see Mo because we talked about going fishing. You follow me so far, Dick Tracy?"

"I'd say you better watch your mouth, boy!" the sheriff snapped.

"And I say you better clean out your ears, sheriff, or listen to the tape recording of this conversation that's been going on since Christ was a baby in swaddling clothes. Now, look. I'm an ex-cop. Do you think I'm going to move into town and, within the first week, go down, hack up a guy I go fishing with and shove him into little see-through containers? Then, am I such a freakin' idiot that I'll drive over to your facility and tell you about it, first thing in the morning?"

"I don't know how smart you are, Mr. Potters. This here, comin' forward on your part, could be a real clever trick that's maybe worked for you 'afor. Up in Maine, say. We been on the phone to your chief, up 'air, tryin' to see if any similar type crime scenes have tookin' place while you was workin' up 'air."

"GOOD! You are one smart sonofabitchin' law enforcement thinkin' machine, sheriff." Darryll said, slowly, watching his interrogator return the smile. "And what did my former boss, the chief of the Washington County Mounties tell you?"

The sheriff was stunned. Speechless.

"Well, what the hell did old Tom Henry say?" Darryll snapped, referring to his ex-boss and chief of police in Maine. "Did he tell you that there were dozens of similar human crabpot fishbait serial killings up there? Huh? I know the answer, sheriff. The answer is, 'NO!' No he didn't, you freakin' moron! And do you know why?"

The sheriff still didn't respond, his scattered thoughts obviously somewhere else.

"I'll answer you then. No. He didn't find any crimes like that because they never happened—not when I was there and not before or after. But, I figure, just to be safe, you had better call him back and ask if they found any little kids—say about 3 or 4 years old—full sized and all complete and not hacked up, stuffed in the larger lobster traps they use up there. That's because, they don't have midget-size, freakin' blue crabs up in Maine. They've got man-eating lobsters. And our bigass, meaner-than-hell lobsters will beat the pincher-snapping shit out of your pip-squeak, good-for-shit, blue balled Chesapeake freakin' Bay crabs. Now, what do you think of that?"

Behind a glass wall, observing the interrogation, Rolph and Craig Dire watched with smiles of delight.

"This is quite entertaining. Don't you agree, Rolph?" Craig asked.

"Very much so, sir."

"I hope we have a video of this. Melinda would enjoy it immensely."

"I've already taken care of it. I'll bring it home with me tonight."

"Good work. Now, I've got to get back to the bank. It's already well past noon. Give them another 15 minutes, then tell my cousin, Saxton, to let Potters go. No sense beating a dead horse. They should be out there looking for the real killers, don't you think?" Craig laughed as he patted Rolph on the shoulder and prepared to leave the station.

Inside the inquisition room, Sheriff Saxton Dire raised a hand and asked, "What county did you just say, Potters?"

"WHAT?" Darryll shouted, jumping up from the table. "I said Washington County. WASHINGTON! Like in George and Martha and the chopped down cherry tree and the freezing, ball-busting winter at Valley Forge. Why?"

"Well, is sure no wonder we ain't got the right details down here yet. Our little girl out there, she's been callin' up t' Walda County. They ain't never heard of you up there. A little mix up, I guess," Saxton added with a weak smile.

"WALDO is two counties over, you incompetent nitwit!" Darryll screamed. "I've had enough of this horseshit! I am out of here and out of here now!" Darryll started to walk toward the exit, and the sheriff jumped up, moved his back against the door to block the way while reaching for his gun.

All movement stopped.

"What are you going to do, sheriff? Kill me? That will make two in one morning. But, in this town, from what I hear, that's still a slow day."

A rapping on the mirror, coming from behind the glass, broke the tension.

"You wait right here, Potters," the sheriff said, leaving the room and locking it from the outside.

Darryll returned to his seat and stared at the glass wall, imagining Craig Dire and little Rolphie looking down at him. The sheriff, some kind of relative of Craig's who was on the payroll, would be inside, taking orders from the town's main man. Darryll knew he would be released soon. They couldn't pin anything on him, even though they would have liked to do so. The whole morning was a slap around session designed to keep him in check. He was very glad he hadn't brought along the folder on Sarah Small. Before he left, he had hidden the filebox under a stack of crates in the smokehouse—just in case anyone might decide to go through his place while he was gone.

After what he'd seen, you had to cover your tracks real well in Dire's Mill.

Sheriff Saxton Dire re-entered the room, smiling and taking a seat. "Well, Potters, seems like we're jest gonna have t' let ya go. But, I'm givin' ya a strong warnin'. Stay outta trouble. Ya ain't been in town for a whole week, an' already you an' me has met. I don' recall me meetin' any other newcomer as fast as I done met you. I find that jest a bit concernin'. Now, maybe what ya's say is true. If so, that's real good. But, I'm in the business to find out things, an' I'm gonna do my job. As ya can tell, I'm good at what I do. So ya jest head on outta here, an' keep your nose clean and stop buttin' into trouble. Understand me, boy?"

Darryll smiled, eager to leave, but he was also still annoyed. He decided to jerk the country lawman around a bit before departing.

"I understand completely, sheriff," Darryll said, nodding appreciatively. "The way I view your current situation and sound advice, you find yourself in a position here, trying to satisfy a variety of conflicting constituencies. The political, economic and social pressures of the community and unbridled progress in the region are moving at an accelerated, exponential rate. This rapid change is taking you to an elevated plane of existence and concern. Therefore, you have an earnest desire to maintain a delicately balanced equilibrium that allows you to focus on the external environment but, simultaneously achieve an inner harmony that you will find both pleasant and financially rewarding. Correct?"

After a long pause, Saxton answered, "Yes."

"And I, through no effort of my own I add, today stand before you as a fly in your ointment. Right?"

"Right again," Saxton replied weakly.

"So, sheriff," Darryll extended his hand, "I am out of here. But, before I go, please accept my sincere appreciation for a memorable stay. Your facility is pleasant, your staff hospitable and your professional demeanor exemplary. If ever I am contacted by a national survey organization, I will give your agency the highest rating."

"You're playin' with me now, ain't ya, boy?" the sheriff asked, narrowing his eyes.

"About what, sheriff?" Darryll replied, "the facility, the staff or your skills?. Oh, no, sir. I have never been more sincere. Here, take my hand." Darryll reached across the space that separated them and shook the sheriff's right hand firmly. "And, one more question, sheriff."

"Yeah?"

"If I come across any leads, have any ideas about this crime, may I come and speak to you personally?"

"Hell, yeah, boy!" Saxton said, nodding, his mind now clear that Darryll wanted to be a friend of the Dire's Mill Sheriff's Office. "Ya come on by any ol' time. We'll have us, jest you and me, a cuppa hot Joe, talk about crimes and such. Our door here is always welcome t' ya. Hell, boy, we's in the same business— fightin' crime."

Nodding, Darryll replied, "I couldn't have said it better myself."

⤳   ⤳   ⤳   ⤳

"A Mr. Potters to see you, sir."

"Wonderful! Show him in," Craig Dire replied into the speaker of his phone. *This was indeed a surprise*, Craig thought. *Fresh from the interrogator's box, the ex-policeman has come to see me in my headquarters*.

Following the events of the morning, Darryll was not in top shape. His clothes were a mess, his hair a greasy mat and he was still angry and annoyed. But, for the last 25 years, throwing off his adversaries was what he had been trained to do, and this was as good a time as any to try to confuse Craig Dire.

Walking from behind his desk, Craig extended his hand and cheerfully greeted his surprise visitor. "Well, to what do I owe this pleasant surprise visit?"

"The papers," Darryll said, "you said I should come by and sign them."

"Oh," taken slightly off balance, Craig replied, "I'm a bit embarrassed. I don't believe they've been delivered from my attorney. Let me check."

Pressing the intercom, he said, "Loretta, call Mr. Wheeler and find out the status of the documents he was preparing for Mr. Potters' signature. And call me back with the information immediately!"

"So sorry, Darryll, but a lot has happened these past few days. Have you heard about poor Mo the Know?"

"Heard about it," Darryll replied. "Hell, I was there."

Taking a seat and indicating that Darryll do the same, Craig said, "Whatever do you mean?"

"I mean, Craig, that I was in the damn fish hut and was the one who discovered Mo's body."

"My God! That must have been horrible!"

"Horrible isn't the word," Darryll said, leaning forward and lowering his voice. "There is no word I can think of that can describe what was in there."

"Do you mind sharing it with me? What you saw and your reaction?" Craig asked, rubbing his hands in anticipation.

"You want me to describe it? I mean, I can. But why?"

"Well," Craig said, waving his hand in the air, "one can only get so much from the newspapers, and the police are of no help. They keep everything to themselves. If you don't mind, I'd appreciate it. I have bit of a fascination with this sort of thing. Being a police officer, you can understand, can't you?"

"Yeah, I sure do," Darryll replied while thinking, *You are one sick bastard, and one day soon I am going to put you in my own little chop box and watch you squirm.* Smiling, Darryll nodded and began.

"I pulled back the tarp and there he was, Mo the Know in about two dozen crab pots, chopped up in little hunks. I'd never seen anything like it in my life."

"Was there any blood?" Craig queried.

"Good question, Craig. Not really. From the looks of it, whoever did the hacking performed the butchery someplace else, then brought the parts over and stuffed them into the pots."

"Quite an ingenious idea, don't you think?" Craig said, smiling at the former policeman's apparent awe of the style of the crime.

"Most would think so, at least at first, but it's not the least bit original. Hell, they've been doing the same thing, hacking away body parts, since Count Dracula decapitated and impaled thousands in Transylvania in the 1400s. This was not anything that will be considered a major league breakthrough in the annals of crime. Most experienced cops would laugh at the amateurish nature of the job. But down here, where it's mostly death by drunken beatings, a jealous spouse, road kills and staged hunting accidents, I'd say it will be considered sensational."

The intercom buzzed, and Craig, annoyed at the interruption, ran to his desk. "What?" he snapped.

"I'm sorry, Mr. Dire, but the papers won't be ready for a few more days."

"Thank you. Now, no more interruptions." Smiling, Craig turned and walked back to the chair. "So sorry, but we'll call you when the papers arrive."

"Can't," Darryll said, "don't have a phone yet. But I can stop by another time." He began to get up out of the chair. "Sorry to have bothered you."

"On the contrary," Craig said. "This has been most fascinating. Do you have a few more moments for us to chat . . . about the crime?"

"Hey, Craig, I'm retired and no longer a suspect," Darryll said. "That makes this my lucky day. Hell of a lot luckier than Mo the Know, get it!"

Craig laughed at Darryll's joke. *Maybe I've been wrong about him after all*, he thought.

"Why were you there so early?"

"We were supposed to go fishing. Man, that was a rough start. Tossed my guts into the river."

"But," Craig redirected the conversation to the body parts.

"Yeah, back to Mo the Know in miniature. Let me see," Darryll said, "where were we?"

"You were commenting on your opinion of the unsensational nature of the crime—relatively speaking, of course—when viewed by the trained eye."

"Yes. But, if you're interested," Craig said, again lowering his voice, "I can share a few tips about how I know they're going to catch this sick bastard—a few things I noticed that I didn't tell the sheriff."

"Why not?"

"Because he never asked, the dumb bastard," Darryll said, laughing. "Hell, Craig, I worked in homicide. That means murder was my specialty for a dozen years. Instead of asking me the same thing for five hours, old Saxton could have saved himself a hell of a lot of time if he drew on my expertise. The fact is, I discovered four major clues that can be used to lead directly the killers—and I know there was more than one person directly involved."

Craig stared intently, his ears wide open.

Responding to a nod that said "Go on," Darryll continued, "There were skin fragments under Mo's nails. That means he put up a good fight. Now, I don't know if it was the killer or someone who snatched him up and later delivered the goods to the butcher, but somebody around here is missing a good chunk of body skin. Could be from the face, the arms. Hell, it could be outta their ass, but the lab will pinpoint that quick enough, but only if Saxton and the boys pry it out soon. That's number one."

"And two?" Craig listened while wondering which of Rolph's incompetent guards had been clawed during Mo's abduction.

"Second is the material I pulled off the crabtraps. On four of the wire traps, there were strands of the same color of distinctive material—none on any others in the hut. Whoever was ordered to toss scraps of Mo into the metal bait boxes got his shirt or jacket caught on the rusted ends, and more than once.

Match the clothing and you have a suspect. Maybe it's not the hacker, but it will be a major link. It could have been a flunky who was paid to bait the traps. But, for that job I hope he got a bundle, 'cause I wouldn't take that assignment unless the pay was sky-high. But, I'll add this, he did a good job. Setting Mo's severed head in just the right direction, so whoever found it would get a faceful, was good work under the circumstances."

"Number three?"

"This one is 'Elementary, my dear Watson,' as Sherlock Holmes used to say," Darryll quipped, smiling at Craig, who was leaning so far forward that a sudden disruption would cause him to hit the floor. "There are fingerprints on the straight hunks of Mo's arms. The idiot who held him down pressed his hands so hard into Mo's limbs that the impressions are imbedded into the victim's skin. Any coroner apprentice will look for that first, and he should be able to lift them within minutes."

"Don't they disappear when the pressure is relaxed?" Craig asked, not overly bothered by this development, since he had worn a pair of plastic surgical gloves.

"Yes and no," Darryll said, casually. "If the crime is committed in the fall or winter—not late spring or in the heat of summer—the prints will usually remain for up to 24 hours. The fact that all of the puzzle pieces of our local boy Mo were shoved into that cold hut while the weather was just below freezing last night—then add the chill breeze blowing off the water—hell, I'd say if he's on the examination table now, they probably are running a print check through the FBI computer system. They might even have a match by tonight.

"Also, even if the killers wore hospital gloves . . . . "

"The latex type?" Craig asked, innocently.

"Right. They're so thin that prints can still get through if someone had been applying intense pressure to hold Mo down. An experienced executioner would have doubled them up, worn two pair."

"And there's one more item?" Craig said, afraid at this point to hear anything else. But, he was unable to ignore Darryll's statement that there was one more clue leading to the killers.

Darryll smiled and laughed aloud. "This is the best one of all," he said, shaking his head and watching Craig, who he could tell was in a very delicate, agitated state, anticipating the final bombshell. "Most people outside law enforcement have no idea this technique exists—and the development is so new that some in the field still don't believe it's possible. It's in the last steps of the experimental stage—not yet ready to go commercial—but in the lab it's worked in more than 70 percent of the test cases."

Darryll paused, staring Craig in the eye, trying to get a glimpse of the murdering bastard's black soul. "It's called Sight Trauma Photography—STP," he said. "Ever heard of it?"

Craig shook his head, unable to talk, and then waited for more bad news.

"Think about this, 60 years ago, they thought Dick Tracy's wrist radio was an unbelievable gadget that would never get off the pages of the Sunday funny papers. Today, hell, cellular phones, satellite communication, vibrating beepers. Technology just doesn't stop. What we use today is outdated within the year."

He paused and made Craig wait a little longer. Taking a breath, Darryll started up again, this time using a conspiratorial tone. "Look, Craig, I'm telling you about something that is cutting edge. So I need your promise that you won't discuss this with anyone else. Not even your wife. If criminals ever heard this is already available, well, you can just imagine the consequences."

"Of course. You have my word," Craig whispered, perspiration forming above his lip and at the edge of his hairline.

Suddenly, the phone rang, shattering the calm.

"DAMN!" Craig shouted. Jumping up, he ran to his desk and grabbed the receiver. "I said no calls!" he hissed.

"It's Mr. Rolph, sir. You know how he demands to be put right through. He just won't be denied access. I'm sorry. I had no choice."

"Well, tell him I said I'll call him back in 15 minutes, and if he doesn't like it, or calls me back first, he's fired!"

Breathing hard, trying to regain his composure, Craig slid back into his seat next to Darryll. "I'm so sorry. Please continue."

"Hey! I understand. You're a busy man, Craig, and I'm in here taking up all of your valuable time. I had better go."

"No. Please." Craig almost sang the words. He was trying to be sweet without showing it. It didn't work. "Now, share with me this interesting information about the new STP, the details, please."

"Yeah! As I was explaining, STP—Sight Trauma Photography—refers to a new, secret, state-of-the-art laser technology that enables someone to see the last thing that the murder victim—or any dead person—saw before he was killed or died."

Craig was motionless, too afraid to believe, too afraid not to. "I don't understand."

"Neither did I at first," Darryll said. "They can take out the victim's eyeballs, cut them open, insert some microcomputer chip device a hundred times smaller than the head of a pin. It roams around, taking muscular retinal impressions with a little camera strapped to its back. These are transferred into a computer that translates the impressions through some type of digital laser scanning conversion. The process is amazingly rapid—takes less than a minute per eyeball. Then, they put the captured residue through a warp speed film processor and, presto, they flash a picture on the screen and it's essentially a photograph—in living color—get the pun? They say it's what the victim viewed last. What do you think of that? Are we into the space age, or what?"

"Amazing. Truly unbelievable," Craig whispered, his mind still evaluating the possibility of such advanced and unheard of technology.

"Hey. I can't explain how it works, but it does. Can you tell me how your computer delivers e-mail, or how your car starts, or how an old Brownie camera with 120 film can take a picture? No, and neither can I or 95 percent of the people walking around. We just want to be able to get in the seat, turn on the ignition and CD and hit the gas and go." Darryll was enjoying himself.

"Hell! They went to the Moon and back a few times without knowing how the rocket was built, so who's to say STP isn't the latest tool in law enforcement's arsenal against crime? Besides, I saw it work in Quantico with my own two eyes, right here in these sockets.

"Plus," Darryll lowered his voice, "an instructor told me there are only three STPs in existence—one down at Quantico, another at the CIA headquarters, in Langley, and, imagine this, one at the DelMarVa State Police Crime Lab in Dover, right up the road in our very own state. I mean, we are in the big leagues. So, if the state boys get called in on this crime, if it isn't solved by Saxton's department, hell, it'll probably be wrapped up in an hour—that's as long as some-body doesn't steal Mo's eyeballs. Well, that's enough morbid talk for today. I'm taking up far too much of your valuable time."

Darryll was on his feet and shaking Craig's hand. "I'll come back next week to sign the papers, all right?"

"Fine," Craig said, walking him to the door, his mind several blocks way. "What happens if someone has the eyeballs? If they were missing?"

"As long as they're in a cold place, stored at between 10 and 32 degrees Fahrenheit, I believe they still will maintain the image. But, it's been a year or so since the course. You have to excuse my memory."

"Of course," Craig said.

"Well, whoever has Mo's eyes can blackmail the killers. That's they way I'd see it. Get it?" Darryll laughed at the pun. "Don't you think that's a fair assumption?"

"Yes. Good idea. Very obvious," Craig said, his voice devoid of conviction. "Well, have a good day."

"And remember," Darryll whispered, "I'd appreciate it if you'd keep the details about STP between us."

"Of course, thank you."

Once the door closed, Craig raced to his desk, nearly dropped the phone and hurriedly dialed

Rolph. Listening to the ringing cycle—once, twice—
Craig muttered aloud, "Hurry up. Answer the damn
phone, you miserable little asshole!"

"Rolph here!"

"Where the hell are Mo the Know's eyeballs?"
Craig hissed.

"What?" Rolph said. "Who the hell is this?"

"It's me, you idiot! And I want to know where
Mo's eyes are?"

"In his goddamn head, I guess. Jesus Christ, you
ought to know. You where the one hacking and saw-
ing on his neck, last I can remember. But then, there
was a hellava lotta blood in my eyes," Rolph said,
laughing at the joke.

Craig was squeezing the telephone. "Don't ask
any questions," he ordered, "just get down to the
funeral parlor and carve out the eyes, and do it now.
Then bring them right over here as soon as you get it
done. I don't want them leaving town when the county coroner claims the body."

Before he could ask the obvious question why,
Craig cut off the connection. As Rolph hung up his
phone, he wondered, *Man, is there no end to this
guy's sick obsessions with the human body? But, he's
the boss.*

In his car, driving slowly toward Gobbler's Knoll,
Darryll smiled as he imagined the conversation that
Craig Dire was most certainly having with his little
aide Rolph. That should keep them busy a while,
tracking down Mo's head and eyes.

"Sorry, Mo," Darryll said aloud, looking up
toward the sky, "but I know you understand. It had to
be done."

12

Early Friday evening

D arryll had spent several hours downing quite a few at the Bay Wolf. After entering his front door and making sure it was locked, he tossed his jacket across the nearest chair. Exhausted, he fell onto the living room couch. Stretched out, his body formed a straight line as if he were lying in an oversized bathtub.

Darryll closed his eyes and tried to relax.

When was it going to stop? he wondered. The evil forces in the town were all around, closing in, everywhere. His main contact was dead, he hadn't had a free moment to think about the Sarah Small situation. He had to find a phone booth and call Pentak, but first, just a few minutes of shuteye.

He was only out a minute when he heard a sound. Darryll couldn't decide if it was the footstep in the kitchen or the voice that he noticed first. They arrived at his senses at about the same time. It didn't matter, someone was in his house, and he was unarmed, his gun under his jacket across the room.

"I knows ya needs your sleep, but we's gotta talk, an' fast," the voice said.

Opening his eyes, Darryll turned to his left, facing the kitchen. It was dark, early evening, and no lights were on in the house. A glow from the moon passed through the open window to his right, illuminating the lower portion of a large man with dark skin. Darryll could barely make out a bald head and a full white beard.

"Who the hell are you, an African Santa Claus?" Darryll asked, his voice weary, his body tired.

"Might just be, afta' ya hears what I gots t' tell ya."

As Darryll raised his body into a sitting position, he asked, "You got a name?"

"Full name's Moses Abraham Neigel Jefferson, but everybody seems t' call me Mose or Ol' Mose. Any of 'ems fine wit me."

"How'd you get in here?"

"Gots me a key, Darryll."

"Damn! It took me three calls to the real estate agent to get an extra key to my own house and here a complete stranger's got one. Anybody else have one?"

"Not that I knows 'bout. But I don' much care 'bout that. We got talkin' t' do. So get up and come in the back kitchen. An' don' turn on no lights. We'll sit ina dark and use my flashlight."

Darryll followed Father Christmas of Dire's Mill into the kitchen, grabbed a seat in a corner of the table farthest from the windows and listened as Ol' Mose told a tale of murder, money and madness.

"I's here 'cause of Moreece," Mose said. "He was a good man. Too few a them 'round nowdays, 'specially in these parts."

"So you know he's dead?"

"Hell, Darryll, I knowed it 'afor you did."

"That's impossible. I found the body."

"Sure's right, but me, I saw who put 'em there."

"WHO?"

"One a Dire's army boys. Couldn't see what one. But, he works for that mean fella, Rolph. Saw him drop off the boy in a big Jeep. He and Rolph, they drugged a big canvas sack over t' Maurice's fish house. Broke the lock open. I was in the water, doin' some night fishin'. Nobody noticed me. Moved in close, an' could see it all. Them stuffin' them traps. Then I rowed on outta there. Never seed nothin' that bad in all my days. Helped me make up my mind t' come to you."

Darryll's eyes widened. "Hey, how'd you know my name?"

Mose laughed, shook his head and turned out the light. "I bes' start at the beginnin', then we can gets up t' speed."

Ol' Mose explained that when Darryll was growing up, he was a regular visitor to Blacktown and played with some of the children there. His mother, Gertrude Merrille Potters, was a good friend of Yvonne, Ol' Mose's niece. Gertrude and Yvonne worked together in the oyster packing house at Dire's Mill Dock. They would start at 4 in the morning and be done by noon, unless there was a heavy run. Then they'd work until they finished.

Usually, Darryll would be dropped off at Yvonne's mother's house, where he'd play with Yvonne's boys, Dexter and Clarence and Martin. Gertrude would pick him up after work. She and young Darryll would arrive home in time for her to cook supper for Darryll's father. He worked as a school teacher by day and as a farmer by night and weekends. But he died young, and that left Gertrude alone and in need of help.

Lenny Shamp was a drunken waterman, looking for an opportunity and he found it at Gobbler's Knoll, in the form of a widow with a young boy and, more importantly, free and clear prime property. He came on as a field hand, oiled his way into the kitchen, then slid into the parlor and eventually moved into Gertrude's bedroom, permanently. She felt soiled after they had relations, did the right thing—according to no one except the Methodist minister—and married Lenny Shamp. It didn't take long for her to realize she was hitched to an alcoholic and wife beater. The physical abuse began within the first month of Gertrude's second marriage, and it never stopped.

"You mother could never come back over t' Blacktown after she hooked up wif Lenny, no way. He hated us people, called us monkeys an' such. But," Mose paused and smiled, "you daddy before him, he was a good man, like you. Tried to teach us to write an' read an' such. That's part a what got 'im kilt."

Darryll's interest flew off the chart.

Mose noticed the response. "You don' know? Hell, boy. Your momma didn't say nothin' t' ya?"

"We didn't talk much when Lenny was around," Darryll replied. "He was too busy beating me up or slapping her around."

Taking a deep breath, Mose added more to the background than he had planned, including town history and the sad Potters family saga. He explained that Craig's father, Jasper, didn't want black youngsters from Blacktown learning how to read, so he refused to let them go to Dire Elementary School, where Darryll Potters Sr. was a fourth grade teacher.

Since there was no bus to take the black children to school in the next town, they had to quit, which was exactly what Jasper Dire wanted.

Darryll Potters Sr. saw what was happening and decided to teach reading and writing classes for free in Blacktown on Sundays after church.

"Your momma and daddy an' even you'd come over t' our services and then we had a big supper meal after he was done teaching. It was good times," Mose recalled, smiling. Then the grin vanished. "One Sunday, when you daddy was done wit' his lessons an' the boys an' girls has jest wen' home, he was headin' back to here, yo' house, an' Jasper Dire an' 'bout six men, they stop't his car. Beat you' daddy up real bad, an' drugged his body down the back roads. Then . . . I can' tell ya no more." Mose lowered his eyes, shaking his head.

Darryll, breathing heavily, ordered Mose to continue. "I have to hear it. What happened?"

"Jasper and them men, a few was his brothers an' their kin, they took yo' daddy's dead body and strung it wit rope, under his arms, from the wooden bridge that runs 'crost Blood Gut Creek. Wouldn't let nobody cut it down. Said if we did, they'd come back an' whip our youngin's real good. So, that poor good man stayed there a whole two days. Then, you' mamma, she marched down there, carried a big kitchen knife, an' cut 'im down, wit' them lookin' on. She was a brave woman, she was. Then the whole town, they wouldn' have nothin' to do wit her. She worked the farm alone for a full year, takin' care a you, tendin' the fields. They thought they could run her off, but she was a strong woman, she was." Mose paused to rub a tear from his eye.

"She would come over t' Blacktown, kep' in touch. Would give us vegibles when we was down an' havin' it rough. Some of our boys, who you daddy helpt to read, would go over at night an' do some work for her, when nobody could see. Helpt keep her goin'. So, when Lenny come along, she had no choice. Understand? It weren't 'bout love, it was jest need. To keep the farm, to raise you up."

Darryll was silent, his head hung low, his eyes looking at the table.

"You never knowed," Mose said, shakin' his head. "She was a good woman. She gived me the key to the house, not too long before she died. Askt me to check on it after she was gone, make sure Lenny din't burn it down, let it go to seed. Was savin' it fer you, she was."

"I never knew anything," Darryll said. "She told me my father was killed in a car crash and his body was thrown into a river and he drowned. How could I live all those years in this town and not know? How could it be that no one said one damn thing to me, during all that time? That's just not possible."

"Damn, boy. This ain't the real world. This here's Dire's Mill. If they say don' talk 'bout it, you don' talk 'bout it. You was but hartly three years old when you' daddy was kilt, Darryll. People shut it out. They shut their mouths real good back then, even more than nowdays. They seed what Dires can do, how evil they was, an' still is. You seen it, too, jest in the short time you been back wit us. Don' try t' make no sense o' nonsense, boy. It ain't possible, is wasted effort's all."

"So, what now?" Darryll asked.

"So now, boy," Mose said, "is the time come to git even."

"How?"

"Sit back and listen to Ol' Mose. I got the ammunition in here. You's the cop, you can takes it from there."

Mose pulled nine, black-and-white composition style notebooks from a beaten leather satchel and laid them out on the table. In the weathered pages, worn from dampness, storage and time, were stiffly printed dates, letters and names. The entries started in 1949, when Mose was a handsome, young 20-year-old man and buried his first body for the Dires.

He had been working with his father and uncle, putting family and friends in Old Place for 11 years, "But," Mose said, shaking his head, "1949, after the Big War, that's when it begun, me workin' wit' the devil Dires."

Darryll scanned the pages, using his finger to focus on the markings.

The drop-offs to Ol' Mose were irregular during certain times of the year. At other times, the number of corpses appeared as regular as a clock striking midnight.

Explaining his basic code, Mose pointed to May 1953—with the entry: "WM-3-May 22, 1953."

"Three white males," Mose explained. "They was fed'ral moonshine agents, as I can recall. They was at the ginmill in town snoopin' one afternoon. Next mornin'," Mose gave a brief grin, "no more snoopin', no more bodies, no ev'dence. I had orders to bury them boys real quick."

"How many do you figure are in here, Mose?" Darryll asked.

"Well," he said, stroking his beard and squinting his eyes, "dat's real hard t' figure. There was some dry spells, then business would get kinda brisk. Could never tell what was comin'."

"Give me a guess," Darryll urged him.

"Well, a slow year could be 10 or so . . . ."

Darryll breathed in softly, "And in a good year?"

"Could be 20 or mo', best I can recall."

Doing the calculations quickly, Darryll made a rough estimate. "If we said 15 a year, since 1949, that's 60 times 15, over 900 bodies. That's impossible," Darryll said.

A bit annoyed, Mose pointed to his books, "My records don' lie. It's all in them pages. Coun' 'em up if ya wan'. But I kep' me good records."

"I believe you, Mose. I'm not questioning your story; I'm just in shock, I guess."

Shaking his head, Mose looked at Darryll, "Ya find a good man chopped up and his pieces in crabpots like a butchered hog, an' ya think all this jest started this mornin'. Listen t' an ol' man who can go anytime now. Sure as dirt on the ground, there's evil walkin' wit' us here on earth. It's jest that a lotta it sorta got together here in Dire's Mill. Don' know why, that's not for us t' figure. It jest is. An' it didn't start up here today, with Maurice. Been here before I come, an' will be here after I go, unless you work t' stop it now."

"What did you know about Maurice?"

"Jest that he was a good man, kind to me an' my folks. Gave us his extra catch of feesh and crabs, an' towed us in offa bay a few times. That an' that he weren't no waterman forever. That I knowed."

"How did you know that?"

"Ya been down here long as me, ya talk t' people, ya hear places in their voices. Little snips and snaps o' things."

"Like what?" Darryll asked.

"Like Army talk. Southeast Asia GI talk. Real big, educated words at times, too. Moreece, he didn't learn all them little funny things an' such readin' books alone, neither. He was a travelin' man, Maurice was, an' he was here in Dire's Mill to git dirt on Dires. I figured that out real soon."

"You think the Dires ever knew."

"Nope, not in all this time he was here. Not 'til last night. Then, they done took care o' it like always. An' if he wasn't shoved in dem pots, I'da got me a delivery this mornin'."

~~~ ~~~ ~~~ ~~~

Craig Dire answered the phone and heard Rolph's voice. It was a little after 5 p.m., at the same time Darryll was meeting with Ol' Mose.

"I finally caught up with your town undertaker, your Uncle Elrod," Rolph said. "Damn, how old is that fossil? I thought it was a lost corpse that had gotten out of its coffin, roaming around and trying to get out the front door."

"And . . ."

"And he said they took the body parts away just before I got there."

"So?"

Rolph was getting irritated with the monosyllabic question routine, but said nothing.

"And, feeling like a goddamn idiot, I asked your walking dead uncle if he looked at Mo's head, and, specifically, if the corpse still had its eyes."

"Dammit, hurry up, what did he say?"

Rolph shouted the answer. "The old bird freaked out, said he didn't bother to examine the parts, said that's not his job. In this instance, he was just a holding facility. Said I insulted him. Then he started bitching 'cause people are always asking him if he ever screwed a good looking corpse. For the record, he didn't. Never even thought about it. Wants to know why anyone would ever think about something like that? And then he wonders why I think that he would want to look into the eyes of a head that was hacked off and shoved in a crabtrap. That about covers my entire enjoyable and embarrassing encounter with your undertaking kin. Satisfied?"

"NO!" shouted Craig. "You need to get me those eyes, and possibly his arms, too."

Rolph couldn't restrain himself any longer. "Look, how about telling me what this is all about. Do you mind? Then maybe I can get some idea of what to do next, and how important this bizarre assignment is."

"All right," Craig said, his palms sweating, "it has to do with STP and fingerprints."

"The oil treatment? What the hell does NASCAR have to do with Mo the Know?" Rolph demanded, holding his head in disbelief and staring at the telephone receiver.

"Not oil treatment, you idiot! STP is Sight Trauma Photography! It's new technology. They can put the bastard's eyeballs in a laser, do some high tech magic with microchips and get a photograph of the last person the victim saw."

Rolph didn't answer. To Craig, the silence on the other end of the phone was deafening, annoying and insulting.

"HELLO?" Craig shouted. "Did you hear me?"

"Yeah, I heard you," Rolph replied. "Did you have a lobotomy since I saw you last, or have you been reading you new subscription of *Future Cop Monthly?* That's the stupidest damn thing I've ever heard! Who the hell told you that one?"

Now it was Craig's turn to keep quiet. Embarrassed, he did not want to reply. Had he been set up, right in his own office, by the wiseass cop?

"WHO?" demanded Rolph.

Craig's voice was a whisper, as he simply uttered one word, "Potters."

The laughter at the other end was the highest insult. "I guess I have your permission to call off the police cars chasing the box of Mo's body parts that are heading, as we speak, to County Hospital?"

Rolph's mocking continued, so loud it filled Dire's office. Craig dared not mention his concern about their fingerprints on Mo's lifeless arms. Seething, Craig was enraged by Rolph's taunting. It stopped suddenly, when Craig took the fashionable, multi-buttoned speaker phone, yanked it from the cord and threw it across the room—breaking the glass and frame that held his Dire's Mill Rotary Club "Outstanding Man of the Year" award.

Friday evening

Troopers Higgins and Merrick, the oversized state cops who had welcomed Darryll back home a week before, were waiting for his arrival on the highway 12 miles outside Dire's Mill. Following a payphone conversation with Michael Pentak, the commissioner sent an escort to make sure Darryll and Mose reached the helipad safely and quickly. From there, they would be delivered to the Liberty Manor safehouse in the midst of Deep Creek Refuge. Apparently, quite a few people wanted to hear what Ol' Mose had to share.

Never stopping, Darryll followed the first trooper. He pressed the accelerator past 75 on the straight-away to keep up with the lead Ford Queen Victoria sedan and the matching tail vehicle joined in, offering protection from behind.

"You always drive this fast, boy?" Mose asked Darryll, shouting at him from the passenger seat.

"No, but I got hot cargo by the name of Moses Abraham Neigel Jefferson with me today," Darryll said, "and some big shots want to talk to you real soon." After a moment, Darryll asked, "You ever been in a helicopter, Mose?"

"Hell, boy, this is 'bout only my fift' time in a car. Ain't ever had no need to travel from Blacktown or Dire's Mill. An' them Dires don't want Ol' Mose outta view. Mighta missed me a dropoff," he said, smiling.

"Well, tonight we are going to be traveling in style, Mose," Darryll said. "Up there, see that light in the field," Darryll said as he turned off the main road and followed the state police car toward the soybean field landing strip.

"Yeah. Like one o' them UFO things ya see on the TV."

"Right, well, that's our ride."

"Where we goin' in that black bird?" Mose asked.

"To meet some important people," Darryll said, slowing the car to a stop. "In fact, it seems like one of them has come to meet you." Pointing out the window, Darryll aimed his finger in the direction of a solitary figure dressed in a black suit, his clothing flapping from the wind coming off the rotating chopper blades. "That's DelMarVa Police Commissioner Michael Pentak, came here to meet you and go with us to the big meeting."

"Ain't he Gov. McDevitt's right hand man?"

"Right."

"I hear the gov'nor's a mean sumbitch. That right?" Mose said to Darryll.

"You'll be able to ask him yourself, Mose. He'll be there tonight to talk to you."

Mose couldn't believe it. Shaking his head, he wished his mother could see him now—a gravedigger from Blacktown being treated like a celebrity, and he

also knew he had the power to help bring down the
entire Dire Dynasty. Who would have imagined such
a thing? Only in the 21st century on DelMarVa.

～ ～ ～ ～

McDevitt was waiting in the main hall of Liberty
Manor as Pentak, Darryll and Mose arrived. The governor greeted Mose, who was carrying the worn
leather satchel tightly under his right arm. McDevitt
expressed his appreciation for Mose's willingness to
cooperate in the investigation. Accompanied by two
security staff members, the four men rode the elevator down to Level D. Entering a conference room at
the far end of the wide tiled corridor, the four new
arrivals settled into empty seats around a large, oval
wooden table. Already in place for the meeting were
Vice Governor Lydia Chase; Sgt. Randy "R.J." Poplos,
the governor's bodyguard; and Chief State Prosecutor
Matthew Gordon.

A few of the staff smiled and exchanged nods as
McDevitt took his chair at the head of the table. A
large, brightly-colored official seal of the State of
DelMarVa served as an appropriate backdrop for the
meeting.

McDevitt began, "I'd like to introduce Detective
Darryll Potters and Mr. Moses Abraham Neigel
Jefferson."

The two men nodded, acknowledging their names
and remained silent as the governor continued.

"We're here because of a series of rapidly devel-
oping events and some critical information that has
just come into our possession, courtesy of Mr.
Jefferson and Detective Potters, who you will hear

from in a few moments. First, I'd like to have Matt quickly review our efforts and the cases we've tried to build against the Dire operation over the last several years."

Matt Gordon pressed a button on a hand-held, remote control unit and all eyes watched the wall behind McDevitt disappear into the ceiling. In its place was an oversized, detailed map of the peninsula state, showing major and mid-size cities, bodies of water, county boundaries and sites of the casinos, theme park and commercial and industrial complexes.

With a gold-tipped laser pointer, Gordon drew a wide circle around the town of Dire's Mill and indicated the Dire family's substantial land and business holdings that stretched well beyond the town limits.

Taking a moment, Gordon stopped his glowing gold dot on an area a few miles outside town. "This is Gobbler's Knoll," he said, looking at Potters, "Detective Potters' place is one of several family farms that Dire is attempting to buy, at ridiculously low prices, to expand his empire and increase his control of the area's economy. We also suspect he somehow has discovered very preliminary discussions about future joint federal and state interest in this area."

Gordon continued, painting a verbal picture of a well-organized, highly paid, mob-like operation that is and has been involved in illegal gambling, moonshine liquor production, wide scale prostitution, state and federal tax evasion and, more recently, the sale of black market babies.

"Dire has the local court system in his pocket," Gordon said, "and several of his relatives sit on the municipal and county benches. They've consistently overruled us during those few times we have been able to make a case. We have 16 cases in various stages of appeal at present. Litigating against the Dires is our white collar crime division's worst nightmare. If I mention the name Dire in the office before a case assignment meeting, a half dozen prosecutors head for the restrooms to hide or call out sick. It's frustrating, because we just can't get anyone down there to talk.

"There's a very strict code of silence among the people in the locale. And, those who we think are ready to cooperate just, frankly, disappear. Over the years, legal proceedings, intense surveillance, heavy state police oversight and covert infiltration have produced minimal results.

"Also," Gordon paused, "it saddens me to report that our agent Michael Webster, operating for the last two years in Dire's Mill under the cover name Maurice Knowles, was killed quite savagely last night. His dismembered body parts are in the county hospital and the Dire's Mill Sheriff's Office is currently in charge of the murder investigation."

A few groans were heard. Lydia Chase slammed her hand against the tabletop, showing her strong disappointment and frustration.

"However, we may have a major breakthrough. As you know earlier this evening," Gordon said, "Mr. Jefferson came forward voluntarily with records of people he has buried for the Dires over the last 60 years."

Several heads turned to face the gravedigger.

"His notebooks, I've been told, detail at least 900 deaths in Dire's Mill of local citizens and strangers from beyond DelMarVa. All of these individuals, that Mr. Jefferson buried in a remote site called Old Place, located on Dire property near Blacktown, are believed to have been murdered by members of the Dire family and its gang. We have reason to suspect that several more murders are imminent, and we must act very quickly.

"The Dire Dynasty's influence includes corrupt politicians and dirty cops, too—but not just in DelMarVa. The family also has a vast network of underworld connections and a larger number of legitimate business associates. This makes it imperative that whatever we decide tonight has to be carried out with utmost secrecy and speed. We cannot let these animals slip away this time. That's all I have at present."

McDevitt looked at the map. "The Dires own nearly every business in town and, as Matt explained, they've been making serious efforts to buy more property, possibly to expand the city limits, which would legally increase both power and influence. That's how we were aware of Mr. Potters' situation, through our secretarial source at the bank who informed us of the letter he received," McDevitt said, pointing to Darryll.

"In addition, the Dires' business interests extend far beyond our region. They've gone global, and a lot of cash is flowing in and out of that little town and through the coffers hidden inside Dire's Mill Mansion."

McDevitt paused, and looked at the others. "I'm afraid we might find that the multiple murders listed in Mr. Jefferson's book are just the tip of the iceberg. But, until now, we've had no proof of the killings. People just disappeared. Now we have dates, descriptions and burial sites. Tangible evidence."

∽   ∽   ∽   ∽

Mose sat in the room, half listening to the conversation and half looking around at the impressive surroundings. He'd lived in Blacktown his entire life and never imagined there could be a place so important looking. And, he thought, he was there, at the table, being treated with respect by all these people in fancy clothes.

Eventually, Ol' Mose gave a summary of his involvement with the Dires, explaining how, in exchange for a burial site for the poor residents of Blacktown, he agreed to lay to rest bodies delivered by the Dire family.

"They'd jest drop one or two off at a time," Mose said. "In the old days, they'd leave 'em in my backyard, near the kitch'n door, so's I'd see 'em soon as I got up."

"Would they be out in the open, just lying there in back of your house?" Gordon asked.

"Well," Mose paused, thought a few seconds, then replied slowly. "Yessir. That's how it happens. But it wasn' like nobody was gonna take 'em an' drag 'em off. They just was there, waitin' fer me. Dires knowed I was an early riser. So, if I saw a body or two, I'd go an' plant 'em that day. Unless it was win'er. Then they'd have t' wait for warm weather, 'til the ground got sof' again."

"Where would you keep them stored, Mr. Jefferson?" Lydia Chase asked.

Smiling, he answered, "Mose, ma'am. Jest Mose is fine."

She returned the smile and nodded. "Where, Mose?"

"In my fish house, most time," he said. "I got me a good size ol' shack for my boat an' tarps an' traps. Jest move some stuff t' one side and stack 'em up.

They don' take up that much room, if ya knowd how t' pile 'em."

Several of those at the table shook their heads in disbelief. Mose, sensing they were bothered by his apparent casual reference to the dead, addressed the topic without being asked.

"I see how ya might be thinkin', right now, 'bout what I done," Mose said. "I ain't proud of what I hads t' do. But, the way I figured, my folk needed a place to rest, an' these bodies, them souls was gone already. Ya can' know what it was like, livin' under the Dires. I seen them beat people, kick 'm for lookin' the wrong way. They kilt that boy's daddy in front of me," Mose said, pointing at Darryll. "Nobody messed wif them Dires, 'specially not black folks, is how I guess I can explain it best. So ya do what ya can t' survive, an' try not t' git the Dires more upset than they was already.

"One time, I even called the state police from a pay telephone in Chippers Corner, was 'bout 10 years back, to try to get us some help." Mose shook his head, recalling the response. "Lady on t'other end said I was drunk an' cut me off. I figure' twas the Lord's way of sayin', 'Time ain't right, Mose.' But, I think now 'tis."

Mose paused, looked up a second, then continued, "As for dealin' wit' the dead, that's been my job since I was 9 years old. For 80 years, I been buryin' folks. People who don' touch the dead with their hands, they jest can' understand how 'tis. Think it's scary. But, to me, is the most peaceful an' natural job of all. Feel I's doin' them a good service.

"Lot of them bodies had been good folks in life, maybe some was bad now an' then. For me, it don' matter. Them ones the Dires dumped in my place, I figure they come to me 'cause there was some kinda good in 'em. That's prob'bly why they was kilt in the first place, 'cause they caused the Dire's trouble. Them bodies deserved a good buryin', jest like my folks. An' that's what I did. I jest wanted to get that clear t' ya all settin' here."

McDevitt looked at Mose. "Mr. Jeffe . . . Mose. No one at this table bears you the slightest ill will and, let me be very clear on this, what you are doing is helping us greatly. We are extremely thankful to you. You will be protected, and your people in Blacktown will be helped by us for your courage. We don't forget our friends. Because of the grace of the Good Lord, we have not lived the hard life that you have. We are not making any bad judgment about how you existed. So, please, tell us more about the Dires."

For about 15 minutes, Mose leafed through his books. With Darryll by his side, he pointed out dates and explained the codes he had developed to identify the bodies.

To say those present were fascinated was an understatement. It had already been decided that copies would be made of Mose's records. The dates and cryptic descriptions would be matched against missing persons reports from the counties of the former three states that had formed the peninsula. Following that, DelMarVa authorities would see if there were similarities with missing person reports from New Jersey, Pennsylvania and mainland Virginia.

Darryll pointed out that the latest burials were at the beginning of the month and earlier that day.

"Today?" Lydia Chase asked.

"Yes ma'am," Mose said. "Two white folks. A big man and a lady. She had a bullet in her head. He had a hole in his back. Shame, he had a nice new Raven's football sweatshirt. Musta been a gif'."

Darryll perked up. "Those two were at Halloween House last night. They had some trouble with Dire, were complaining about the press cutting into line. Damn! I saw them walking off with his little buddy Rolph."

"Mr. Craig don' like nobody arguin' wit' 'em, Mose said. "I'd seen 'em kill folks fer alot less. That's what happens t' outsiders, 'cause folks 'round here knows a lot better.

"Them three earlier this month was two locals an' one stranger. Pretty lady wasn't from 'round here. She was beat up real bad, 'fore somebody shot offa back o' her head. The two men, I seen them 'round at times. Done grass cuttin' and limo drivin' work for Mr. Dire. One o' them was shot in the head, too. Other one, he was a mess. Real bad. Lookt like some animal gotta holda 'im. A hunk a raw meat was all he was. Real bad one. Seems t' me they's gettin' worse."

Eyes met around the table and all present suddenly understood how the number of burials in Mose's books probably weren't too exaggerated after all.

In the few cases when he knew a person, Mose had listed the identity of the victim.

When he read out the name Charlotte Ann Meredith Dire, Craig's first wife, Matt Gordon nearly jumped from his seat.

"You buried her?" Gordon asked, excitedly.

"Yessir," Mose said, softly adding, "She was a good woman. Gave her a real fine restin' place, overlookin' the field wit a view of the bay. I was real sorry when she showed up."

"You know where she's buried? You can lead us to the grave?" Gordon's excitement couldn't be controlled.

Mose stared at the prosecutor, noticeably surprised by the question. "I know where they's all planted, sir. I can take you to Miss Charlotte Ann Meredith on a pitch black night. Hell, 'scuse me ma'am," he said, nodding at Lydia Chase, "I could pro'bly get ya to her if I turned blind," Mose added.

"Do you have a date there, in the book?" Gordon asked quickly.

"July 5, 1994," Darryll read aloud.

Leafing through Craig Dire's file, Gordon found what he had been seeking and read an entry, his voice a bit shaky, "Charlotte Ann Meredith Dire. Missing in a boating accident of suspicious nature in the late afternoon of July 4, 1994, during an Independence Day celebration at Dire's Mill Mansion."

Gordon looked around the table and said, "Listen to this sworn statement by her husband, Craig Dire, given during a formal inquiry in his attorney's office. 'My wife took the speedboat out into the bay late that afternoon. I was concerned, because she had been drinking heavily and didn't have much experience on the water. We tried to stop her, but she ran off and jumped in the boat, gunned the motor and was well into the bay before three of my employees could even get into another boat and follow after her.'

"Remember, these are Craig Dire's very own words, under oath," Gordon stressed. Continuing, he read, " 'We headed out as quickly as possible but, when we found her boat, it had overturned and she was nowhere in sight. We searched that day and the next. The Dire's Mill Sheriff's Office and Fire Company dredged the bay for the rest of the week, but, unfortunately, with no luck. My darling, beautiful Charlotte Ann was gone forever.'

"That statement from a grieving husband—plus the sworn accompanying affidavits by three employee witnesses and the town sheriff and captain of the Dire's Mill Fire Department—enabled widower Craig Dire to collect on a $3 million insurance policy within two months of his first wife's empty casket funeral."

"That ain't true," Mose said.

"Excuse me?" Gordon said, his head snapping toward the old gravedigger.

"Miss Charlotte Ann didn't drown. She was beat in the backa the head. Was crushed real bad. I looked in the bag when she come t' me. Didn't drown, that's fer sure."

No one spoke, realizing that the exhumation of Charlotte Ann Dire's body alone was enough to march Craig Dire to the gallows. The smashed skull would seal her husband's fate.

Mose continued going through his hand-written books, pointing out patterns and, in particular, an annual dropoff that had occurred each fall for the last eight years.

"Early November's a steady time," Mose said. "Get a lotta work right after Hall'ween. These years now, they come in black rubber bags, all zipped up. Don' have t', but I tak'a look inside, t' see if it's anybody I know. Most o' them in November's strangers. An', I think them Hall'ween bodies is from Mr. Dire's big party."

Darryll explained Mose's opinion that Dire was killing off some of the actors at the end of his Halloween House showcase. Asking for a moment of consideration regarding an unrelated matter, the retired detective referred to his file and explained the unsolved missing persons cases from Washington County, Maine. After describing Sarah Small, he immediately explained his sighting of the girl with the palm pentagram he saw being whipped by Melinda Dire.

"I think this is my runaway," Darryll said, "and I want to go in and get her out."

McDevitt looked at Pentak.

The police commissioner spoke directly to Darryll, "From what we've heard and seen in Mose's records, and the fact that Craig Dire has been in direct contact with Mose regarding burials, we have enough to go in and dig up Charlotte Ann Dire. We can put the cuffs on Craig Dire and search his home and businesses and use whatever we can find as extra leverage. Who knows what we'll find? We should be able to get the young woman when we close down his operation."

"How soon will that be?"

Everyone looked at Matt Gordon, who said, "Two days, max. We'll prepare the paperwork and get a judge to sign off, and then . . . ."

"And by then that girl could be dead and dumped in the bay, or maybe shoved into another set of crab traps," Darryll said, forcefully.

"Listen, there's something else here," he added, pressing for a different solution. "I've been in this business a long time, too. I have a strong feeling there's more to these actresses than just a Halloween show. Where has Sarah Small been the last seven years? How did she survive? How did she end up with Dire? I tell you, I believe she might be able to lead us to the big money, the source of the heavy cash, you people also are after."

"We can't go on hunches, Mr. Potters. We're in the fact finding business," Gordon the attorney said, obviously a bit irritated with an outsider giving his opinion and pressing his own interests.

"Well, if it wasn't for me, Mr. Gordon Esquire," Darryll snapped, "that file on Craig Dire, resting in your manicured hands, would still be covered with dust and buried deep inside a dead vault, waiting for divine inspiration to resurrect it to life."

A few at the table smiled, and quickly looked down.

Lydia Chase spoke up. "I tend to agree with Detective Potters. I say we hear him out. I sense he wants to go in and release Ms. Small and, if he's right, she may provide us with valuable information in a totally different area. I'm particularly interested in the disappearing girl's connection to our operation. There must be a lot more to this, and the sooner we get her here the better. If she doesn't give us anything new, we can go in to get the first wife's body on a warrant that can be prepared in the meantime."

"But," Darryll said, "I hope you have a judge you can trust and who's not on the take."

"Yes, we do, Detective," McDevitt said, signaling his annoyance at the last comment. "I think I've heard enough. It's your call, Mike," he added, looking at DelMarVa's police commissioner.

Pentak leaned forward, a page full of notes spread on his desk. Looking down at what seemed the beginning of a plan, he said, "Matt's approach is the safe one, and I like it a lot. Makes good sense."

The attorney tossed a proud smirk at Darryll.

"But," Pentak said, "I never seem to take the sensible, safe approach. With the wealth of information that this girl might provide us, I'm going to have to go with Detective Potters' recommendation."

Darryll nodded his thanks.

"What I'd like to do is go in tonight, with a small force, and bring back the Small woman and her two associates. From the sound of what they've been through, we should get to them as soon as possible. In the meantime, I'll place Mr. Jefferson in the hands of a debriefing team. We'll use the CIA alumni who've come on board. Our FBI hires can go over Mose's records, there's too much in those books for us to digest here.

"With file satellite photos that we can obtain within minutes from our Global Web Files, some topo maps of Dire's Mill and the countryside, and Mose's excellent memory, we should be able to pinpoint Charlotte Ann Dire's gravesite without Mose even having to go back with us at this time. We'll take him to Old Place later, after the situation is stabilized.

"About tonight, since Detective Potters has been on the estate, we can make good use of him on this mission. If you're agreeable?" Pentak looked across the table, not expecting a negative answer.

"Affirmative, sir."

"Good," Pentak continued, "we'll also get recon photos of the mansion complex, and I'll call in Chief Lively from the Salisbury Barracks and Carlton Buxton from Rehoboth. They're good men. Lively knows the area and Buxton's good on the water. They can select a few men each. We'll hit Dire's very early in the morning, about three hours before dawn. That's the best time.

"We also have several years worth of photographs and intel from Mike Webster—Mo the Know—that will be very useful. He identified a few rarely used deepwater coves that run behind Dire's mansion

property. We won't have too much trouble develop-
ing a plan, entering by water. Our objective is to get
in, get the ladies, and move back out with no loss of
life—on our side anyway.

"In a best case scenario," Pentak added, "we'll get
the ladies out, do the debriefing and be moving on
Dire with a second roundup, hopefully, before they
discover the women are gone."

"They keeps 'em in the old guest house," Mose
said. "Least, that's what I hear from a few young boys
who does some caterin' up at the big house from time
t' time. Gots four or five bedrooms, on the second
floor. Downstairs, he gots a garage an' workshop.
Only saw it one time, myself."

"Thank you, Mose," Pentak said. "Again, you provide very valuable information." Pulling out a photograph of the guest house structure that was labeled in
one of Mo's files, he passed it to Darryll Potters.

Pentak added, "If that's the case, we can come up
in one of the guts, cut through the woods, hit the
house and have them out without anyone knowing a
thing. That would give us the important lead time we
need for debriefing."

"Will you bring them back here for that?" Lydia
Chase asked.

"No. I'll have a interrogation team on standby
aboard *The Pocomoke,* which will be our point of
departure about five miles out in the Chesapeake. On
the outside, it looks like a floating scrap heap, inside
it's high-tech heaven. As soon as we get the women
on board, we'll give them any needed medical attention and have a team question them to get our prior-
ity info needs ASAP."

When Pentak ended his overview, all eyes turned to McDevitt.

"All right. That's it for now. I assume you're along with them on this one, Mike?"

"Good guess, Hank. Wouldn't miss it for the world."

"Will you at least stay on *The Pocomoke*?"

Pentak didn't reply; apparently he didn't hear the governor's question.

14

Early Saturday morning

The eight-man rescue party gathered on the main deck of *The Pocomoke*, a 10,000-ton rusted container ship on the outside and a high tech command center within. The former Lithuanian tramp—460 feet long and 70 feet wide—had been seized in a drug deal at the Port of Wilmington two years before and was converted into a floating police barracks with the very latest in communication, security and navigational equipment. It was on 24-hour duty, prowling the bay and ocean with a crew that was essentially a DelMarVa version of the U.S. Coast Guard.

Conference and meeting rooms, plus officers' and crew quarters consumed one deck. A small, but well-equipped, hospital ward, several interrogation rooms and two jail cells were located two levels below.

Following a signal from Michael Pentak, the men moved forward and climbed down the dangling rope ladder, descending from the main deck into the two waiting 31-foot, shallow-draft speedboats that would carry them to the coastline and up the narrow inlet behind Dire's Mill Mansion.

The two black craft, constructed of composite materials, were part of DelMarVa's 26-boat Coastal Patrol Craft (CPC) fleet that the state used to monitor the waterways of the Delaware and Chesapeake Bays and Atlantic Ocean. Nearly identical to the Patrol Boat River (PBR) craft used by U.S. Navy Seals, the craft were powered by two 6V53 Detroit Diesel engines, which drive water pumps rather than propellers, making the PBR capable of speeds in excess of 35 knots in less than 15 inches of water. Highly maneuverable, the boat's shallow draft allowed it to follow suspects into coves and guts believed to be unnavigable and surprise even the most cautious smugglers.

Each member of the two attack squads carried a 9 mm Smith and Wesson automatic with silencer and three extra clips, an AR 15 semi-automatic rifle and three 15-round magazines, one concussion and two smoke grenades, a razor-sharp Para Edge throwing knife, 50-feet of nylon cord and a multi-channel radio. Throughout the operation, all team members would be in continuous communication with the command center on board *The Pocomoke*.

Dressed in black fatigues and thick-soled jump boots, the assault team would blend in well against the darkness of both the water and the brush of the forest. The lead CPC—designated *Maurice 1*—transported Salisbury Barracks Chief Dean Lively and Troopers Higgins, Stiles and Stanley. The four troopers in *Maurice 1* were very familiar with the area and all were members of the DelMarVa Hostage Response Team. They would take the lead in the attack, with those in

Maurice 2 serving as backup. The second craft carried Michael Pentak, Darryll Powers, Rehoboth Barracks Chief Carlton Buxton and Trooper Merrick.

According to the nautical chart and topographic map, a quarter-mile overland trek through the dense brush would deliver the attackers to the rear of the main building complex and open grounds of Dire's estate.

Maurice Knowles' photographs showed that the carriage guest house was located only 100 yards from the woodline. There were two entrances, one through the downstairs garage and the other up a metal stairway that led to the second-floor bedroom and living area. With luck, the landing party could surprise the three women and carry them off without notice.

The CPC pilots placed the engines on low and moved slowly away from *The Pocomoke*, heading north. The swift current was flowing in, so they made good time gliding along with the tide. Clouds concealed the moon, providing added cover. Moving up the bay at 0330 hours, they passed well beyond sight of the lone sentry pacing the main dock of the estate. The pilots told team leaders Pentak and Lively that their ETA was 0355 hours at current speed.

Everyone was quiet, hoping they could move in and out of the building and grounds without firing a shot. There was no time for a dry run, but they had reviewed the plan several times in the captain's cabin of *The Pocomoke*. Darryll, never really at ease on the water, carefully stared over the starboard side of the small boat. Looking into the black depths of the bay, he wondered how many bodies Craig and the rest of the Dires had drowned in these waters over the centuries.

The shoreline wasn't far off and the CPCs, opening up the engines to a mere 25 knots—covered the five-mile distance to shore in about 10 minutes. The occupants grabbed for the sides of the crafts as the pilots turned east and pointed toward the narrow inlet.

"Down!" Dean Lively signaled through his radio and eight figures, resembling Ninja warriors, hunched over to reduce their silhouettes.

Pentak, bent over between Darryll Potters and Carlton Buxton, looked at Trooper Merrick, who had to practically lie on the deck to reduce the size of his tall body. "It's times like this that I'm glad I'm so short," Pentak quipped.

The other men smiled, trying to show they were relaxed, knowing the trip up the narrow gut was the most dangerous part of the mission. If the pilots got stuck, they'd be forced to leave their craft and the entire team would have to be choppered out. That would ruin any opportunity to exit unnoticed. But grounding didn't happen often. Lively was more concerned about being discovered in the inlet. If so, the boats and attack teams would be easy targets, subject to fire from the higher banks of the wooded shoreline.

"This is as far as we go," the lead pilot announced as he ran the nose of the boat onto the soft marsh-like beach. Following Lively's hand signals the landing party moved over the side and headed for the steep incline to the right, their black boots pressing deep tracks in the beach. As both squads scaled the sandy bank, the two pilots checked their watches and surveyed the area, preparing mentally for the swift exit that would occur when Lively and his men returned.

"Look for us well before 0500 hours," Lively told the pilots, then disappeared into the woods.

Troopers Stiles and Stanley wore night vision goggles and moved swiftly through the brush, leading the way for the others. The trip from shore to the end of the woodline took only 15 minutes.

It was 0413 hours.

"Here we are, sir," Lively whispered to Pentak. "Stiles says his scope indicates there are no guards, no dogs—no human or animal security. We can't tell about electronics, but I'd bet that's concentrated on the mansion. They probably don't expect a hit this close to home, and especially not on the guest house."

"Let's hope not. Okay, we'd better not waste any time," the commissioner said. "Proceed as planned."

Lively raised his right hand and signaled his squad to advance. The four shadow figures covered the 100-yard distance to the guest house in less than a minute. When he saw they had reached the building and stood with their backs pressed against the wooden walls, Pentak turned and whispered the command, "Let's move!" A minute later, when both squads reassembled, the individual attackers proceeded without orders, following the preset plan. Stiles and Stanley moved in a clockwise motion, responsible for checking the area around the carriage house. Meanwhile, Merrick jimmied the downstairs door of the garage and entered with Higgins close behind. Buxton, carrying a leather case with medical supplies across his chest, followed them and disappeared into the garage.

Lively led the way up the outside stairs, which fortunately faced the woods rather than the main house. Darryll was close behind while Pentak stood watch outside.

Without incident, five intruders met in the upstairs parlor—Darryll and Lively arriving from the outside stairs, Merrick, Higgins and Buxton entering from the interior staircase. Moving his hand rapidly, Darryll pointed to two rifles and a fatigue cap, lying across the couch of the parlor.

Seeing the weapons, Lively nodded. Suddenly, the rescue party heard a voice from one of the bedrooms. It was a woman, obviously shouting at an intruder who was trying to get some free action.

Buxton waited behind, resting his medical kit on a table and preparing some of the contents for use.

Lively held up two fingers, and Merrick drew his throwing knife. Darryll did the same, and the three men moved toward the bedrooms. The noise was coming from the chamber farthest from the parlor.

With two rifles on the couch, all of the rescue team knew another guard was probably hiding somewhere on the second floor.

Their bodies tense, their eyes roaming, they moved forward slowly.

Silently, with razor sharp knives held a safe distance from their bodies, the men advanced. Suddenly, the horrors of hell arrived with a vengeance.

As Lively pushed open the last bedroom door and rolled inside toward the bed, Angeleen screamed at the sight of three more men, probably thinking they were going to take a sexual shot at her as well.

One of Dire's guards, his clothes half on, was stunned by the intruders. Pushing himself off Angeleen's body, he reached for his belt, but only felt bare skin. Then, he uttered two final words, "What the . . ." before Merrick's cold Para Edge blade entered the rapist's heart and sent him to the next world for keeps.

Darryll jumped on the bed, covered Angeleen's mouth and shielded her with his body as Lively, moving with the swiftness of a panther, slit the throat of the second guard who was exiting the bathroom.

Angeleen was biting Darryll's fingers, clawing at his body and tossing like a wildcat.

To calm her, he kept repeating her name, "Sarah Small, Sarah Small, Sarah Small," until Buxton entered the bedroom, knelt by her side and administered a hefty injection of midazalam hydrochloride in her thigh to knock her out.

It was his third joy juice application of the evening, having already given doses to Tina and Nannette, who had been sleeping through the assault and knife fight.

"All secure," Lively said into his radio. "Two bad guys down and out. *Maurice 2*, you'd better get up here, sir."

Leaving Stiles and Stanley at the bottom of the stairway, Pentak raced up the steps, moved through the parlor and entered Angeleen's bedroom.

After receiving a quick report, he said, "Get out a bigass kitchen knife from downstairs and cut through the same wounds again, just like you did the first time."

Lively nodded to Merrick, who ran down the hall and came back within seconds with a piece of fine cutlery that would do the trick.

"Good," Pentak said, as Merrick lifted up the bodies and traced through the raw slashes a second time. "We'll make it look like she kept it under her pillow and killed the first one, then got number two as he came out of the bathroom."

Darryll shook his head, indicating disapproval.

"You've got a better idea?" Pentak said, a bit irritated and concerned about the time.

"Not really," Darryll said, "but it's going to be a stretch for them to believe she got both of them. At the moment, and with time a bit tight, I'd say it's the best we can do. Unless," Darryll paused, "you take the hunting knife out of bed boy's belt and stick it in his hand. Make it look like there was a jealous scene and he offed the bathroom boy as he came through the door."

"And then the broad got him in the heart with the kitchen knife on her own when he tried to jump her in bed. It's a stretch," Pentak agreed, "but better than the first idea. All right, Merrick, carve them up again and make it look real good. Then shove the kitchen knife in bed boy's heart and leave it there, sticking out. The rest of you, pick up your gear and let's get the hell outta here. Anything else Dean?"

"No, sir. You get 'em movin' and I'll have me a last look 'round. Gotta make it look like them girls left in a hurry. I better find some purses and such that they'd take with 'em. I'll keep Stiles with me, Stanley'll get you movin' with his night eyes. We'll be right on your tail."

"Hurry it up," Pentak said, "It's already 0434."

It took them longer to make it to the woods, Darryll carrying Angeleen, Merrick responsible for Tina and Higgins hauling Nannette.

The women were clothed in nightgowns and Buxton had grabbed some sweat clothes to give them when they came to. There were blankets on the boats that would help keep them warm for the return trip on the bay.

The men moved through the dense woods slowly, taking measured steps, careful not to drop the women or any equipment.

As Lively and Stiles reached the clearing they looked back. Everything was in order. The doors were locked and lights shut off. They performed a quick sanitization and no one, on first glance, would know the house had been visited by nearly a dozen intruders. Later, someone would find the two dead bodies and think the room had been the scene of a brutal rape and murder. Hopefully, Dire would believe his men were killed by a wild woman who ran off with her friends through the woods.

The two canvas bags taken by Lively and Stiles contained jewelry, clothes, pocketbooks, money, IDs and assorted personal items. But there were plenty of clothes and belongings left behind. That also should help add to the believability of a hasty escape.

As Pentak's squad reached the waiting boats, the pilots had their engines running on low and were eager to cast off. Just as the drugged women were settled on the wooden decks, Lively and Stiles descended the steep bank. There was no time to cover footprints or tracks, daylight was approaching. Lively looked over at *Maurice 2* and Pentak waved a thumbs up.

"Let's move out," Lively ordered, and the two boats moved cautiously out of the inlet and headed for *The Pocomoke*. About 500 yards offshore, Pentak asked if "these toy boats could go any faster?"

The CPC pilots nodded to each other and smiled. In a loud voice, they turned to face their passengers and shouted, "Hang on!" Immediately, they shoved the engines forward to the max. The assault team had not expected the mean jolt as the bow of each boat raised up in the water—like a dolphin jumping in the air—and the boats headed at top speed back to the command ship.

There, several teams of doctors and interrogators were waiting to talk to the three sleeping women and pick their brains for details about Dire's operation.

~ **15** ~

Pentak was on the phone talking to McDevitt. It was 5:50 in the morning and everyone had returned safely to the ship. The commissioner explained the smooth entry into the house, the rape scene and justified killings and how Darryll Potters had suggested a creative cover up for the stabbings.

The three women were just coming around, and the doctors said they would be able to be released to the interrogation teams within the next half hour.

Potters was in the room with Sarah Small. He wanted to talk to her to confirm his theory about her real identity. Pentak had given him permission to sit in on her questioning over the strenuous objections of the interrogators.

McDevitt agreed with the decision and left word that he was to be interrupted as soon as they discovered anything useful.

Since the three persons abducted from Dire's Mill Mansion were women, Vice Governor Lydia Chase was on board *The Pocomoke* to assist in any way possible.

If breakfast was served at the Dire residence around 8 o'clock, Pentak estimated that they had about two hours before the girls were discovered missing. Add about another 45 minutes before they realized the women were rescued, and not simply runaways. This would give Pentak and his teams a maximum three-hour lead time to get critical information and start to move accordingly. Not a lot of time at all.

Pentak suggested that McDevitt make himself available for the rest of the day. When things started to happen, they were going to happen very soon and very quickly.

~ ~ ~ ~

Darryll Potters was seated on a low stool only a few feet from the bed where Angeleen—who he believed was Sarah Small—rested. Lydia Chase had just entered the small cabin and asked the detective about the young woman's condition.

"She's still asleep, but Chief Buxton said he gave all of them just enough drugs to keep them out for an hour, so she should be up any minute."

Suddenly, the woman in the bed moved her right arm, blinked her eyes and began to stir slightly.

"It's good you're here," Darryll whispered to Chase. "You'd better talk to her first. It will be best for her to hear a woman's voice, especially after all she's been through. I'm sure last night was no picnic for her, before or after we arrived."

Lydia moved near the hospital bed, leaned over the stainless steel frame and spoke softly, being careful not to startle the woman. "Hello! Hello! Can you hear me?"

As her head moved from side to side, Angeleen saw a blurred figure hovering over her head. The whiteness of the room and bright overhead lights were unexpected. She let out a short scream and huddled, forming her body into a large ball.

Shuddering, she focused on the attractive older woman. She also noticed a man in the background dressed in casual clothes. Darryll and the others had changed from their assault clothing and, seeing the injured woman's reaction, he realized the good sense of that decision.

As Darryll left the room to get a nurse, Lydia continued to talk softly, trying to see if Angeleen could comprehend even brief comments.

"Relax. You're safe," she said. "I'm Lydia Chase, vice governor of DelMarVa. You were rescued. The two men who were attacking you are dead. Do you understand what I'm saying? Can you hear me? If so, please, just nod your head."

Angeleen stared hard at Lydia and—still gripping her own arms and staying as far as possible from the stranger near the bed—she nodded her head.

"Good!" Lydia smiled. "I'm going to step back, sit in this chair. You can relax. You've been through a lot. Please. Lie down. You don't have to be frightened."

Just as Angeleen began to return to the center of the bed, Darryll and a nurse entered the cabin. Reacting to their intrusion, Angeleen screamed and jumped back.

The nurse moved forward slowly. "Hi. I'm Martha. I'm here to help you. Please, come closer. I want to see how you're doing."

Angeleen didn't move.

"You'd better step outside now, detective," Lydia

suggested. "I think we can get her moving along more quickly if you're not here right now."

Darryll hesitated. He had waited so long, but he also knew the vice governor was right. Smiling at Angeleen and then at Lydia, he walked out and shut the cabin door.

"Good," Lydia said. "Now, we can have some privacy and get you taken care of."

After the nurse took Angeleen's blood pressure and temperature, she examined the bruises between her legs and asked the young woman to turn over.

Angeleen slowly moved onto her stomach.

Several rows of fresh, white gauze bandages covered a large portion of her back.

"We noticed the skin on her back was raw," the nurse told Lydia. "It was as if someone hit her with a belt or . . . ."

"A whip," Angeleen said, turning a bruised face toward the nurse and Lydia Chase.

Taking advantage of the opening, Lydia asked, "Who did this to you? Do you know?"

"Yes," Angeleen said, having difficulty moving onto her side to face the vice governor.

"Melinda Dire whipped all of us. It was part of her Halloween act." She paused and coughed. The nurse handed her a small paper cup of cold water. "She whipped us all, for her sick show . . . for kicks." Angeleens' voice was low, soft but filled with hatred.

"Listen to me. What should I call you? What's your name?"

"Angeleen."

"Okay, Angeleen, I am going to get to the point, because time is critical. If you understand me, just nod. All right?"

The woman moved her head slightly.

"Good," Lydia replied. "Here's the high points of the story. You and your friends were rescued last night by police from the state of DelMarVa. The two men who were attacking you are dead. Our men made it look like the three of you ran off and escaped on your own. Do you follow me so far?"

Again a slight nod.

"We have to find out as much information as we can from you as quickly as possible—how you met Dire, where you came from. Anything you tell us will help us put him and his wife in jail for a long time, or . . . ."

"I want them dead," Angeleen snarled.

"There's a very good chance we can arrange that," Lydia said confidently. "We have a team of very experienced interviewers waiting to talk to you."

"Cops?"

"Sort of. Why? Is that a problem for you?"

"I don't trust cops, never have. What if I don't want to talk to them?" She held her head, trying to steady a brief dizzy spell.

"I'm afraid you'll have to," Lydia said. "I'm being honest with you. We need your help to get these bastards. And we don't have time to be diplomatic and polite about what we need or beat around the bush. I'll stay with you, if you want, but we have to get them in here to question you and we need to start right now. All right?"

"Okay. But I want you here, through the whole thing. Is that a deal?"

"Yes. No problem."

"Also, I'll tell you all I know, but I don't want to go to jail. Understand?" Angeleen's coughing returned, and the nurse was there immediately with another cup of water.

"I'll say this," Lydia replied, "unless you murdered someone in cold blood, I don't see jail in the picture. You've got my word that you'll have immunity concerning anything you tell us. Is that good enough?"

"For now," Angeleen said, wincing as she shifted onto her back. "Okay. Let's get started."

～　　　～　　　～　　　～

Pentak saw Darryll leave Angeleen's cabin.

"How's she doing?" the commissioner asked.

"Just coming around. Vice Governor Chase is with her, I figured it would be better if she didn't see any men for the time being."

"She's going to have to talk to our people real soon," Pentak said, getting a bit concerned. "It's already 6:35 and time isn't going to give us a break. So far, we've got nothing new to work with. One of the other girls is still out, and the other one is too scared to say a word."

"All right," Darryll said, nodding. "I think your vice governor is trying to get her going."

Both men turned as they heard a door open. They saw the short, skinny grim-faced nurse heading toward them. Darryll thought she looked like the nurse he had in school who hated all the boys, and smiled only at the girls.

Nurse Martha stopped and snapped, "She's ready to get started. But I suggest you get in there fast. The pain killers will last just so long. With that raw back and the damage from the assault, well, when the drugs wear off, there's no question that she'll be screaming and begging to get knocked out again."

"How long do you think we have?" Pentak asked.

"I'm not a psychic," she said, rolling her eyes. "But I'd guess no more than 20 to 25 minutes."

"That should do," the commissioner replied.

"It'll have to," the nurse snapped. "When the pain meds wear off, it doesn't matter who you are or what you're doing. But, you don't have to believe me. You'll find out for yourself, fast enough, young man." Then, she turned brusquely and walked back into the cabin.

"She's a real charmer," Darryll said. "I wonder if they teach that caring, how-to-deal-with-the family technique in nursing school or do these nurses just develop it over the years?"

Pentak rolled his eyes. He wasn't being insensitive, just realistic in trying to find out the status. Pulling a small radio from his pocket, he pressed a red button and said, "Send the first team of interrogators down to Cabin 2, and make it fast. She's ready, but we just got word that she won't last very long."

While waiting for the inquisitors to appear, Pentak knocked on the white wooden door and asked permission to enter. Getting an okay from Lydia Chase and a curt nod from the guardian nurse, he and Darryll entered the room.

By 6:45, the questioning by A, B and C teams was under way. Both John Nomoth and Judy Alexbund had spent 20 years doing the same thing for the CIA in foreign locales and, occasionally, in the U.S.

They had worked the last five years as a team. The pair accepted a generous offer and joined DelMarVa's Criminal Investigation Division 18 months

earlier. In 2007, they debriefed all of the survivors of
Charles Bettner's kidnapping spree on the Peninsula.
One of the kidnapped victim's was Stephanie Litera, a
state social worker, who, after the rescue, eventually
married the governor and now served as DelMarVa's
First Lady.

This October morning, their subject was a tense,
troubled and agitated woman named Angeleen.

Pentak had given all three interrogation teams a
list of questions suggested by Potters, Mose and spe-
cialists in the DelMarVa's Area Intelligence Division,
but the inquisitors knew they had leeway to follow
any significant leads. They were instructed to get per-
tinent details from the women to determine if they
were connected to Dire's illegal operations in any
way. The teams also were to use their experience to
obtain details that could be acted upon very quickly.

In addition, their long-term objective—to be
secured in additional question-and-answer sessions
during the coming week—was to analyze, summarize
and assemble all the information and present it to the
governor. Ideally, the final report would satisfy his
one, clear aim—to get enough proof to hang Craig
and Melinda Dire from the Gumwood gallows.

As Angeleen was meeting John Nomoth and Judy
Alexbund at 6:45, Rolph was driving toward Dire's Mill
Industrial Park to check on a shipment of material.
Following that brief visit, he would head to the other
side of town for an 8 o'clock breakfast meeting with
Craig Dire. They were going to review the status of the
latest Asian pickup, any new developments in the Mo

the Know murder, and how the pain in the ass Darryll Potters was going to be eliminated.

At the same time, four Dire security officers scheduled for the 8 a.m.-4 p.m. shift were waking up and getting dressed in their respective homes. They would arrive at the guard house at 7:55 to relieve the graveyard shift that had been working since midnight.

In the office of the NoTel Motel, Snarky Jack was cooking a microwave breakfast and looking at the small TV in the office. It had been a very slow night. The only activity was the long black limo that picked up the five young "passing ladies" about 3 in the morning.

Coming out of his shower, Craig Dire walked past his lovely, wife who was still asleep in their king-size bed. He opened the second-floor window, looked down on the manicured lawn of his beautiful family estate and smiled. Stretching his arms high above his head, he shifted his body from left to right several times, then leaned over the wrought iron railing of his spacious balcony.

To his left was the perfectly painted red-white-and-green Victorian carriage house, temporary home of his unappreciative guests. To his right, in the distance, the gravel lanes leading up to Halloween House, his pride and joy.

Another successful year, Dear Craig, he said to himself. *Hundreds of appreciative visitors—well, most anyway, except for the fat idiot in the Ravens' clothes.* But, he smiled, thinking, *Rolph took care of that pinhead and his ugly wife. Too bad. Guilty by association, same thing as a coconspirator. Well, you should be careful about the company you keep,* he thought, laughing. *That slob won't be rude to anyone ever again. Unappreciative lout.*

Then, turning again to face the guest house, he thought—*such beautiful bodies, such pathetic uncultured minds.* He certainly wouldn't miss any of them after the weekend. But, he still had to decide who to kill off and who to ship out. *Well, for sure,* he thought, *that redheaded bitch was going to Mose's. No questions there. The little blonde, she might live through it and take a long trip. And the older, dark-haired slut, he'll let Melinda decide about her.*

God, what stupid women, he thought again, staring at the quiet, sleepy guest cottage. *If only the dumb bitches realized that to get ahead all they have to do is what I say and they'll be fine. Maybe I'll give them another chance, walk over with Rolph after our meeting and see if they've had an attitude adjustment. Yes,* he told himself, *That's what I'll do, go see them and have a little friendly chat.*

As he dressed, Craig thought of his father and the good advice Jasper Dire used to dispense at the supper table right after a lengthy blessing.

Make your own luck, Craig. No one will help you.

Never look back, Craig. Make a decision and never question it, even if you find out you were dead wrong.

Never apologize, Craig. Saying you're sorry is the first sign of weakness.

Better to become irrational rather than let people get the best of you.

The only happy people are winners, Craig. Have you ever seen a smiling loser?

There are no such things as tears of joy, Craig. There are only tears of failure.

Revenge rules, Craig. If you let your enemies get the best of you, you'll regret it forever.

Think like a winner and you'll be a winner, Craig. Think bad news is coming, and it won't disappoint you. It'll hit you like a Mack truck without brakes heading downhill

Completely dressed, Craig looked at his watch. Plenty of time before Rolph arrived to relax and enjoy nature. He would take a half hour and walk the grounds, breathe in the bay air, listen to the birds. A rejuvenated, positive master of the house leaned over his still sleeping wife and kissed her forehead, whispering, "My dear, today is going to be a perfect day. I, Craig Dire the Fifth, Lord and Master of Dire's Mill Mansion will that this is one wonderful day and absolutely everything is going to come our way."

At 7:10 on Saturday morning, Pentak huddled in a corner of the hallway, holding his phone and waiting for McDevitt to answer his private line.

"Yes?" the governor said, speaking from the phone in the Woodburn kitchen.

"Clear your calendar and get ready to move quickly," Pentak said, holding the small black phone to one ear and his hand over the other to keep out external ship noise.

"What's up?"

"More than you can believe. She's jumping all over the map, giving us tons of intel but not in any order. We can piece it all together later, but I had to get this to you right away. Potters is still inside taking notes and will be out if something comes up while I'm on with you."

"So?" McDevitt asked, "what have you got?"

"These girls are part of an escort service located in an old warehouse in Philly, near Vets Stadium, run by some German or Austrian guy. The women arrive there from all over the country, picked up by guys who promise young high school beauties and runaways lots of dough and the good life in the city. Some are put on the street, like this one, serving very high priced clients."

"How high?"

"How about City of Brotherly Love judges, top state and city cops, local and U.S. congressmen and even a fair number of frustrated clergy, of both sexes? This girl, Angeleen, the one Potters identified, said she heard the entry fee was at least $20,000."

"Got a name?"

"Chez Cheveux. No security on site, as far as she can tell. The girls will visit occasionally, pick up bonus cash and get their limo rides to their gigs. But they get most assignments over the phone. She said she's been working there four years and is making in the six figures—tax free."

"How's Dire fit in?"

"This girl, Angeleen—that's the name Potters' little runaway is using. She said Dire and Melinda were up there and personally picked her out for the job. She said, Theo, the manager, was falling all over himself for the Dires. She thinks that they might be more than just regular customers, maybe even part owners. What do you think?"

"I think we'd better get somebody up there to close up that shop and pull their files, so we can see what else we can find and who owns the operation," McDevitt said.

"That's going to be real tough if word gets out and somebody on the take puts on the stall and alerts the place," Pentak said.

"Right, and we also have Dire to worry about. How soon do you think we have before he discovers his girls are gone?"

"About 45 minutes if we're lucky. Wait! Potters just came out with some more info." Pentak pressed the phone receiver against his chest and listened while Potters brought him up on the latest details."

"Potters says the girl has heard rumors that Theo also was involved in some kind of overseas operation, possibly supplying girls to foreign countries. She said that's only hearsay, a few of the women talking, and she never saw anything herself. Sometimes, girls would just disappear and never come back. When asked, Theo would remark that they've gone on a slow boat to China or that they are off learning a new language."

"Our vice division gave a report about two months ago, to the chiefs meeting," McDevitt said. "He reported that young, attractive white girls could bring up to 10 grand each in Asia and the Middle East."

"And Dire could be selling them overseas for cold untraceable cash."

"And the records could be with Theo at the office in Philly," McDevitt said. "I've got to make a few quick calls. You get back to me if anything else breaks, but tell our interrogators we need the address, layout and anything else she can tell us about Chez Cheveux."

Pentak and Darryll headed back into Cabin 2. It was 7:20 in the morning.

≈　　　≈　　　≈　　　≈

In an industrial park, just on the edge of Dire's Mill, Rolph parked his Ranger Turbo SUV and walked across the lot, heading for a large orange building that looked like an airplane hanger. The words Dire Storage were written on the side in black letters.

A small, thin Asian man with dark hair closely cut and tiny strong hands nodded as Rolph approached.

"Mr. Tsu Chan Wrie, I trust everything is satisfactory?"

"Very nice, Mr. Rolph," he replied, pointing to a tall man who was the warehouse manager. "Again, Mr. Shepperd has shown me a fine shipment of merchandise, one that my superiors will be quite pleased to accept. And, here, as usual, is the payment. All cash, $15,000 each, times five is $75,000, plus a bonus of $20,000 for Mr. and Mrs. Dire, from my uncle— who was very pleased with the fine young lady that they sent to him as a gift last month. My uncle kept her for his own."

"Very nice," Rolph smiled, accepting the black leather satchel and bowing slightly.

"You may want to count it?"

"You can be trusted Mr. Chan Wrie. Mr. Dire wanted me to ask about the possibility of adding a third delivery a month. Are your buyers interested?"

"Very much, but we need a few months to make arrangements, such as the enticements and travel plans. It takes a small effort, but please inform Mr. and Mrs. Dire the answer is yes, absolutely. We have many clients, so we want to have more of this fine, beautiful merchandise to spread around our country. Now, one more thing. When will I see Mr. Dire again?"

Rolph shook his head, "Next month, for sure. He has his Halloween House going on now, and he is very busy. But I trust you will tell him that Mr. Shepperd and I have served you well?"

"Indeed," the Oriental buyer said, smiling. "Come, before we close them up, let me show you my favorite. Please?"

"Of course," Rolph said, following the man toward a large 18-wheeler. On the red door of the tractor cab, white script letters proclaimed: "Mort's Egg Farm, Denton, DMV." The full-sized trailer was dull gray with no markings except, "Farm Fresh Eggs" in large red block letters that were scraped and marred from years of travel and battling the elements. A refrigeration unit was mounted on the top, it's engine already running.

Rolph and Chan Wrie walked up the temporary wooden steps leading toward the trailer's 8-foot-wide, narrow back end. As they opened the tall metal doors, hundreds of tan cardboard boxes, marked "Mort's Egg Farm" filled the unit to the back edge. Smiling, the Asian pulled a remote control unit from his pocket and pushed a button, signaling a two-row section of boxes to move inward, toward the tractor cab.

"After you," Chan Wrie said, pointing Rolph toward the narrow passageway. Dire's assistant walked proudly into the hidden section of the false-backed trailer that he had designed. The interior could hold up to six women, each with her own separate cubicle containing a single bed, small chair and lamp. A half-dozen stalls had been built on the left side of the trailer. The stalls, that consumed most of the tailer's length, were separated by side-wall partitions with no doors. All six of the 5-foot-wide, three-sided living areas opened toward a long, narrow aisle that extended the length of the 40-foot-long trailer.

That hallway ended at a doorless toilet facility built at the end of the trailer opposite the rear cargo entrance.

As his escort walked over to the attractive red-head, who looked like a young Reba McEntire, Rolph thought back to the meeting five years earlier when he presented the plan to Craig Dire. Instead of relying on the percentage off the top of each escort service performed through Dire's Chez Cheveux, Rolph suggested a well-operated, white slave trade enterprise, where large sums of money were received up front by eager foreign buyers.

Rolph supervised the modification of three large trailers and set up a cash payoff system to the port guards in Salem City, New Jersey.

The guard would alert Dire's manager, Orville Shepperd, the day before the ship was scheduled to depart. That's when Mort's tractor would drive the human haul—hidden behind the egg crates—over the DelMarVa Memorial Bridge to Salem, making delivery a few hours before the ship left the dock. The guards allowed Mort's egg truck to enter the port yard and drop off the customized trailer. It stood unnoticed when it was placed next to hundreds of others, all waiting to be loaded by crane onto the departing container ships.

For maximum surveillance, there was no privacy among the half-dozen occupants. During each ocean crossing, built-in video cameras were connected to four monitors, in a closet off the side of the pilot house. But even with the lack of privacy, the women's cramped accommodations offered slightly better comfort than the ship's crew quarters.

Bathing and showering would be done in the facilities of the ship on which the captives sailed.

When the human cargo was shipped out of the Jersey port, Mort picked up an empty trailer that arrived on the foreign ships that returned to the Salem port at two-week intervals. In this way, there always was a filled trailer leaving for the Far East and an empty one arriving back to be prepared for the next human shipment. In addition, the third customized container was a backup that could be used if necessary.

Customs inspectors at both ends were easy to buy off. For a flat $500 tax free in the U.S. and as little as $50 American overseas, the underpaid civil servants could care less what came in or went out.

The girls were no problem. Throughout each year, Dire's scouts were supplying Chez Cheveux with an endless supply of eager young beauties. Theo kept those with the highest potential for that business and shipped the rest south to DelMarVa.

The girls all believed the story about being sent to a private party with Washington bigshots on an Eastern Shore estate. So there was no trouble having them delivered to Snarky Jack's motel, where they waited for limo pickup to the big party, where some thought they might even meet Mister Right.

After the operation began, Rolph realized that there was a large number of foreign customers who were particularly interested in young girls in the 13 to 17 age range. Since they were too young to work as escorts in Philadelphia, they filled a growing need overseas where the motto was: The younger the better.

Everyone was a winner in this operation, Rolph told Craig Dire years ago, and the enterprising Neo Nazi had been right.

Walking toward the pretty redhead, Rolph complimented Chan Wrie on his excellent taste. The girl was no more than 16 and a knockout. She was in her cubicle, sedated and strapped in the stiff metal chair that was bolted to the floor. They usually awakened by the time the ship left the Delaware Bay and was just into the waters of the Atlantic. Of course, Rolph knew, the girls had no idea of where they were when they first opened their eyes.

The night before they had been lounging at the NoTel, expecting to attend a first-class reception. All dressed up, they took their small bag of belongings and eagerly entered into the stretch limos. Enroute, they were given drugged champagne. Upon arrival at the industrial park, while asleep, they were carried into the warehouse—where they were bound and gagged.

On each ship, the well-trained crew medic made sure they remained sedated until they were well off-shore. Rolph had made one trip early in the operation, to observe his master plan in person. He noticed that by about the third day, the girls realized where they were going and that they had no options. Eventually, they were released from the trailer for three hours each day, to bathe and walk the decks. They knew their only options were to enjoy the cruise or jump over-board—and that had only happened once.

Most people, Rolph knew, would accept practically any humiliation rather than die. The rational human maintained hope longer than one might expect. There might be an accident, they might be rescued, someone would arrive to help them. He knew what they thought, what the captives hoped.

When Craig said he was afraid that a large number would jump ship and drown in the ocean, Rolph bet him that during the first year there would be less than five jumpers. Craig had smiled, thinking he would be sure to win.

Final score after the first 12 months—Girls Safely Delivered: 132; Leapers: 1. Total received for the overseas delivery service during one year: $1,980,000 in cash. Winnings of Rolph's bet with Craig: $5,000.

Of course, Rolph made a lot more than what he won on that meager wager, which was chicken feed, compared to the $1,500 a girl he got from Dire. And that rate would continue, as long as nothing went wrong, and he planned to make sure nothing stopped the flow of women heading east, which insured the flow of cash into his pocket.

Looking at the trailer's occupied cubicles, Rolph glanced at the other four girls. They were run-of-the-mill, good looking American kids that had been dissatisfied with life, bored or seeking a fresh start. Well, Rolph thought, that they would get. The two blondes, they would go fast; a brunette and a black haired girl rounded out the shipment.

None was bruised or scared in any way, and that was important. Chan Wrie, or one of his representatives from New York, was on the scene before each departure to inspect the quality of the merchandise and verify that they were in top level condition upon shipment.

Chan Wrie's associates in Asia would sell the cargo for much more than the $15,000 per article investment. The highest prices would come during invitation-only auctions, where the women would be paraded in a boxing ring stage and bought by the highest bidder. Others were already spoken for, purchased in advance by eager businessmen and corporate executives awaiting arrival of their young American brides.

During early discussion of the business, Rolph had once told Craig how lucky these girls were. "What do they have to lose?" he asked, sincerely. "They're either poor white trash, homeless tramps or runaways, most of them hustling their bodies for next to nothing on the streets. They're on a one-way fast lane to drug addition, AIDS or an abusive relationship. Over there, they'll be bought by the elite—doctors, politicians, military officers, even warlords and millionaire sheiks. Many of the girls will do better than they ever could have done over here. If you think of it that way, we're doing them a favor, probably giving them the biggest break they've ever had in their sorry lives."

In China, as in other Asian and Middle Eastern countries, getting identity papers for the women would be no problem, for their new owners had all the necessary contacts.

When he took time to review his master plan, Rolph smiled, for every aspect of the operation was working very smoothly. On more than one occasion, he had compared himself to a proud father who was sending his little ones off to a better life.

Once on board the ship, any damage to the goods was the responsibility of the captain, who knew what he was carrying and the physical and financial penalties he would receive if the women were hurt or marred. He also received a generous bonus from the Asian brokers when the trailer and its precious contents were off loaded and the women were released in perfect condition.

During an early voyage, and only once, two crewmen decided to have a go at one of the girls. Fortunately, they were caught before any serious physical contact was made.

The captain gave the crewmen a choice: They could continue the voyage without one hand, which was to be cut off, or they could jump overboard.

The pair arrived in Hong Kong minus left hands. The official reports said each was lost in a "machinery accident" in the engine room.

Back on the warehouse floor, Rolph and Chan Wrie shook hands as the rear doors of the trailer were locked and the sleeping cargo sealed behind the false wall of egg crates. Mort, a Dire Storage employee who earned nice bonuses for his safe driving record, started up his rig and headed out, bound for New Jersey.

It was 7:30 a.m. The *Yang Jiang Star*, a small combination cargo and container carrier, was already in port and scheduled to depart early that evening.

"See you again in about two weeks," Rolph said, smiling and holding the leather bag.

"Yes, two weeks," Chan Wrie said. "As always, we will call before our next ship arrives. And soon," the Chinaman smiled, nodding, "we will see each other even more often."

＊　　＊　　＊　　＊

DelMarVa Gov. McDevitt was speaking to David P. Hornsby, second term governor of Pennsylvania. It was a call McDevitt hated to make. The Keystone State's crime and unemployment rates were both five times that of DelMarVa's. Hornsby was not hesitant to blame some of his state's crime problems on his successful neighbor to the south, and the two men had not been on good terms for some time.

"We need your help, Dave," McDevitt said.

"That's a switch, isn't it, Hank?" Hornsby's tone was sarcastic and he did not hide his annoyance at being called at 7:25 in the morning, especially by a colleague who was a recognized political folk hero. "What could an on-the-ropes, old time politician from a dying industrial state like mine do for the country's media darling?"

"We need to have permission to cross over your border and pick up a resident who has information that is critical to an ongoing investigation. The criminal activity is being conducted in Cecil County in DelMarVa and in your state near York and Gettysburg."

"I didn't think you had a crime down there, ever since you started hanging eight year olds for stealing money from bubble gum machines," Hornsby said, laughing at the comment.

McDevitt ignored Hornsby's third insult in two minutes. "Time is of the essence in this situation," McDevitt said, "and we need your cooperation immediately."

"Are you going to tell me what type of criminal activity we're talking about, Hank? Or am I going to have to play an early morning guessing game version of *The Crime Is Right?*"

"I'm afraid I can't do that, Dave. You see, our informant tells us that there are a number of high level politicians and law enforce . . . ."

"You damn showboating bastard!" Hornsby shouted. "You have the balls to call me and ask for my help and then you have even bigger gonads to tell me you don't trust me!"

"Not you, Dave," McDevitt said. "We don't know how high up this can be. All I want you to do is fax me an executive order giving us clearance to come across the border and get this guy. It will be a simple operation. I'll send two troopers up and your guys can assist with the apprehension. Then, when we wrap it up, we'll give your officers some credit for . . . ."

"I'm not going to listen to any more of this, McDevitt! The answer is NO! Hear that, governor? No! And, even if you send up a request through channels to my attorney general and the colonel of my state police, I'm calling to tell them to put it at the bottom of the pile. If they ever see it, the answer will still be NO! Got it? NO!"

"Thanks for your consideration," McDevitt said, smiling, as he gently replaced his telephone onto his desk.

"Screw you, asshole!" Hornsby said, slamming his receiver down so hard that the entire phone fell off the wall near his refrigerator.

Running into his den, Hornsby picked up another phone and called his state police colonel, warning him to watch for unauthorized DelMarVa police personnel entering into Pennsylvania off Route 896 north of Newark and in the area of Route 1, near the Conowingo Dam.

"If you see them," Hornsby said, snarling, "I want them stopped and searched for proper paperwork. And if they don't have it, which they won't, ship them back to that goddamn redneck state where they belong."

Hanging up the phone more gently, he smiled and felt good, finally having the upper hand over McDevitt.

~ ~ ~ ~

"Pentak here!"

"This is Hank. Do you have the address and the rest of the information on the office of Chez Cheveux?"

The answer was affirmative.

"Good," the governor replied. "I need you and Potters back here in Dover, immediately, along with the entire assault team. You're going up to hit the escort office and retrieve all the information you can. I also want that manager in for questioning as soon as possible. What time do you think he gets in?"

Laughing, Pentak said, "Hank, in that business they never sleep. It's an around-the-clock operation. The girl said she thinks Theo has an apartment right there. If we're lucky, he'll be there when we arrive. By the way, what did you have to give to get permission to go into his state?"

"Don't ask." McDevitt said.

"He wasn't excited to help you out?" asked the commissioner

"If I know the Hornbugle," McDevitt said, "he's got his police cars parked at every border crossing leading to York and Gettysburg, waiting for our people to try to cross his state line."

"You and the colonel have a plan?" Pentak asked

"We're putting it together, and I've got a call into Claymont Barracks Chief Tom Brennan."

"He's the one who always complains in my chiefs meetings that there's not enough crime for us to fight."

"Well, his day has come," McDevitt said. "I'll see you in Dover, within 30 minutes. Get to shore somewhere and get choppered in, fast."

Pentak closed his phone and said to Darryll, "We're heading to State Police Headquarters for a briefing, and then it looks like we're going to invade Philadelphia. You still want in on this?"

"All the way. No way I'd bail out now," Darryll said. "I just want your promise I can get back to Angeleen and ask my questions when your people are done with her."

"That won't be a problem," Pentak said. Then, the former detective thought back to his days working Philadelphia's streets, discovering bodies and searching for murderers in the best and worst sections of the town. When he agreed to work for McDevitt, Pentak had never thought of returning to the city where he had spent more than 25 years on the job.

The City of Brotherly Love was where he had gotten the idea for his best selling cop thriller—*He Got Away With Murder*—and his follow-up expose on unfair promotion practices—*Quota Cops in Command*. While his fellow cops liked the books, they were not appreciated by those who occupied the most important offices in the Round House—the nickname of police headquarters.

If he was heading back into Philadelphia, one of Pentak's main objectives was to get in and out unnoticed. There were several top level administrators—including the commissioner and chief of police—who would love to get their hands on Michael Pentak and toss the former officer in a Philadelphia jail cell for a few unpleasant days.

Who said you can't go home again? Obviously, life was full of surprises.

A t 8:15 a.m., Craig Dire was seated in his breakfast room, having a cup of coffee that had
been served by Sadie, his maid. An older black
woman close to 80, she had been in the Dire family
service for more than 50 years. One could only imagine
the stories she could tell. But she knew she wasn't
ready to leave this world yet and end up in Old Place,
so she kept her eyes straight ahead and her mouth
shut.

The Dires paid her well, and she used that money
to help her granddaughter get through college. So, if
it didn't affect Sadie or her family, the Dires could do
whatever they wanted. There were a lot of other people waiting in line for a good job like hers, and Sadie
knew it.

"You seems t' be in a good mood this here
mornin' Mr. Dire," Sadie said, keeping her eyes low
and bending her shoulders to show her place. "If'n
you don' mind my sayin' so."

Smiling, Craig, who had gotten off the phone a bit
earlier with Rolph and heard about the smooth transfer

of money and bodies, said, "Yes, I am, Sadie. Indeed I am. In fact, today, your master has decided, it's going to be a good news day. What do you think of that?"

"Sounds t' me like a good plan, Mr. Dire," she agreed, heading for the kitchen.

As she pushed through the swinging door leading from the breakfast room, two men appeared, almost knocking her down.

"Where's Mr. Dire?"

Sadie rolled her eyes and pointed toward the adjoining room.

Without knocking, the pair ran in, rushing toward the small table where their boss was enjoying his coffee.

"Mr. Dire. We've got bad news, sir."

Craig stopped lifting his cup and lowered it slowly into the white china saucer. His eyes, cold and lifeless, stared at the young security guard who dared speak and intrude on his wonderfully calm morning.

"NO! There is no bad news today. Understand?"

The guards stood silent, motionless.

"Now! Tell me good news first. I don't want to hear anything bad. I want good news! I demand it! Do you hear me, you two pinheads?"

Neither man said a word.

Annoyed at the lack of a response, Craig demanded an answer. "I said talk to me and tell me something good! Right now!"

The chubby man, standing in the back, figured he had to say something, so he spoke up. "Mr. Dire, I've got good news for you and some not-so-good news, sir."

Craig stood up and walked toward the speaker, trying to get a better view of the speaker. "That was very good, very creative. What's your name?"

"Mitch. Mitch Meggels, sir."

"Well, Mitch Meggels, what is the good news?"

The other guard stood by nervously, hoping his partner didn't set Craig off.

"The good news is, it is a beautiful day and the outside of the carriage guest house is in perfect A-1, condition," he said, waiting for a cue to continue and complete his report.

"Good," Craig said, nodding his head and heading back to his seat at the table. Then, seated, he took a sip of coffee and asked, "And the not-so-good news?"

"The not-so-good news, sir, is that inside we've got two dead security guards and no women. Looks like they've run off."

Screaming, Craig raced past the two men and out the back door. Reaching the building, he took the outside stairs two at a time and entered the top floor of the building. Two of his other guards were inside, and they tried to stop him from touching anything until Rolph arrived. They told Mr. Dire that his assistant was expected soon.

When Craig saw the knifed men in the back room, he turned away and raced into the hall bathroom, splashing water across his face.

"Where are they?" he screamed. "How did they get away?" he shouted at the two guards who were speechless and praying Rolph would make a miraculous arrival through the ceiling.

"We don't know, sir," one guard replied. "We just came on this morning at 8. Then we rushed over here, because Ned and Chas, the dead ones in the back room, didn't report at the guard shack to punch out."

Meggles and his partner had run over from the mansion and were outside talking to Rolph, who had just pulled up. They gave him a quick report and he headed into the building, walked past Craig and went immediately into the back bedroom.

For five minutes, everyone waited in silence. Then Rolph appeared. "It looks like the two of them were trying to get some free action and got into a fight. Then, from initial appearances, our little wildcat took out the winner. That's my first guess," he said. "But, why did the three bitches all run off? They could have called us. We could have taken care of it. Was your wife beating the shit out of them this early this year?"

"I don't know," Craig said. "Does that matter? We have to find them, and quickly. We can't have them running around the town, showing their wounds and ⸱ises."

⸱Relax," Rolph said. "If they ran off, they can't get .. They're probably hiding in the woods or lost in the marsh." Turning to the guards, he said, "Call the other two who were working last night in here. I want to talk to them. Meanwhile, the four of you bag these idiots and one of you drop them off in Blacktown, at Mose's place."

❧   ❧   ❧   ❧

Two CPCs ripped across the bay at 38 knots, delivering Pentak and his team at a deserted dock south of Easton. There, three unmarked vans trans-ported the occupants to twin unmarked choppers waiting in a nearby field. By 8:15 Pentak, Lively and heir men were racing across the helipad behind ⸱elMarVa State Police Headquarters.

McDevitt, along with Col. Frank Edwards, commander of the DelMarVa State Police, stood in the front of the large briefing room. A tall man with a buzz cut, Edwards looked like a model for a U.S. Marine Corps recruiting poster.

Standing against the back wall, the recent arrivals joined another dozen troopers seated around the main conference table listening to Edward's plan.

On the wall behind his podium was a detailed road map of the northern edge of DelMarVa, focusing on the routes leading from Claymont into Philadelphia. Using a wooden pointer, he indicated critical points of the operation in both states.

"We'll be choppered to the Claymont Middle School football field," Edwards said, using the tip of his stick to mark the spot. "There, four white Philadelphia Gas Authority (PGA) vans will pick us up and transport the team along Interstate-95. We'll take the Broad Street Exit and head behind Vet's Stadium to the Chez Cheveux warehouse complex."

As he signaled for the next slide, Edwards said, "We'll all be wearing white zip coveralls and PGA hard hats. Underneath you'll be fully equipped, with assault gear and bulletproof vests."

Pentak stepped from the rear of the room and intruded briefly, "We've been informed that our objective employs no human security, strictly electronic surveillance, but we have to be prepared. Also," he paused, "this is a black operation, ladies and gentlemen. That means we have not received authorization from the state of Pennsylvania."

A few heads turned and more than a few troopers raised their eyes in amazement and worry.

Gov. McDevitt spoke up before the questions arrived. "I've personally authorized this operation, and time is ticking, people. This is a critical mission and many lives are at stake. We asked for permission to cross the border and that request was denied. We have no other option. We have to hit the site now. Therefore, gunfire is a last—and I repeat—final option, to be used only in case of a life threatening incident. You've all been qualified in hand-to-hand and knife techniques. Use them first."

"Also," Edwards stressed, "any bad guys killed or injured come back with us. That's imperative. A sanitization van will enter the site immediately after your departure, but we don't want them to find anything to do."

"What if we're stopped?" Tom Brennan, Claymont Barracks chief, asked.

All eyes turned.

"Make sure you're not," Pentak replied, then told Edwards to wrap it up.

Referring to hand-drawn diagrams of the exterior and interior of Chez Cheveux, the colonel said all records, computers and files were to be removed. Also, the manager, who lived on the complex, and any office personnel, were to be returned to DelMarVa for questioning. That would take place at the Claymont Barracks, which was being prepared for debriefing. Also, two vacant office complexes nearby were already rented and would house interrogation teams that were moving into place.

"Any questions?" Edwards asked.

No one spoke.

"All right," Edwards ordered. "Let's move!"

It was 10:45 a.m. and Theo had just finished his second cup of coffee and settled behind his desk. Answering his buzzer, he thanked Katlin, his secretary, and picked up the call she had put through from Craig Dire.

"Good morning, Mr. Dire," Theo said pleasantly.

"I need three more women, and I need them today!" Craig screamed. "They ran off last night!"

Theo didn't understand. "Please, sir. Can you explain?"

"What's to explain, you idiot? The bitches you sent down here killed two of my men and ran off. They're gone! Can you understand that, you stupid Nazi shithead?"

Theo breathed heavily, then spoke calmly, "Yes. I understand. I can send three more girls. I will have them flown down this afternoon. Is that satisfactory?"

"As long as they get here on time. And, Theo," Dire said sarcastically, "this time, can you make sure you hand select the kind of women that don't kill anybody?" Then the phone went dead.

The conversation troubled Theo. He knew all three women. Tina and Nannette were younger and had not worked as long as Angeleen, but none had ever presented him with a problem. Dire had to be crazy. No matter what his employer told Theo, none of his girls was capable of killing, unless they were attacked and did so in self-defense.

Whatever problems had occurred, Theo knew they were Craig's and Rolph's doing. To a certain degree, he was glad the women had escaped. He hated sending girls down there. In fact, he actually thought the ones who went overseas had a better chance of surviving than those who performed at Dire's Halloween horror show. But, there was nothing he could do. Ever the faithful employee, Theo opened his computer and scrolled down, selecting "United States," then "New Hires." Hitting the search command, he waited for his choices to appear.

While his PC conducted its search, the phone's intercom rang again.

"Theo," Katlin said, "look at your gate security camera. There are several white gas trucks at the entrance, and the driver is on the line. He says we have a leak in the building, and they say they must enter to find it. He sounds like it's serious."

What a mess, Theo thought, then told her to put through the call.

"Yes? This is Theo Athanor, manager. What's the problem?"

"Sir. We have a serious gas leak reported in your complex somewhere. We need to get in there fast and locate the problem. Please let us in."

"I don't smell anything."

"You wouldn't," Trooper Tom Brennan said, ad libbing his responses. "The line feeds are well below the surface, beyond the range where you would notice an odor. We have detectors in our trucks that we will place at several points in the building."

"Are you sure?"

"Who can be sure, sir? Our computers at the main plant show a blinking orange dot, indicating a leak on your block. You've got the only building in the area. We have to check it out, and if we don't get in there soon, I'm not letting my men inside. If the dot moves to red, we can all forget about ordering lunch. When we hit the red zone level, that means we don't even enter."

"How long will it take?"

"Within 10 minutes of placing our gas sensitivity meters, we'll know if you're clear or not. Look, we need to get in right now. Please. I don't want to alarm you, but you could be in danger, and so could we."

Theo thought for a moment, then said, "All right. Come in. I will open the exterior gate and also our garage entry doors. You can drive directly up to my office tower. Take the stairs to my secretary's room."

"Thanks. I'll have my people place the meters while I check in with you."

On the security camera, Theo saw the three large PGA trucks move into his parking lot. Switching to intercom, he informed his secretary that the gas people would be arriving and to show them directly in. As a precaution, he opened his safe, retrieved a metal box containing his backup computer files and placed it into his knapsack. As an afterthought, he took two dozen stacks of $100 bills and shoved them on top of his files in the same dark blue canvas bag.

While the rest of his men wandered the interior of the massive garage, checking for security, Brennan, Potters and Pentak, entered the secretary's office. They presented a threatening appearance, clad in white environmental-style suits with gas masks dangling.

"He said you can go right inside," Katlin said, pointing to the small stairway behind her desk.

Potters and Pentak took the steps. Brennan waited in the outer office, making sure the secretary took no incoming calls and verifying there were no other employees on the premises.

"You better get your important files together, Miss," Brennan said, noticing the stack of folders she already had assembled atop her desk. "Do you need me to help you?" he asked.

Smiling, she thanked him and Brennan began filling large cardboard boxes with three-ring folders, manila files and plastic boxes containing computer disks. Luckily, the phone did not ring as he helped the young, attractive woman.

When everything was secure, he suggested they walk downstairs and move her and the documents to safety, while they completed their tests. Noticing her head turn toward Theo's office, Brennan said, "Don't worry about him, Miss. I'm sure he's in good hands and will be out very soon."

As Brennan handed the girl off to two associates at the bottom of the steps, he returned to the office, disconnected the phone and radioed for a squad to empty the entire room. Fortunately, there were no other employees in the area. They received no resistance as they carried everything out of the outer office—including file cabinets, bookshelves and telephone. All they left behind were three potted plants and an empty, disassembled desk.

    〚   〚   〚   〚

Only 15 feet away, Mike Pentak held a knife to Theo's neck as Darryll Potters asked the manager a series of quick questions.

"How long have you worked for Dire?"

No response.

Pentak pressed the point of the blade harder against Theo's soft neck.

"What do you know about Angeleen, Tina and Nannette," Darryll asked

Again no reply, and Pentak carefully applied more pressure.

"They're gone," Theo whispered, deciding these crazies were serious. His voice was little more than a squeak as he tried to get the few words out of his restricted throat.

"Now we're getting somewhere," Pentak said releasing the knife and stepping back, taking a seat on the desk. "Look, Theo," he added, "we know you work for Dire, we know this is a high priced hooker hotel and we know there's a lot more going down that you may or may not be involved in. Am I right?"

When Theo didn't reply, Pentak raised his knife and Darryll took a step forward.

"Wait. All right. Yes! I work for Mr. Dire." Theo couldn't figure out who his attackers were. He paid big money to city police commanders to be sure his women weren't hassled as they came and went from the warehouse. The money also was to insure that the office complex was protected.

The entire incident was strange. He was genuinely frightened, both for his safety and for the effects the situation would have on his business.

As he waited for the next question, several more white coated men and women entered his office, many with hand trucks. Swiftly, they began carting out his file cabinets and bookshelves. A pair disconnected wires and picked up his computer and printer. As Darryll rolled Theo's chair aside, the detective stumbled over the blue knapsack.

Pentak picked it up and looked inside. "Going on a little trip, Theo?" he asked, noticing the metal box underneath the small fortune in bills.

As the office dismantling continued, one trooper discovered a wall safe, hidden behind a photo of a castle in Theo's Austrian homeland. It only took two small cuts below his right ear before Theo agreed to open the mini-vault. Seconds later, he watched helplessly as the intruders bagged and labeled its remaining contents.

Pentak, looking at his watch, turned to Darryll, and said, "We've got to go. We'll continue this conversation when we get him and her back." Then, speaking into his radio, Pentak gave the order, "Time's up. Get ready to move out in three."

Darryll pulled Theo, whose hands were cuffed behind his back, out of the empty office and led him down the stairs. A white van, with its back doors wide open, waited at the bottom of the stairs. Darryll shoved Theo in and took a seat on the bench beside the recently unemployed pimp.

〜   〜   〜   〜

Melinda, noticing the confusion at the Carriage House earlier in the morning, drove off the grounds in her gray Mercedes sedan. Slighlty before noon, just beating the bank's Saturday closing hour, she stopped in Salisbury Savings and Trust and retrieved her passport and $700,000 in cash from her safety deposit box. She had much more in overseas bank accounts, but, she thought, a woman needed a little walking around money.

She had no fear that her husband would discover she was gone. He and his little assistant Rolph were out running around looking for the runaway witches. Over the last few days, her concern had intensified, and she wanted to be sure she was prepared for a quick exit if it became necessary.

Before she returned home, she stopped to see Belcher at Blood Gut Marina. Her documents and money remained hidden beneath the spare tire in the trunk of her car.

It was nearly 2 o'clock when she pulled into the circular driveway in front of the mansion. Craig ran out and started shouting, demanding to know where she had been, telling her Theo was sending three more girls, telling her the Austrian manager hadn't returned his follow up calls and that the answering service didn't know when the manager would be back.

"Relax, Sugar Babe," Melinda said, reaching up to stroke Craig's head, but he would have none of it.

"Stop! I'm ready to kill somebody," he shouted, pacing three steps back and forth. On the porch, Rolph smiled at Melinda, nodding toward her husband and rolling his eyes.

Rolph also had his own escape plan. Despite the wonderful operation with Tsu Chan Wrie, Craig's practical lieutenant realized one had to be breathing to spend one's fortune. Besides, if his little DelMarVa operation crumbled, there were plenty of other opportunities for a bright, energetic criminal genius with guts, drive and imagination.

Craig Dire, on the other hand, had his connections firmly rooted in the past and would have to fight to the end on his native soil.

"I'm going to wait inside for a call from Theo!" Craig shouted, ascending the stairs to the mansion. "We'll have to pick them up as soon as they arrive, in order to have them here in time for tonight."

"Yes, Baby Doll!" Melinda called to her husband. "I'll be right in to sit beside you, Sugar," she added, as she got into her car and drove it to the rear of the house and locked it in the garage.

≈   ≈   ≈   ≈

Theo's eyes focused on Michael Pentak, who introduced himself as DelMarVa's police commissioner. The Chez Cheveux manager was seated in an uncomfortable chair, with several electrodes from a lie detector attached to his left arm.

Up to this point, he had been less than cooperative. Pentak, explaining that he represented the full authority of the governor, spoke firmly and slowly, making sure Theo understood his limited options.

"We are not interested in you, or your secretary," Pentak said. "Our focus is getting enough proof to prosecute the Dires. Do you understand me?"

Theo nodded, looking at Pentak, and then to Darryll Potters and the lie detector technician and the two other interrogators in the crowded room.

"Here is the status. At present, we have a dozen computer geeks reviewing your files. In short order they, and the teams of accountants and ex-IRS personnel who are working with them, are going to hit paydirt. When they do, we are going to have the option of turning you over to the feds, Pennsylvania authorities and maybe Interpol. But, you may find this hard to believe, we don't give a shit about the Philadelphia operation of Chez Cheveux."

Theo waited for more.

"We hope you will voluntarily give us as much information as you can on the Dires. If so, you and your secretary can walk out of here, with no questions asked. You can keep whatever assets you have. We will give you a 48-hour lead to put your affairs in order and leave this area of the country."

Pentak paused, and Theo sat silently.

"What we want," Pentak added, "is your complete cooperation. Essentially, you will save us time. Eventually, we will find everything we need, but your assistance in speeding up the process will be looked upon favorably and rewarded." Looking at this watch, Pentak said, "It is now 2 o'clock. I see no reason that you can't walk out of here before midnight. What do you think?"

"And if I don't talk?" Theo asked, already deciding that he would take the generous offer, but he wanted to know his alternative.

Pentak moved closer and said, "We start asking questions and, if we don't like what we get, you start hurting. We've got innocent lives at stake and we intend to get what we need. No one knows you're here, and there's no reason we can't make you disappear . . . forever. Also, that young secretary out there's fate is linked to yours. You can do yourself and her a favor if you're smart. One more thing, the Dires are going down and nothing you can do will save them. But, you can save yourself. What's your decision?"

"How much time do I have?" Theo asked.

"Like I said, we need your answer now. Your thinking time's up. What's it going to be?"

Theo nodded. "All right. What do you want to know?"

Pentak explained that Theo would remain connected to the lie detector and that his team would ask him a number of preliminary questions. After that, they needed details, very quickly, about the women who were sent to Dire's Mill and the overseas operations."

"How did you find out about that?" Theo asked, astounded.

"We know more than you realize," Pentak added, continuing his bluff.

"Including the girls shipping out tonight?"

Pentak looked quickly at Darryll. Neither could contain his surprise.

Theo smiled, then nodded. "I should start there, as a sign of good faith. If you move quickly, you can stop tonight's shipment. Then I can fill you in about the rest. Agreed?"

"Fine," Pentak said.

"I am trusting that Katlin and I will be able to leave without prosecution," Theo said, verifying the deal.

"You have my word, just give me the Dires, and quickly."

After more than a half-hour of non-stop conversation with Theo, Pentak emerged from the conference room and headed for a secure telephone line in Tom Brennan's office in the Claymont Barracks.

Gov. McDevitt and Col. Edwards were in the state police commander's office, speaking to Pentak. The two men already had been informed of the successful raid and preliminary details of the files the troopers secured from Chez Cheveux.

Pentak concentrated on the imminent loading of the five young women in the trailer that was to be placed on the deck of *Yang Jiang Star*.

Based on Theo's cooperation, Pentak had secured details on Dire's white slave trade operation from its Philadelphia beginnings to its U.S. end in Salem City. But, there was no question that the central exchange took place at the warehouse in Dire's Industrial Park in DelMarVa.

According to the Philadelphia Maritime Exchange, the *Yang Jiang Star* was scheduled to leave its New Jersey dock at approximately 7:30 p.m. This allowed plenty of time to rescue the women and pick up the ship's crew.

Within 30 minutes, McDevitt called Pentak and reported a very cooperative offer from New Jersey Gov. Sharon Kannedie. She agreed to have her police guard the exits of the Salem City Port Authority and Boat Yard, insuring that none of the crew or guards escaped.

DelMarVa officers had her permission to enter the area by sea and air, rescue the women and capture the crew. She also suggested the arrests and prosecution take place in DelMarVa.

"We have enough business over here, Hank," Gov. Kannedie said. "Besides, your laws are quite a bit more stringent and you'll be able to make sure these foreigners don't get shipped back. And," she added, "your involvement will insure that none of my people are placed in harm's way."

Sharon Kannedie's response at 3:30 that afternoon was exactly what McDevitt had hoped for.

18

Tension was thick in Dire's Mill Mansion. Craig had to get ready for his first big Saturday night of the season, but he faced significant problems. His three female guests had not been found, Rolph had noticed unsettling boot tracks leading through the woods, the replacement witches for Halloween House had not arrived, the security guards were nervous and Melinda had locked herself in her room.

Rolph decided not to tell Craig about the footprints that led to the inlet behind the mansion. The assistant had already determined it was time to plan a quick exit from the Dires' employment rolls. At 4 o'clock, Rolph told Craig he would run into town for a few items they needed for the evening performances, but he would be back by 5 p.m., in plenty of time to help with the opening and operation of Halloween House

Craig planned to meet his assistant in the barn and went upstairs to speak to Melinda, who he found in a distressed state. Complaining that she had no actresses, his wife refused to go through with her act and had locked herself in their bedroom.

Breaking down the door, Craig entered the room and they had a heated argument, with one tossed lamp and several broken knickknacks. Enraged, Craig left the mansion and walked to the tobacco barn.

As he stomped across the lawn, he told himself that he knew his wife. *She would never miss an appearance, and she would perform by herself if necessary.* He also knew Melinda would appear at the last moment, just before they opened the doors, to make him suffer.

As Craig entered the empty tobacco barn, proudly looking at his grand masterpiece, he checked his watch. It was 4:30. The crowds would begin forming soon, usually an hour before the first tour, beginning at 5:30.

He smiled as he passed the Witch Trials stage and Alien Invasion space ship, *My two brainchilds,* he thought, proud of his creative mind. Heading into his office/dressing room, he closed the door, opened the top desk drawer and pulled out a dull black 9 mm Glock automatic.

You never know what kind of nut will be out there in the crowd. There could be thieves, kidnappers or even worse, he thought. Unfastening his belt, he attached the black holster and rebelted his pants, with his pistol holder pressing against the small of his back.

Verifying that he had a full clip, Craig slid the Glock into place and put on his tuxedo jacket and cape. *One could never be too careful,* he thought.

The barn office had been built during the Civil War. A wooden trapdoor, hidden behind a false panel below a built-in bookshelf, led to a cramped, underground passageway. Inside the tight alcove, an 8-foot ladder descended to a low, narrow tunnel that ended about 200 feet away, inside an old camouflaged boathouse. There, at a secluded inlet, *Vampyr*, a sleek, black and red speedboat with a pair of 200 hp Mercury outboards, waited to take Craig away at top speed.

Tonight, is going to be a very good night, the Master of Dire's Mill said, smiling into the mirror and waiting for the arrival of Rolph.

〰️ 〰️ 〰️ 〰️

At 4:45 p.m., Melinda Dire waved to the guards at the main gate, leaving word that she would be back in just a few minutes. Then, turning south, she drove away from Dire Drive and, 20 minutes later, stopped at a deserted farmhouse outside town.

Parking her Mercedes to the side of the garage, she opened the battered doors, walked inside and drove out in a black 1999, slighted dented, four-door Ford. After locking the Mercedes inside, she transferred her bags into the Ford and followed several back roads, heading for Blood Gut Marina. In her trunk were two suitcases—one filled with precious jewelry, stock certificates, bank books and false identity papers. The other was filled with warm weather clothing, several wigs and sunglasses that would help with the disguises she knew she was going to need. By her side was the smaller bag she had carried out of the Salisbury bank earlier in the afternoon. And, under her seat, was a snub-nosed Smith and Wesson .38 caliber Detective Special.

At 5 o'clock, Rolph drove away from his small cottage in a two-door, unwashed, rented and dented green Honda. His three small satchels were filled with money, a minimum of clothing and assorted weapons that he hoped he would not have to use.

~~ ~~ ~~ ~~

Craig Dire was frantically pacing the area outside Halloween House, searching the forming crowd for Rolph, calling his assistant's car phone and shouting at his security guards to bring Melinda over from the mansion.

It was 5:40 in the afternoon and several people in the front of the line at Halloween House stepped forward to ask Craig, clad in costume, when the doors were going to open.

"Get back in line, you ungrateful chislers! All this is free! Understand? We'll open when we're ready, and not a moment earlier, and don't ask me again!"

By 5.50 p.m., the crowd was starting to shout. Then, a mocking chant rippled like a growing ocean wave of discontent. "O-PEN UP! O-PEN UP! O-PEN UP! The chant grew louder, annoying and taunting.

Craig grabbed a bullhorn and announced that if the crowd didn't shut up, he would close down the operation.

Boos and curses drowned out the end of his announcement.

Slamming the bullhorn to the ground, Craig rushed inside the tobacco barn and locked the door. With his back to the entrance, he waited, breathing heavily, his mind trying to convince himself that he could still salvage the remnants of his anticipated good day.

Where was Rolph? Maybe there was an accident, he thought, hitting his assistant's car phone number again. At the other end the line chirped inside an empty car, intentionally submerged in a wetland off a deserted dirt road.

And where's my Melinda? What's taking her so long? Craig wondered, still waiting for a report from the security guard he had sent to the mansion. He swore he was going to rip her beautiful throat out as soon as she appeared.

     ∽   ∽   ∽   ∽

At 6 p.m., several legally-endorsed documents had been signed, approving operations that commenced simultaneously. From the Delaware City Barracks dock, four CPCs headed across the Delaware River, bound for the Salem City, New Jersey. At the same time, an equal number of the high speed boats were heading north from Lewes at a full 40 knots, prepared to board the *Yang Jiang Star* if the Chinese ship was lucky enough to get past the dock assault units.

Members of the New Jersey State Police had taken up positions around the perimeter of the Salem City Port Authority and Boat Yard. They were prepared to nab anyone who tried to escape during the siege.

A half-dozen DelMarVa detectives in unmarked cars surrounded the Dire's Mill Sheriff's Office and arrested Sheriff Saxton Dire for aiding in the cover-up of the murder of Mo the Know.

Several troopers stopped to talk with Snarky Jack at the NoTel and checked out Rooms 4 through 7, just to make sure there were empty. On the way out, one of the officers informed Snarky that he could begin renting out the rooms. There would no more special deliveries of the pretty "passing ladies."

Eight DelMarVa State Police patrol cars sped past the brick-columned entrance of Dire's Mill Mansion, while two DelMarVa State Police helicopters landed on the estate's front lawn. As four troopers subdued members of Craig Dire's security force, other officers and detectives armed with search warrants entered the main house. At the same time, another squad worked its way through the interior of the carriage guest house.

Within a half hour, state police personnel were loading marked and sealed boxes into a half-dozen black vans parked at strategic points throughout the grounds.

Two other teams of investigators were inside the spacious office of Dire Federated Equity Savings and Loan, confiscating Craig's bank and personal files.

Salisbury Barracks Chief Dean Lively directed a dozen troopers through the mansion and outbuildings, searching for Craig and Melinda Dire and Rolph. Pentak, Darryll Potters and an armed squad moved through the waiting crowd, trying to get inside Halloween House and secure the site in their attempt to locate the three ringleaders.

Inside the barn, Craig heard the sirens and could tell there were problems outside. Racing to the second floor window that offered a view of the pathway leading to the old building, he stopped and peered through a dirty window pane. About 100 feet away he could see police approaching, some with rifles held high and others carrying searchlights. And there, in the lead, was Darryll Potters, the recent arrival who had become a royal pain in Craig's ass.

"Damn!" he said, cursing his luck. Quickly, he ran to the electric control panel on the first floor of the barn, hitting a switch that activated all of the mechanical and musical features inside the building. A cacophony of discordant music began, with lights flashing and images bouncing off walls and ceilings throughout the barn.

Running through the ground floor, he shouted for all the actors to leave as quickly as possible, causing a mad rush of confusion as they raced out the single side door exit.

There, waiting police officers caught the escapees, trying to identify each person and check them against the photographs of Rolph, Melinda and Craig.

"What the hell's going on in there?" Pentak asked, halting his squad outside the main entrance.

"Looks like he knows we're coming in, and he's turning on his lightshow to add to the confusion," Darryll said. "But, on the bright side, he's letting us know that he's inside and not out here, slipping through the crowd."

"So, he's not so smart after all," Pentak said.

Darryll responded seriously, "At the moment, Craig might not be that smart. But he's still as dangerous as hell. We'd better break in as fast as we can. God knows how many ways there are out of that old place."

Pentak agreed and ordered six troopers with a battering ram to break through the main door. Meanwhile, helicopters and cops on the ground were directing the people who had come for the free evening show back to their cars.

As the ram hit the door a second time, Craig pressed a switch that controlled the fireworks display that he had planned to set off next week, at midnight of Halloween night.

As clusters of light, distant sounds of cannon and multicolored sparklers filled the air, screams of surprise were mixed with sighs of admiration. Some of the escaping spectators paused to applaud and cheer.

"Jesus God!" Pentak shouted, "get us inside before this guy drops rocks down on us from the sky. Hurry up! Do it!"

On the fourth attempt, the ram splintered the huge, hundred-year-old, oak doors. One of the smaller troopers climbed between a broken panel and released the lock. Immediately, a stream of searchers flowed into the barn, their rifles ready, their flashlights blazing.

Potters and Pentak each led a small group, searching every corner, checking out each rafter, lifting pieces of scenery and inspecting all the rooms and stalls. Finally, they ended up on the ground floor outside Dire's office.

The thick, wooden door was locked, but a small explosive charge easily blew down the sturdy barrier. When they entered, the 20-square-foot room was as empty and as the devoid of life as the rest of the barn.

"Check this room from top to bottom!" Pentak said. "This is an old place. There's probably another way out."

Troopers began tossing books off shelves, pulling up rugs and turning over furniture.

"Keep looking," Pentak said. Then, turning on his radio, he called the search party in the mansion, "What about you, Dean? Any luck?"

Reporting from inside the main house, Chief Lively replied. "Negative, sir. The wife and Rolph are gone. We've got men searching the woods and choppers with searchlights scanning the area, but they may have slipped through. Out."

At 6:20 p.m., the four speedboats arrived slowly, drifting silently toward the dock of the Salem Port Authority and Boat Yard. Unnoticed, Troopers Merrick and Higgins reached the guard shack and surprised the single security officer.

With very little prodding, the middle-aged rent-a-cop placed a fake radio call to the bridge of the *Yang Jiang Star,* explaining that Mr. Dire himself had arrived and wanted a word with the captain.

Excitedly, the Asian seaman assembled his crew on deck to greet their generous benefactor. As the Chinese sailors stood in a straight line, facing the pilot house, a police boarding party arrived on deck—just as three black helicopters flew low overhead. Whether the crew looked up, forward or behind, their eyes were staring down the barrels of loaded guns.

The five sedated girls were transferred quickly to CPC's and transported to a hospital across the river in DelMarVa. The member of the Pilots Association of the Bay and River Delaware, who had no idea that the ship was transporting illegal human cargo, had been smart enough to remain on the bridge until after the arrests were made.

The experienced, white-bearded Delaware River pilot—who had been assigned to guide the ship down river to Lewes—agreed to sail the *Yang Jiang Star* to the Port of Wilmington, where its modified trailer was to be off loaded and the ship itself was to be seized for use or sale by the state of DelMarVa.

19

W hile search parties combed the grounds above, Craig Dirc crawled through the insect infested, muddy tunnel that would lead to his escape. He had always prided himself on planning ahead and insuring a way out of the worst possible situation. The fact that he was still on the run, proved that he hadn't lost his touch. This time, as always, he had pulled an ace from the bottom of his magic deck.

In this case, the old Underground Railway tunnel that had aided so many of the slaves his family had abused would rightfully serve their master in the end.

Along the winding, dark earthen walls, he had tossed off his cape and tuxedo jacket. His white cuff-linked shirt was almost totally brown; his polished black oxfords were covered with green sludge and wet mud. But, he thought, there would be plenty of time for new clothes, a new name, another start. He had the money put away. All he had to do was get to it. In a compartment of the *Vampyr* was enough cash and sufficient identification to get him out of the immediate area. He would race across the Bay into Maryland, wait a few weeks in a fleabag motel, hop a train to Canada and stay there a few months. Eventually, he'd fly to Europe. Once in Switzerland, he'd secure money from one of his numbered accounts and start over. He had contacts, plenty of cash. This was nothing more than a temporary setback. All he had to do was make it across the Bay.

Following the beam of his thin-handled flashlight, Craig came to another turn. He estimated that in another 25 feet he would be inside the boathouse. And he was right.

The tunnel ended well above the water and dock, behind a window that looked down into the small building. From inside the boathouse, the tunnel entrance appeared to be a vent or window about eight feet off the wooden floor.

The building was dark. Absolutely black.

Craig laid down on his back, pulled his knees toward his chest and with all his force smashed open the wooden grate with his feet. Immediately, he turned on his stomach, held onto the damp earth and let his legs hang over the side of the opening. Dangling, he extended his body. Slowly, he relaxed the tension on his arms, until his feet were closer and closer to the boathouse deck. Then, letting go, he dropped the last four feet to the solid surface.

The sound of his body hitting the wood echoed along the empty walkways. Turning quickly, Craig raced to the boat, using his flashlight to locate the ignition. It only took seconds to find the round metal receptacle that, when turned, would start the boat. But, there was no key!

Where was the goddamn key! Craig wondered.

WHERE IS THE GODDAMN KEY! his mind screamed.

Frantically, he looked on the deck of the boat, beneath the ignition. Nothing. On the walkway of the deck. Again nothing.

Frustrated, he began to beat his right fist on the top of the fiberglass black boat.

Then, from the shadows, he heard a sound . . . a chant . . . a mocking, taunting, sing-song, repetitive phrase.

"Bobby Bottles! . . . Bobby Bottles! . . . Bobby Bottles!"

Craig drew his gun and shut off his flashlight, squinting to see in the darkness.

"Bobby Bottles!"

The sound was coming from the shadows to his right. Craig fired, but the bullet hit nothing but the earthen wall.

"Bobby Bottles!"

This time the voice was from the other side of the room. Craig turned, couldn't see anything and shot twice. Still, there was only silence.

"Bobby Bottles!"

"STOP!" Craig shouted, holding his hands over his ears. "Who is it? Is it you, McDevitt. You asshole. You cowardly, saintly, holier-than-thou bastard? It's got to be YOU?"

From the darkness came the answer.

"I have the key to your boat in my hand, Craig. Do you hear me? If so, nod your head. I can see you."

Craig nodded, his gun and flashlight sweeping the room, his eyes squinting to catch a glimpse of any clue to the location of his stalker.

"I am going to toss the key to you, Craig. If you catch it, you can go on your way. If not, too bad. Understand? I think you know how this works. Remember when you and your friends played the same little game with Bobby?"

Craig didn't respond.

"Do you remember, Craig?"

Angry, Dire shouted his reply. "I can't catch the damn key in the dark, you asshole!"

"Too bad, Craig. But this time I'm in charge, just like you were when you made the rules for Bobby, when we were at Salisbury. If you don't want to play, I can just toss all three copies of the boat key in the water at once. How's that?"

"NO! I'll do it. Okay."

"Good. Now on the count of three, here comes Key Number One. ONE! TWO! THREE!"

PLOP!

The sound indicated that something hit the water only a few inches from Craig's left hand.

"Too bad, Craig. Here's your second chance. ONE! TWO! THREE!"

PLOP!

Again a precious key found its way into the water.

"LAST CHANCE! ONE! TWO! THREE!"

This time Craig waited, but there was no sound, nothing landed. He started to scream, when suddenly, all the overhead lights came on and, kneeling about 10 feet away—on the dock near the opposite end of the boat—was Henry McDevitt.

The governor was holding a .38 caliber revolver in his right hand and a longneck, brown beer bottle in his left.

"Drop your gun, Craig," McDevitt commanded.

As the businessman hesitated, a sound came from the dock to his rear.

"He means right now," Randy Poplos said, aiming a Smith and Wesson revolver down at Dire's head from his position on the elevated wooden walkway.

"How did you know I'd be here," Craig asked, as he placed his gun between his feet, on the flat deck of the boat.

"A little gravedigger friend told me," McDevitt said, smiling as he climbed into the boat with Craig.

"That old black bastard. After all I did for him," Craig said, snarling.

"Right," McDevitt said, now on the boat deck less than 10 feet from Craig. "I keep forgetting. You're a real give-back-to-the-community type of guy. Well, let me provide you an update on today's hectic events, 'Scarface.' "

Craig's hand reached up to the spot on his cheek that Bobby's bottle had cut so many years ago.

"Your white slave trade operation is closed down, along with Chez Cheveux. Your converted, mobile slave trailer is at the Port of Wilmington dock. We have Mose's records of each body he's planted for your family since 1949. Your pal Theo turned on you, and we have all the documents we need to send you away for several lifetimes. So, other than that, Craig, how's your day going?"

Dire's head was swirling. *Could what McDevitt said possibly be true? How? What happened?*

"Oh, and the three women from your little guest house are in our custody. Actually, they have been with us since last night. Now, I'd say your options are quite limited. You have nothing to deal with. I'd guess that the guys at the Gumwood gallows should start working on knitting you a rope for the hanging. What do you think? Any comments? Any interesting thoughts, Craig?"

Silence.

"You know what, Craig? I always wondered how the hell you could have lived with yourself after kicking Bobby Bottles to death. All those women you shipped overseas to lives of hell. The people you killed each year from your little haunted house. Then, most recently, Mo the Know."

"That no good rat snitch deserved everything he got," Craig snarled. Even if he wanted to, the businessman couldn't control his emotions. His entire world was crumbling. The pressure on the deck was intense, unbearable. It was all because of McDevitt. For years he'd hated the pompous bastard. Trapped, Craig decided that if he were going down, he would take McDevitt with him.

"Kick your weapon toward me," McDevitt ordered Dire.

Slowly, Craig's foot directed his 9 mm across the deck, in the direction of the governor.

"So what are my options?" Craig asked, sarcastically.

"I don't see any, Craig. I think this is where your world comes to an end," McDevitt replied. "Unless you sprout wings or are able to get the last key out of this little bottle in my hand, I'd say you're going in, tonight.

"And you just can't imagine what your roommates do to you in prison nowadays. I hear life in the slammer is absolutely awful, especially if you're unlucky enough to get put in with the wrong element—which," McDevitt said, smiling, "I can make sure you will."

"I bet you will, you bastard," Craig said, looking from the governor to Poplos, the bodyguard.

"Enough talk!" McDevitt said. "Randy, cuff him and let's take this piece of human filth in. I'm tired of talking to someone who's already dead."

"Right," Randy said, stepping down carefully from the dock aiming his foot for the edge of the speedboat. But, as his smooth soled shoes hit a wet spot, Randy's body fell forward.

Tumbling, McDevitt's bodyguard's head hit the deck and his weapon slid toward Dire, who, in a quick move had Poplos' revolver in his right hand and the injured man's head in his left.

Using McDevitt's bodyguard as a human shield, Craig pressed the tip of the officer's gun barrel against the side of the unconscious trooper's head. Dire smiled at McDevitt and, in a taunting tone, said, "Oh, how quickly fate can change the course of life and the ebb and flow of any given situation. One moment you're in charge. The next moment, you're under the gun."

"This makes no difference," McDevitt said, moving a step closer to Dire. The governor's arms were extended, his elbows locked. His gun was aimed directly at Craig's forehead.

"Are you crazy, Henry? I'm going to pull the trigger and kill this bastard friend of yours if you take another step. Do you hear me?"

"And do you hear me, Craig?" McDevitt replied. "Do you know how much I hate you for what you did to Bobby and to all those other people? You're not getting out of here alive. Tonight, I intend to exterminate the ultimate evil that you are. Do you understand me?"

"You're crazy! You can't do this. I'm going to kill this poor bastard, RIGHT NOW!"

Continuing to point the gun at Craig's head, McDevitt said, "If I were you, Craig, and I had a chance to get off one shot, I'd take it at me. If you shoot him, I'll nail you. But, if you shoot here, right in my chest, and get me first, then you'll have a chance. You can shoot him second. He's unconscious right now, so he won't feel anything at all. Then, with us both dead, you can come over and take the key out of this bottle and sail off to freedom."

Waiting, giving Dire only a brief moment to think, McDevitt continued, "I'm your only shot, Craig. Right?"

Craig was sweating. He was getting tired of holding up Poplos as a shield.

"RIGHT?" McDevitt shouted. Then, laughing, the governor added, "But you can't shoot a man by yourself. You've got to have help when you do your killings, like when you kicked Bobby to death and hacked up Mo the Know, and when you beat your first wife's head in with a shovel. You're a gutless piece of shit. That's what everyone knows. That's how everybody remembers you, Craig. They would call you Chicken Shit Craig. Remember that one, you . . . ."

The gun Craig had been pointing at Randy suddenly was aimed at McDevitt's chest. "Click!" But when Craig pulled the trigger, the weapon didn't respond.

The sound was a pathetic excuse for a shot.

Again, Craig pulled the trigger, but the sound was another tiny, useless, pitiful "Click."

McDevitt smiled, pointing his loaded gun toward Craig Dire's body. "If I kill you, Craig, it will be over very quickly. If I take you in, you'll be in jail for a very long time—and that, I'm sure, would be a living hell for you. But, during those days, you'll have hope. You'll hire the best lawyers. You'll cost the state needless expenses and tie up our limited courtroom space. So, now I have to decide what to do."

McDevitt paused, and Craig stared, silent—in a frozen state of fear.

"Long ago," McDevitt added, "I vowed to make sure you paid for all you've done, Craig. And tonight," the governor paused, "I intend to fulfill my promise. Actually, I'm doing you a favor, you won't have to endure a long trial and then a horrifying march to the gallows."

Dire's mind snapped. He knew his world would end in the next few seconds. He had no more options. His hourglass had run out of magic dust.

Losing total control, Dire gripped Poplos' empty gun and charged toward McDevitt. With the revolver held high above his head, Craig planned to beat the governor to death with the useless weapon. Waiting calmly, McDevitt aimed the first shot at the center of Craig's chest, very close to where his black heart should be.

Craig was stunned.

Without hesitation, McDevitt had delivered the killing round.

Craig's body jerked, stumbled. His face a death mask in shock. Then, as the dead attacker fell back onto the deck, the governor looked down and calmly emptied his pistol of the four remaining bullets— one for Bobby Bottles, one for Mo the Know, another for Charlotte Ann Meredith Dire and a final purifying slug for hundreds of other nameless victims who had waited so long for vengeance, for justice, for their avenging angel to arrive.

Getting up off the far end of the deck, Randy Poplos casually brushed off his clothes and walked over to McDevitt. "You okay?" the bodyguard asked, gripping the governor's left shoulder.

"Fine," McDevitt said, looking down at Dire. "I've wanted to do that for a long time. Finally," McDevitt added, matter-of-factly, "Craig gave me a legal opportunity—self-defense."

Sporting a smile, Randy said, "If you don't mind my saying so, I think you were cutting it a little bit close. Suppose he had a back-up gun somewhere? And what was that comment about me not feeling anything if Dire shot me?"

Looking at Randy, McDevitt ignored the questions, patted his bodyguard on the back, and asked, "When are you going to start keeping bullets in your gun?"

Epilog

"This is WDMV-TV reporter Diane Kramer, reporting live from just outside Dire's Mill Mansion, home of Craig and Melinda Dire, wealthy DelMarVa businesspersons and philanthropists. The Dires also are known throughout the region for their annual Halloween House extravaganza.

"But, the big story tonight on *Your Eye on DelMarVa* is the arrest of dozens, and perhaps as many as 30, suspects in a far reaching operation that is believed to involve political corruption, scores of murders and a white slave trade operation, where young girls were shipped and sold to buyers in the Far East. Approaching the microphone is Police Commissioner Michael Pentak, who we're told will be making a statement."

"Good evening," Pentak said. "I am pleased to report the successful completion of a multiyear investigation involving dozens of agencies from throughout DelMarVa and the excellent assistance of members of the New Jersey State Police, with the full cooperation of New Jersey Governor Sharon Kannedie.

"With simultaneous operations at the Salem Port Authority and Boat Yard in New Jersey; on the grounds of Dire's Mill Mansion; at the Dire's Mill Sheriff's Office; and at several other unspecified sites across the state, we have taken into custody members of an international smuggling ring. In addition, we have evidence of possible illegal business practices in Dire's Mill, alleged corruption in the sheriff's department and close to a thousand disappearances and murders that have taken place both on and off our peninsula state during the last several decades.

"As I speak, more than 50 DelMarVa State Police officers and deputies are opening graves in a burial site known as Old Place, near Blacktown. According to reliable information, the makeshift graveyard holds the body of the late Charlotte Ann Meredith Dire, who was believed to have died in a freak boating accident several years ago.

"A long list of charges have been issued against Craig Dire V. Unfortunately, the well-known area businessman will not be brought to trial. He was killed in a gun battle with members of the DelMarVa State Police.

"His wife, Melinda Dire, and his associate, Rolph Kunralt, are still at large and believed to be armed and dangerous. They disappeared immediately before the coordinated assault by state police units throughout the state. Serious charges, including murder, money laundering, kidnapping, prostitution, assault and fraud, have been issued. State Police officials have added the two fugitives to DelMarVa's Most Wanted List.

"Finally, the state of DelMarVa would like to express its appreciation for the cooperation provided by Moses Abraham Neigel Jefferson, a lifelong resident of Blacktown, and Darryll Potters, a retired detective from the state of Maine who had recently returned to Gobbler's Knoll, his family's farm. Their information and assistance were crucial in solving this case. Finally, we're particularly pleased to announce that Mr. Potters has agreed to join the DelMarVa State Police Homicide Division.

"That's all I have at present. We'll take questions during a formal news conference tomorrow morning at State Police Headquarters in Dover."

"That was Police Commissioner Michael Pentak," the reporter said, as Pentak retreated from the bank of microphones.

"Now, in other news," Kramer continued, "this afternoon, Gov. Henry McDevitt's office released a statement announcing a major rural redevelopment initiative in the area of Blacktown. A fact-finding commission will report within six weeks and significant public utility, education and housing improvements are expected.

"Based on projections of major increases from the state's gambling revenues, the Division of Parks and Recreation will receive $10 million for significant structural and programming improvements to Fort Delaware on Pea Patch Island. The national historic site's renovation is nearing completion. Considered one of the state's top five tourist attractions, park officials announced that next year they expect to host more than 100,000 visitors, with most coming during its popular Civil War reenactment weekends and the park's summer Ghost Lantern Tours that are marking their 13th season.

"The Cape Charles Shipbuilding Complex will be launching *DMV Rodney,* its first full-size passenger cruise liner in three weeks. The vessel, named after the DelMarVa patriot and signer of the Declaration of Independence, has been under construction for two years and will sail out of the Port of Wilmington for its maiden transcontinental voyage to London.

"Attendance figures at Pirate's Cove, DelMarVa's popular theme park have outdistanced expectations and major additions are under consideration. In fact, officials at the Accomack County site say the entertainment giant is considering construction of another theme park at the former Bainbridge Naval Training Station, outside Port Deposit, at the northern edge of the state.

"This is Diane Kramer of WDMV-TV, reporting for *Your Eye on DelMarVa*."

                ~   ~   ~   ~

The next morning, Rolph Kunralt and Melinda Dire watched news broadcasts and follow-up reports about the raid on Dire's Mill Mansion from a cheap motel room outside St. Marys City, Maryland, not far from where Belcher had dropped them after their rendezvous at the Blood Gut Marina. In two weeks—Melinda seated in a wheelchair and posing as a wealthy, gray-haired patient, and Rolph, disguised as her matronly nurse—would board a cruise ship in Florida, bound for the Cayman Islands. From their tropical home, the two would continue their successful criminal careers.

≫

Darryll Potters eventually spoke at length with Angeleen and learned that she indeed was Sarah A. Small, the Maine runaway he had been tracking for several years. Looking for a place to recuperate and enjoy the rural setting on DelMarVa, Sarah moved into Gobbler's Knoll, where she rented a room and seemed satisfied with her new surroundings.

≫

Chez Cheveux was back in full operation with Theo Athanor as it's sole owner within two weeks of the surprise emergency gas leak inspection.

≫

With the death of Craig Dire, Gov. Henry McDevitt was able to close the book on the sad tale of Bobby Bottles. Finally, in McDevitt's mind, his promise to collect personally on Craig Dire's long overdue debt to society was fulfilled.

State of DelMarVa
Office of the Governor
1000 Justice Boulevard
Capital City, DelMarVa

Call for Entries

Dear DelMarVan or Visitor to Our State:

Thank you for your support of DelMarVa, a unique regional state that is dedicated to the protection of its citizens and the swift and just punishment of criminals. For the last three years, we have worked very hard to improve the quality of life for those who live and visit here. We have eliminated all state and local taxes. We have made extensive improvements to our recreational facilities. We continue to improve our clean environment, expand our first-rate health care and enhance our excellent school system.

Like other states, we have designated our official state motto, song, tree, bird, fish, and other appropriate identifications. However, we do not have a state poem.

I am seeking submissions for the State of DelMarVa official poem. This 8- to 12-line work must represent our new state in a positive fashion. It may focus on its environment, colorful history, recreational attractions and/or present day political and social climate—or any other suitable focus.

However, it also must rhyme. I am one of those people who believe a good poem rhymes. and that also makes it easier to remember.

Submissions may be mailed to:

DelMarVa Gov. Henry McDevitt
c/o Myst and Lace Publishers Inc.
1386 Fair Hill Lane
Elkton, MD 21921

Be sure to include your name, address and telephone numbers, so you may be contacted with questions or notified of your acceptance.

The person whose poem is selected—and a spouse or guest—will be written into the upcoming DelMarVa Murder Mystery *HOSTAGE* as guests at the State of DelMarVa Poem Awards Ceremony. The event will take place at Fort Delaware next summer. My wife, DelMarVa's First Lady Stephanie Litera-McDevitt, will make the presentation.

The **REAL NAME** of the winner will be used in the upcoming book, and I am told by the selection committee that there is a very good chance that the poetry winner also will be named DelMarVa's first poet laureate at the official ceremony.

Submissions must be **printed or typed** and must be received at Myst and Lace Publishers office by Dec. 1, 1999, to be processed, judged, verified and included in the book *HOSTAGE*.

If there are any questions, please call Myst and Lace Publishers at 410-398-5013. My friends Ed and Kathleen, who reside at the northern end of our state, will answer your questions. They have my complete confidence and authority to make decisions on this important matter for me.

I look forward to reviewing your poems and I am eager to meet the winner and his or her guest next year at the ceremony at Fort Delaware on Pea Patch Island.

With my best regards, I am, respectfully,

Henry McDevitt
First Governor, State of DelMarVa

ort Delaware, a granite-walled garrison that held
thousands of Confederate prisoners during the
Civil War, is a popular getaway attraction.
Located on Pea Patch Island in the middle of the
Delaware River, the state park hosts several thousand
visitors each year. They come from around the world
to experience the hallowed site's award-winning
Living History Program during the day and cringe in
fear during its popular evening Ghost Lantern Tours.

But, during a hostage crisis in the summer of
2010, scenes from the captivity of the past repeat
themselves behind the hallowed walls on Pea Patch
Island.

Turn the page to read an excerpt from

HOSTAGE!

DelMarVa Murder Mystery #3

to be released in Spring 2000.

HOSTAGE

(An excerpt)

The three couples relaxed on mauve-colored, padded lounge chairs spread across the deck of the *Ultimate Escape*, a 48-foot mini-yacht with a small galley and sleeping quarters for six, docked amidst 300 other expensive pleasure craft in Pirate's Cove Marina. The antiseptic boatyard that catered to the wealthy and well off was located on Smuggler's Inlet, which led to the bayside entrance of Blackbeard's Refuge, a five-star, 1,200-room resort hotel. Directly across the narrow man-made channel was Kidd's Haven, a similar buccaneer theme hotel offering an additional 700 luxury suites for vacationers from all over the world.

Both grand hotels were part of Pirate's Cove, a grand theme park constructed two years ago in Accomack County, DelMarVa, and already one of the country's 10 most popular family tourist destinations.

All six of the beautiful people were affluent, childless and in their mid to late 30s. Even their names matched their sophisticated expensive wine and tailored clothing lifestyle. No Stans or Stellas had ever trod the polished teakwood deck of the *Ultimate Escape*. Brice and Heather Healey and Todd and Naomi Sharp were the married twosomes. Nick Trench and Allison Golden had been living together for six years, but had not done anything official. They were "still trying things out," she explained.

The Healey couple's household income was $160,000—the low end of the boating group. The Sharps stood at the top of the trio when it came to paychecks, bringing in a bit more than $200,000 per year. In all three cases, their money was not the result of family inheritance or sweet luck at the Wild Pony Casino. It was payment for endless, pressure-filled, 70-hour-average workweeks endured by each member of the group.

Brice was a financial analyst for Global-Lifestyle Credit Corp., an international credit card monster headquartered in its sprawling suburban campus south of Wilmington. Conveniently, Heather worked for the same corporation in its loan consolidation division. "The family that works together stays together, so they can see each other in the cafeteria," was the bank's unofficial motto. The credit giant—recognized by its distinctive colonial blue and gold colors and logo—was a major player in the Peninsula State, standing tall and proud as its third largest employer.

Todd spent more than 70 hours a week—and the rest of his time attached permanently to an irritating beeper—as assistant director of security at Christina Casino in Wilmington. The U.S. Army combat veteran and graduate of the FBI Academy supervised a staff of 120 guards and undercover agents. He also was chairman of the Security Division of the DelMarVa Casino Control Commission that regulated the state lottery and all six state gambling centers. During his one free weekend a month, Todd traveled more than three hours to Pirate's Cove to enjoy precious little time on the *Ultimate Escape*, which he co-owned with the other five members of the group.

Naomi, Todd's wife, was fitness director of DelMarVa Tourism and Travel Inc. She was responsible for child-care and employee health programs at the private company's 12 statewide locations. Occasionally, she and Todd met in passing at their Wilmington condo, housed in an historic paper mill overlooking the scenic Brandywine River.

Nick and Allison lived in a restored Victorian mansion in Chestertown and were co-owners of DelMarVa Medical Services Ltd. The state-of-the-art medical laboratory offered X-rays, blood tests, stress tests, MRIs and CAT scan services to clients at locations in a half-dozen counties on the northwestern side of the state.

In each couple's case having enough money was never a concern, finding time to spend it was the problem.

It was an unusually warm weekend for mid-April. The women were in scanty bikinis. The men, in comfortable shorts, had shed their monogrammed knit shirts. Empty bottles of imported beer were scattered across the deck and card table.

The wind was brisk, but with late afternoon temperatures close to 80 the weekend offered a glimpse of the upcoming summer—another summer most of them would miss.

Setting his fourth empty of Blue Hen Ale beside his lounge chair, Todd said, "This is the life. The only problem is we only get to do this every six weeks."

"Isn't that the truth," Allison agreed, her head resting on her live-in's lap. "Nick and I have to head home tonight and be in the Cambridge office by 7 in the morning to start training six new assistants. Then we'll each spend the rest of the day racing to three other labs."

"And we might get together in time to watch the 11 o'clock news," Nick said, agreeing with a sigh.

"It's just one goddamn ratrace," Brice announced, seated beside the ship's wheel at the far end of the craft. "You drop out of the womb, crawl for years under enemy fire and then you drop in a hole and they cover you up. Way to go, Todd! Thanks for reminding me! I'm already getting depressed."

Naomi, the health and fitness guru, and Heather, the loan adviser, raised their drinks in a mock toast. "Thanks, Todd!" Heather shouted. "I was just thinking: I sure wish somebody would remind me that another miserable 80-hour week was just about to start."

"Yeah!" Naomi agreed, "we're trying to relax and enjoy a little slice of life with no idiots hovering over our shoulders, and you decide to bring us back to reality and steal our last precious hours of freedom."

"Hey!" Todd said, jumping up, "it's not my fault. Life sucks. That's just a sad freakin' fact. What do you want me to do?"

"Then just keep your stupid mouth shut!" Brice yelled, enjoying the fact that everyone was jumping on Todd, the casino security chief whose main fault was telling the truth at an inappropriate moment.

"Well, to hell with all of you!" Todd said, now standing and waving his arms. "because I'm going to get off of my endless one-way highway to a heart attack or the state mental ward."

"Right!" Allison said, her tone mocking. "There are only two sure ways out of the Monday morning blues, baby—death or the state MegaMillion Lottery."

"Wrong, beautiful thing," Todd said to Nick's main squeeze. "There's a third way to the promised land of financial independence that will enable all of us to do what we're doing now every damn day of the year."

"Oh, God," Todd's wife, Naomi, groaned, "he's going to tell us to go up to his casino and drop our money into the progressive slots." Her tone was defensive, trying to distance herself from her husband's upcoming promotional speech about the Christina Casino.

"You're close, but not a winner, doll," Todd said to his wife. He paused, took a quick sip of beer, and looked at his five friends. They all were waiting for more—hoping to hear a genuine, possible way out of their present never-ending, working lives.

"It has to do with the casino," Todd said, nodding as he looked at his wife. "And it involves enough money to keep us all in a lifestyle far beyond what we have now, for the rest of our lives and beyond. But, we're not going to get the money we need by winning it. That's a sucker bet. We're going for a sure thing. We're going to steal it."

No one spoke.

After a few awkward moments, Naomi announced, "He's just kidding, honest. Tell them, honey," she said, waving her hands at her husband.

After three more silent seconds Todd let out a hearty laugh. Then, in a stuttered, uneven fashion, the rest joined in, until they all were smiling, more from relief than from the humor of the situation.

"I got you all didn't I?" Todd asked, pointing at his friends as they smiled and waved back, Heather giving him a thumbs up sign.

"That was a good one," Brice said, slapping Todd with a high five. "You really fished me in."

"YEAH!" Todd shouted. "I did it, didn't I? Just for a split second, I had all of you. I could tell. You all thought it might just be possible. Right! Answer me! Right?"

Nick broke another disturbing moment. "Yeah. You had me. You did, Todd. But it was all a joke. Wasn't it?"

Todd smiled, walked over to his friend and put an arm around Nick's shoulder. "What do you think?" Todd asked.

"To tell you the truth, for just a second or two, I thought you were serious," Nick replied, uneasily.

Todd laughed, pulled Nick's body closer and slapped the med lab owner on the back. "You think I'm crazy? Hell, only a nut would try to rob one of our casinos. It's impossible, and I'm the one who should know. Damn right, I was only joking. Wanted to see what you would do. But I did have all of you."

As he scanned the group one last time, Todd caught his wife's stare.

Silently, the message passed between the two of them.

They're almost ready, Todd's eyes announced.

I told you they'd go for it, Naomi signaled in silence.

About the Author

Ed Okonowicz, a Delaware native and freelance writer, is an editor and writer at the University of Delaware, where he earned a bachelor's degree in music education and a master's degree in communication.

Also a professional storyteller, Ed is a member of the National Storytelling Association. He presents programs at country inns, retirement homes, schools, libraries, private gatherings, public events, elderhostels and theaters in the Mid-Atlantic region.

He specializes in local legends and folklore of the Delaware and Chesapeake Bays, as well as topics related to the Eastern Shore of Maryland. He also writes and tells city stories, many based on his youth growing up in his family's beer garden—Adolph's Cafe— in the Browntown section of Wilmington.

Ed presents storytelling courses and writing workshops based on his book *How to Conduct an Interview and Write an Original Story*. With his wife, Kathleen, they present a popular workshop entitled, Self Publishing: All You Need to Know about Getting—or Not Getting—into the Business.

Through Myst and lace publishers Inc., he releases up to three books each year. Most—including his novels—are set on the Delmarva Peninsula and in the Mid-Atlantic region.

**The *premiere*
DelMarVa Murder Mystery**

FIRED!

by Ed Okonowicz

It's early in the 21st century and DelMarVa, the newest state in the union is making headlines. There is full employment. Its residents pay no taxes. The crime rate is falling. Just about everything is going right.

But, in the first year of this bold experiment in regional government, a serial kidnapper strikes . . . and the victims are a steadily growing number of DelMarVa residents.

Will the person the newspapers have dubbed "The Snatcher" ruin DelMarVa's utopian state? Or will the kidnapper be caught and swing from a noose at the end of a very stiff rope.

In this first DelMarVa Murder Mystery, meet Governor Henry McDevitt, Police Commissioner Michael Pentak and state psychologist Dr. Stephanie Litera, as they pursue the peninsula's most horrifying kidnapper since the days of Patty Cannon.

WINNER
*Delaware Press
Association
First Place Award
1999
Best Novel*

$9.95
320 pages
4 1/4 x 6 3/4 inches
softcover
ISBN 1-890690-01-5

Possessed POSSESSIONS

Haunted Antiques, Furniture and Collectibles

by Ed Okonowicz

A bump. A thud. Mysterious movement. Unexplained happenings. Caused by what? Venture through these two volumes and discover possible answers. Experience eerie, true tales about items from across the country that, apparently, have taken on an independent spirit of their own—for they refuse to give up the ghost.

From Maine to Florida, from Pennsylvania to Wisconsin. . . . haunted heirlooms exist among us . . . everywhere!

112 pages
5 1/2 x 8 1/2 inches
softcover
ISBN 0-9643244-5-8
$9.95

Each book contains 20 TRUE STORIES

112 pages
5 1/2 x 8 1/2 inches
softcover
ISBN 1-89069-02-3
$9.95

WARNING

There could be more than just dust hovering around some of the items in your home.

*S*pirits
Between the Bays
Series

True
Ghost Stories
from the
master storyteller
Ed Okonowicz

Open the door and wander through these
collections of true ghost stories of the Mid-
Atlantic region.

Creep deeper and deeper into terror, until
you run Down the Stairs and Out the Door
in the last of our 13 volumes.

To order any of the first 7 volumes
see order form on page 322.

Disappearing Delmarva

Portraits of the Peninsula People

THE BUTLER, THE BAKER, THE FISHNET MAKER . . . ONCE FLOURISHING OCCUPATIONS ON THE DELMARVA PENINSULA, ARE A SAMPLING OF THE MANY SKILLS THAT ARE FALLING VICTIM TO TIME.

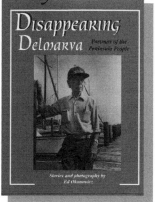

Photography and Stories by Ed Okonowicz

"(This) book will elicit feelings of nostalgia in many, but more importantly, it provides a permanent record of work and traditions that stand on the verge of extinction."

—Carol E. Hoffecker
Richards Professor of History, University of Delaware

"This book is about people who have hung on over a lifetime to a cherished way of life while change boiled around them. It tells us to take stock today of what we cherish and not let change destroy it."

—Russell W. Peterson
former Delaware Governor

WINNER
National Federation of Press Women
2 First Place Awards
1998
Best photojournalism
Best general book

208 pp
8 1/2" x 11"
Hardcover
ISBN 1-890690-00-7
$38.00

Order Form

Name_____

Address_____

City_____ State _____ Zip_____

Phone Numbers (____) _____ (____)_____

_____I would like to be placed on the mailing list to receive the free *Spirits Speaks* newsletter and information on future volumes.

_____I have an experience I would like to share. Please call me.

Qnty	Title	Price	Total
	Pulling Back the Curtain, Vol. I	$ 8.95	
	Opening the Door, Vol. II	$ 8.95	
	Welcome Inn, Vol. III	$ 8.95	
	In the Vestibule, Vol. IV	$ 9.95	
	Presence in the Parlor, Vol. V	$ 9.95	
	Crying in the Kitchen, Vol. VI	$ 9.95	
	Up the Back Stairway, Vol. VII	$ 9.95	
	Possessed Possessions	$ 9.95	
	Possessed Possessions 2	$ 9.95	
	FIRED! A DelMarVa Murder Mystery	$ 9.95	
	Halloween House DelMarVa Murder Mystery #2	$ 9.95	
	Disappearing Delmarva	$ 38.00	
	Stairway over the Brandywine	$ 5.00	

*Maryland residents add 5% sales tax.

Please include $1.50 postage for the first book, and 50 cents for each additional book.

Subtotal _____
Tax* _____
Shipping _____
Total _____

All books are signed by the author. If you would like the book personalized, please specify to whom.

Mail to:
Ed Okonowicz
1386 Fair Hill Lane
Elkton, MD 21921

Make checks payable to Myst and Lace Publishers, Inc.